CHIEFTAIN'S DAUGHTER

VIOLET MOON SERIES
BOOK 2

Alisa Hope Wagner

Chieftain's Daughter
Violet Moon Series Book 2
Marked Writers Publishing
Copyright 2019 by Alisa Hope Wagner
www.alisahopewagner.com
Written by Alisa Hope Wagner
Illustrated by Albert Morales
All rights reserved
ISBN: 978-1-7334333-2-7

CHIEFTAIN'S DAUGHTER

VIOLET MOON SERIES
BOOK 2

Alisa Hope Wagner

Acknowledgements

F'lorna's continuing saga has both plagued and delighted me. When I finally sat down to write, the story would not let me go. I poured it out in less than a month, relishing every character and scene that came alive before my eyes. My imagination sapped all my strength each night, but glimpses of future readers cheered me on.

I would not be able to labor this book without my husband's encouragement and support. My destiny is intertwined with yours, Daniel, and you enable me to live out God's highest design. And to my children who always see the best in me—your love gives me purpose.

Thank you to my editing team who find the little pesky typos that seek to infiltrate F'lorna's story. I'm grateful to Patricia Coughlin, Jennifer Smith, Bernadine Zimmerman, Sunny Reed and Daniel Wagner for helping to make this book excellent.

And to Albert Morales, thank you for bringing F'lorna and her family and friends to life with your illustrations. You bleed your heart with your pen, and I'm honored by your talent and imagination.

Finally, to my writing partner, the Holy Spirit. You have favored me far beyond what I deserve. When I am stuck, You whisper secrets. When I am weary, You renew my strength. And when I am defeated, You claim my victory.

I am a fool made wise because of Your love and guidance.

DEDICATION

To my high school sweetheart and husband, Daniel, my stories live because you cherish me.

To my three loves, Isaac, Levi and Karis Ruth, I write with excellence to make you proud.

To my readers who walk in the magic of their own creative destiny. May this story add possibility to your days.

Thank You, Father, for giving me purpose.
Thank You, Son, for redeeming my world.
Thank You, Spirit, for guiding my journey.

"As for me, I shall behold your face in righteousness; when I awake, I shall be satisfied with your likeness." – Psalm 17.15 (ESV)

MAP OF THE LAKE-KEEPERS

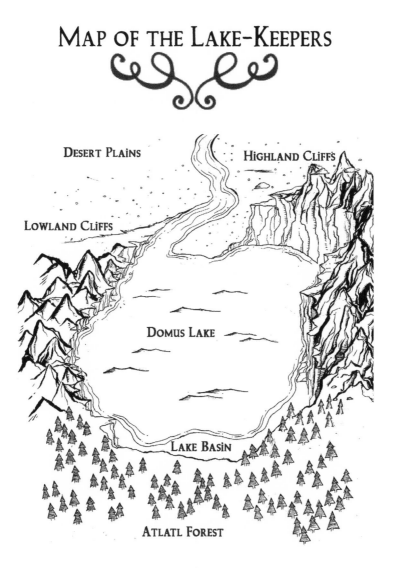

DESERT PLAINS

HIGHLAND CLIFFS

LOWLAND CLIFFS

DOMUS LAKE

LAKE BASIN

ATLATL FOREST

TABLE OF CONTENTS

Prologue

MISSING HEIR

L othar bar Haven rubbed his stubbled chin and
itched at his neck, pushing down the fur from the
black animal pelt he wore around his shoulders. His
gray hair fell loose around his horns, flowing onto the
fur. He knew his guests were awaiting his answer, but
none of the options pleased him. He leaned against the

armrest of his stone-carved throne and looked down at the steel sword by his side. The ruby stones appeared almost black within the dark walls of his rocky fortress. The light coming through sky holes in the stone ceiling was dull due to the cloudy day. The sword he protected had been his father's—passed down through his family's lineage of chieftains. The time to allow his heir to train with it had long passed. All eight of his wives he had taken during his almost forty years as chieftain left him without a single heir. He blamed the women and banished them for being barren. He had just recently become doubtful of who was really to blame. He finally stopped taking wives. Their presence only mocked him.

If his pregnant mother had not run away, he would have a younger sibling who would have given him a niece or nephew by now. Instead, his mother was a coward and a traitor. The Befores had judged her and she died in the caverns with her unborn child. His father died a few years later twisted with rage at his wife's actions. The only surviving kin he had now was his father's sister who was also barren. A cousin had never ruled as a chieftain in his lineage, but even now a cousin would be better than nothing. He eyed his guests. They wanted to merge the Highland Cliffs with the East Basin. A united territory of power to subdue all other chieftains and rule the Lake-keepers. One ruler to finally allow stability in the land instead of the constant territory wars.

"Darmin bar Holthen, I have not found a daughter worthy of adoption. When I find her, I will let you know." He knew his guests wouldn't like his reply.

"Lothar, I understand none of the options I speak of please you, but look at my son. He's been of age for over two years! How can I keep him waiting for a wife? Her youth memories must still be available to learn both our family histories and customs. That will make her at least twelve years old, and that is too young for her to marry. Even if you found her today, he would have to wait yet another two years for her to be old enough!"

"I cannot simply pick any girl from the Highland Cliffs to represent my family line," Lothar scoffed.

"Then look south to my territory. East Basin has many accomplished bowman families with fine daughters who still have their youth memories available."

Lothar stood abruptly and brandished his sword. "How dare you suggest I choose from your territory! Already I am forced to go outside of my family's fortress to find a daughter. I would not dare go beyond the cliffs to anywhere on the basin, least of all East Basin! Next you'll have me choose a daughter from the woodsman in Atlatl Forest! Do you see the Goliathan heads mounted on the wall behind me?"

Darmin looked beyond the throne. "Yes, I saw them on my last visit."

"I killed all five of those monsters with my bare hands and this single sword." Lothar allowed the loose stands of light to glint off the sharp edge of the large, bowed blade. His eyes in a trance of memories.

"I've heard the stories many times. Your renown is well-known, which is why I come to you. I do not want your legacy to end here. Train up a wife for my son who can continue your family's lineage."

Lothar swung the sword inches away from his guest's face. "Not just any girl can wear the crested cuff of the Highland Cliffs on her horn!"

Darmin held his hands out. "Lothar, you have long since established yourself as the strongest chieftain of the Lake-keepers. I would not challenge your demands. But my son is to take over our territory soon, and our enemies are always pushing from the west. Your territory is safe only because you are buffered by us and the desert. If the chieftains of the west unify, we will be overrun and the Highland Cliffs will be next."

Lothar let out a mocking laugh. "No chieftain would willingly give up power to merge territories. I only consider it because I have no heir."

"Yes, and our family is honored to unite with yours. My son is willing to marry whomever you find worthy. All he asks is that she be skilled at the bar Haven swordcraft."

Lothar looked at Darmin's son, Rathtar. He was twenty years old and taller than most Lake-keepers. His skin tanned from living on the lake coast and his hair lightened by the sun. His eyes were a variant of hazel, the standard color for many of the bowman from the basin. Most of the village families of the basin were boatmen and fishermen, building boats and bringing in the fish from Domus Lake. The chieftain families of the basin shot the bow because wood was plentiful around the lake's rim but metals were only found in the west and east cliffs. Another reason Darmin wanted to unite their two families. Rathtar was an accomplished chieftain's son, and he had no scarcity of young women fawning over him. Lothar brought his sword to his side and collapsed in his chair. The enflamed look in his eyes now lessened to frustration.

"You want your children to learn our craft of sword fighting?" Lothar asked, continuing to eye Rathtar. "I think you want to mount Goliathans on your wall and you know the bow does not penetrate their hide."

Rathtar's expression remained stoic. "Yes, Chieftain Lothar. If we are to unite the territories, I must ensure our children can both shoot the bow and wield the sword."

"What of beauty?"

Rathtar hesitated. "I will make up for any lack in appearance that she may have."

Lothar pounded the armrest of his throne. "And that you could! Any young girl I choose will most undoubtedly be enamored by your good looks. And I'm sure that more than one young lady has piqued your interest."

Rathtar's cheeks reddened; though, he showed no emotion. "None of the sages from the Highland Cliffs have your swordcraft memorized?"

"The bar Haven swordcraft is not something that can be learned by the sages. Practice and body memory is required, not simply having it in the youth memories. My aunt and I are the only ones left who know our craft."

"So Chieftess Dalia will teach her then?" Rathtar pressed.

Lothar paused. He could sense the boy's eagerness underneath his cool veneer, not a good sign for a chieftain. "I will decide her schooling. Watch yourself. You reek of impatience."

The young man looked away. "I apologize. Maybe I am impatient. I have much I want to do, but right now my hands are bound."

Lothar rubbed his chin again in contemplation. "As they should be." He looked to Darmin. "Give me a month to search for her. I will send out all my scouts, including my aunt. Pray to the Befores that she's out there. Right now as it stands, there is no daughter worthy of me."

"You know the Befores don't pay attention to us anymore since they covered more than half our lands with sand. They are angry with us for reasons none of us know. It's best to ignore them, so they leave us alone."

"Yes, many Lake-keepers ignore them, but they can show up just as suddenly as they left us hundreds of years ago. It is better to stay in their favor just in case they decide to intervene once more."

"Do as you wish," Darmin shrugged. "My son and I will return in a month." He turned to leave but stopped. "I need to tell you that your stable boy informed me this morning that my Swarve has died. I knew he was close to his time, but I was hoping he would last this trip. Blasted animals. They don't live more than five years and their decline is rapid. If they weren't so easy to train, I would prefer to ride a Goliathan."

"Yes, yes, take one of ours. Just bring it back when you return," Lothar said dismissively. He paid no attention to his guests leaving. The Befores were to blame for his misfortunes. His mother's death, his infertility and now his lineage was about to end. He had gone through all his sages to find a way to please them. But nothing he did worked. The Befores remained silent, and his territory would be given over to enemies.

"So you will give him our lands," a melodic voice echoed off the cold walls.

Lothar looked up as his aunt walked into the throne chamber. Her hair had long since turned silver and flowed loosely over the small fur she wore along her shoulders. The family crest was chiseled into a golden cuff secured to her left horn. Her thick fabric dress was of the same honey color.

"My aunt, you know we've discussed this. We have no heir. Forging an alliance with Darmin and the East Basin bowman is the only option I can stomach. I would rather all of Domus Lake be covered with sand then to let my lands be taken by the insufferable bar Hathway family of the Lowland Cliffs."

Dalia stopped several paces in front of the throne. "I wish I would have known what Tarsha was planning on doing. I could have talked some sense into her before she met her early death and the death of her unborn child."

"If my father would have known, he would have barricaded her to the Forest Room until his child was born and then he would have killed her. Her leaving us has caused the Befores to curse our family line!" Lothar pushed up from his seat, causing the heavy throne to wobble on its back legs. He began pacing the stone floors. "Why of all places would she hide in the caverns? She had Fear of the Cliffs. Her Swarve couldn't help her for long in that environment."

"You were young, Lothar. You didn't see what your father was doing to her. I asked him over and over again to seek the sages, but he wouldn't listen to me. He may have driven your mother just as mad as he was."

"The sages don't need to know our personal business. They already know too much as it is!" he shouted. "Why should my father expose his struggles to them? So they could memorize it and add it to the history of our people?"

"No, need to become so angry with me. I have done nothing wrong. I am not the one who left you."

"I am not angry. I just weary of this conversation. The questions I ask never have answers. They all died with my mother in the caverns, along with my unborn sibling." Lothar went back to his throne, sat down and began to rub his temples.

"She must have assumed there was a land beyond the desert on the other end of the river," Dalia said. "Lake-keepers have always made speculations about hidden lands and distant people. Of course, there is no credibility to those ridiculous theories. I have been deep in those caverns myself as a girl and I never saw lands— just endless tunnels and darkness."

"But to risk her life and the life of the baby growing inside of her on mere speculation? That was not like my mother. She was smart, not a stupid maiden chasing mere fantasy. Maybe you are right. She might have gone just as mad as my father when she left us."

"There's nothing to be done about it now. What's done is done, and there is no getting her or her baby back. Just be glad none of the sages have the stories saved in their youth memories. It was good that your father had the sages bound to the temple after she left."

"And that is why I have made my decision. I will not have my family lineage ending with whispers and rumors of the past. Go, Aunt Dalia, and find me an heir. Maybe the Befores will honor me after all they've taken from me. Find me a daughter who can represent the bar Haven family's legacy."

Chapter 1

RIVER OF WORSHIP

F'lorna allowed her hands to flow along the current, softly swaying in the gentle embrace of the cool liquid. A group of younglings were practicing the tingla before dinner and the wind scattered their sweet music throughout the south tributary. She felt the Heat

Source's dimming rays continue to warm her back and legs. Her skin had tanned a bit from her travels down the River with her aunt. She looked toward the horizon. The Violet Moon would greet Rodesh soon, but she didn't want to leave the wooden raft that carried her around the tributary's endless circle.

The local village had just finished a lengthy project of digging a trench from the endpoint of the tributary to its beginning, allowing the water to move continuously around. They built a bridge to connect the land around the circular tributary to the land within it. The Village Achion cluster was located within the circle, and the family Achion clusters dotted the outside rim with farmland stretching beyond that. Thinner, longer trenches were dug along each family's land, bringing fresh water to their crops.

She had never been to the southernmost part of the River. She had met many River-dwellers and visited several villages. Though they all had the *Divine Oracle* in their Eternal Memory, the villagers were much different than the River-dwellers from her village. She began to realize how traditional Right River Hook was compared to the villages close to the main trunk of the River. Tomorrow they would travel to the stone bridge, so her aunt could inspect the exposed River, cutting down the center of Desert Plains that was exposed after the ground shudders.

F'lorna instantly banished the image. She had seen a drawing of the stone bridge that Weston, her new friend from the marshlands, had made. Her Mountain Terror sickness caused her to faint, and her sickly horn fell off. She reached her damp hand to her left temple.

The wound had only just healed. It felt strange not
having her horn there. She had finally gotten used to the
stares from other River-dwellers, especially the
younglings who didn't know better. She had grown
accustomed to their questions, and she had her routine
answers ready.

"What happen to your horn?" they would ask.

"It broke off when I fell," she would reply.

"What made you fall?"

"I have a sickness called Mountain Terror."

She never mentioned she had first fallen during
the storm that caused the ground shudders while she was
giving her Adoration to Ra'ash. The Mountain Terror,
although not a pleasant subject, was better than
discussing the storm and the night Rodeshian landscape
changed again on a massive scale—something that
hadn't happened since the *Great Engulfing* when many
Rodeshians, specifically the Lake-Keepers, had been
swallowed up. She thought of Lemmeck and gently
clasped the misshapen glass pendant that dangled from
her neck. It held the mane of the White Diamond Stag
that Lemmeck had harvested many moon rises ago. She
wondered if he still thought of her. He said she was
beautiful—even with one missing horn. She struggled to
believe him.

"F'lorna," she heard a voice yell over the
gurgling water. "It is time to head in. There is a surprise
waiting for you!"

F'lorna sat up on the raft and looked for where
the voice was coming from. Her aunt, Eline, stood on the
bridge and waved to her. She waved back. "I'm
coming," she yelled. She let her feet and legs dangle in

the water and then pushed off from the raft allowing her entire body to submerge into the cool water depths. When her head finally popped back up, she grabbed the raft with her hands and began to kick her feet toward the shore. She would miss this village, but she was ready to go back home to Right River Hook. Tomorrow her aunt would inspect the stone bridge while she waited a safe distance away. She knew the harsh land of the rocky cliffs would cause her Mountain Terror to immobilize her. When her aunt was done with her survey of the land bridge, they would make the trek north back home. Her time of banishment from her home was finally over.

When she got out of the water, she carried the raft to the holding compartment on the water's edge. She would miss floating the tributary.

"Guess who is waiting for you at the visitor's Achion cluster?" her aunt asked. The wrinkles around her eyes and mouth deepened as she smiled.

"I suspect with a smile like that Banthem has come with a note from Weston," F'lorna said with a teasing voice.

"Yes, our falcon friend has returned. He's waiting on the leather swatch you keep strapped to the branch of our tree. The parchment tucked into the cylinder around his claw looks thick today. Weston must have a lot to say."

F'lorna wrung out her hair and the fiber fabric of her travel shirt. "He always has a lot to say," F'lorna said. "I best attend to Banthem before the villagers begin to wonder. I want to send a letter to Weston, letting him know that we will begin our journey back home. He should wait a while after we return to Right River Hook before sending Banthem with another letter—two phases of the moon at least. Elder Trenton may have his eyes fixed on my every move for a time. I don't want to give him any reason to cause my parents grief again."

"Yes, it's best not to send a letter right away. Two phases will give us enough time to travel back and get settled again. We don't know what has happened at Right River Hook since we've been gone—over a moon phase it's been. I offer silent words to Ra'ash that all has been made well and forgotten."

They began walking back to their temporary Achion cluster. F'lorna said nothing for a moment, but decided she finally needed to tell her aunt her full plan. "I mean to make more Sand-shaper symbols. I want my mother to have more of the *Divine Oracle*. It is not fair that her Eternal Memory doesn't have it, but now that I know I can write songs and chants down for her, I won't stop until she has all of it."

Eline walked next to her niece in silence. "Yes, I figured as much. I know your mother would want them. She'd easily move away from Right River Hook at a moment's notice. But your father, he's another story. He won't want to leave. Ever since he was a youngling, he loved community. He longs to be in the thick of relationships even though they are messy and difficult. His heart is for the people."

"It's time for his heart to be for my mother," F'lorna said. "She's lived in a community that has ostracized her for long enough—all my life and longer. My dad sees only the good in others, and he's in denial of the rest."

"Your father sees as Ra'ash—loving and tender."

"But Ra'ash is also just and stern. Much of the *Divine Oracle*—even the Forty *Chants of Jeyshen*—speak on enacting justice after long-suffering patience," F'lorna countered.

"Yes, this is true. Your father is unique in more ways than one. Honestly, I knew from his birth Ra'ash had marked him for a purpose. And you," Eline said, looking at her niece who was now several palm lengths taller than she. "Ra'ash has a purpose for you far greater than I could ever imagine."

F'lorna smiled. "My father's birth must have been a shock to Grandmother and Grandfather. You were already Onefold by then. And they were well enough in years. To have another child at such an age...I've never heard of it happening. It's more likely that he would be your son."

Eline looked toward the dimming light of the Heat Source in the distance. "I wish he could have been mine, but Ra'ash has called me to never join. My children are the people I impart the Healing Adoration to. I have many children and grandchildren by now. Your father, though, was like a gift from Ra'ash to me. Your grandparents and I so loved raising him. Even when he was a youngling, we would always find him at the Achion cluster of other villagers. They all adored Jaquarn. He could make the sick laugh and the sad smile."

"I miss him. I miss Mother. I miss Lemmeck and all of my friends. I'm ready to go home. Elder Trenton doesn't frighten me any longer. After so many different villages, I see now that he is ruled too much by fear."

They made their way to the Achion cluster as the Violet Moon peeped over the rolling farmlands. F'lorna saw Banthem's talons wrapped around the worn leather she secured to the branch. He was eating the dried meat she had tied next to the leather. She spied the white parchment. Several parchments ago, she explained to Weston how to make black dye and use River Pine Needles for writing the symbols instead of using smokestone, which was thick and took up too much space on the parchment.

"I will leave you now, so you can get ready for the Shoam-sha tonight. Make sure you are not seen as you write those symbols. Although the villagers here are more open to ideas, they are the furthest away from the Sand-shapers. They won't understand what you are doing, and we won't be here long enough to explain it all."

"Yes, Aunt. I will be careful," F'lorna said.

"Why don't you get yourself packed? Then organize the herbs and plants we've gathered during our travels and pack them into my healing pouch as I taught you. I'm surprised how quickly you are learning the Healing Adoration."

"I believe I picked up more than I thought as a youngling following around Father when he was visiting the sick."

"You sing, dance and now you are learning healing. You are a Spiritual Elder in the making," Eline said proudly.

F'lorna gave a slight smile back. She didn't want to hurt her aunt's feelings, but the last thing she wanted to do with her life was to be a Spiritual Elder for a small village. She felt something greater growing within her, but she didn't know what. She would ask Ra'ash tonight with voiceless words at the Shoam-sha. Maybe He would answer as He did the night of the ground shudders when He told her she would write.

F'lorna sat down on the smooth grass next to the line of Achion trees in the back of the village meeting. Her aunt had left early to attend a young mother delivering her baby. Most likely she wouldn't make the Shoam-sha tonight. F'lorna didn't mind. She wanted to be alone with her thoughts. She was worn out from writing the Sand-shaper symbols in her letter to Weston. She had gotten better at translating the sounds from Jeyshen's Chant to the corresponding Image, and then drawing the symbols on the paper. But writing still took time, and her fingers and mind were exhausted. She wanted to disappear into the crowd and feed on the spirit of the Shoam-sha.

She liked that this Village Achion cluster didn't have the long wooden tables that her village had. The meeting was casual with the villagers sitting on the ground and younglings running and playing on the outskirts. The Heat Source had disappeared for the night and the Violet moon glowed beautifully on the village awaiting the festivities. Unlike the torches at her Village Achion cluster, each family brought a few stone containers that burned with fat, low flames. Yellow lights speckled the grassy floor, causing the shimmer from the ground to meet the glow of the moon. It created an intimate ambiance for the Shoam-sha. With the low light and the soft sound of the flowing circular tributary, she could be almost lulled to sleep. But she wanted to experience Ra'ash tonight. The atmosphere was already energized with expectation. She needed to hear Him speak to her with voiceless words.

She recognized the Spiritual Elder, Limmian. She was older than her father, but not as aged as her aunt. She had umber skin like her friend, Sage, which made F'lorna miss her birth friend even more. Her silver hair was braided around the base of her horns, like the traditional River-dweller style, but she formed it into a knot at the base of her neck. It was windier in South Village because there were fewer trees and more farmland as they traveled south, which was probably why she wanted to keep her hair out of the way. She stood near a large, stone basin that contained a great, effervescent fire at the front of the meeting grounds.

"My fellow villagers," she began. "I know you were expecting a few words from me this evening. However, I sense Ra'ash wanting us to enjoy a time of thoughtful adoration instead. I am only a messenger here. And although I am honored that you listen to my words and consider my thoughts, Ra'ash longs to speak to you individually. Jeyshen was expanded in order to have a relationship with each of you. This relationship came at the highest price, so let us not neglect it. Let us turn our attention to Him. If you have brought your instrument, and feel led to offer your Adoration, please come and play for us as we meditate on the Indwelling. Ra'ash is offering us voiceless words tonight."

F'lorna exhaled deeply. This is exactly what she wanted and needed. To sit alone and allow the world around her to fade into the gurgling of the water encircling their meeting. She heard some movement moving forward as the instrument players stood and made their way to the front of the crowd. Then silence fell for several seconds just before the sweet sound of the leera swirled and hovered over the villagers. Then the tingla joined with its gentle strumming whisper, and finally the rhythmic pounding of the poonga grounded the melody.

F'lorna closed her eyes. Anxiety about going to the stone bridge tomorrow morning tried to bombard her mind, but she used the techniques her aunt taught her on how to seize and control thoughts. Then an image of Elder Trenton with his enraged expression tried to steal the moment, but she quickly swiped his memory away. Right now, she needed to sit in the presence of Ra'ash. He would prepare her for what was to come, and she didn't want to miss this moment of restfulness and reassurance.

For more than two songs, F'lorna simply sat and allowed the atmosphere of worship to surround her and fill her. Several people had gotten up and began to dance the *Images of Jeyshen*. She also heard the sweet aroma of singing coming from soprano and tenor voices alike. She wondered for a brief second if Ra'ash wanted her to add her voice to the moment, but she had the feeling she needed to wait and listen and enjoy. She couldn't help the smile that drew her lips into a wide crescent. Something new lingered in the distance. She didn't know what. She allowed the image of her birth friends to filter through her mind, but none of their faces carried the weight of what was to come. She thought of her mother and then her father. His imaged remained. Something about her father, but not quite him. Maybe a father figure?

"What, Ra'ash? What are You up to?" she whispered.

"You will enter a time of unknowing," she heard the voiceless words say.

"What does that mean?" she wondered.

"I'll will be waiting for you on the other side. You do not have to worry. You will make your way through the darkness to the light."

"I don't understand," she said, opening her eyes.

"I have called you to write. Now I am calling you to gain sight."

F'lorna looked around at the other villagers lost in worship. They did not hear the words she had been given. She didn't know why fear filled her chest, forcing the air out. She couldn't explain it, but she felt like she was falling—not into the open sky—but deep within the belly of Rodesh. Hidden and lost, with only a distant light offering a fleck of hope to find her way out.

Chapter 2

LEAVING AT DUSK

R aecli didn't want to move from the thick, fiber-filled mattress that engulfed her. A colorful assortment of blankets surrounded her like strands of sweet grasses woven into a bird's nest. There was no reason to wake up anymore. Her Grandfather's voice could already be heard shouting orders to the servants. All he talked about was auraium, and she tired of the topic. He brought her south down the River to the land bridge where she knew no one. She had made new friends in the Northwestern Coast—other sons and daughters of wealthy merchants. There weren't many of them, but they had become close in the turn of the moon she had lived in the coastal cities. But here she was now back in River-dweller territory. She had seen them passing by, looking curiously at her grandfather's traveling case and their make-shift home created by wooden poles and sheets of heavy fabric.

She touched the turban around her head. Her wavy, dark hair poured like a waterfall at night from under the layered fabric. She should extract her horns already and be done with it. She would never fit in as a Sand-shaper with them still intact. She had barely memorized the Sand-shaper symbols before her Eternal Memory shut. She thought of the *Divine Oracle*. She hadn't memorized all the *Images and Chants of Jeyshen*. It didn't matter, though. The other Sand-shapers had very little perception of the *Divine Oracle*. She was stuck somewhere between a Sand-shaper and a River-dweller, much like F'lorna's mother was, but on the opposite end of the spectrum. Instead of having to weave twigs in her hair like T'maya, she now covered her horns with a turban.

As they had traveled down the River to get here, they passed Left River Hook. She had drawn the curtain in the traveling case briefly to take a look. She thought maybe F'lorna would be standing by the forest rim with her amber hair swirling in the breeze and her translucent grey eyes looking for her. She wasn't there. Just the rocky, dry ground that lined the River. F'lorna had moved on, and she had finally forced herself to do the same. She waited for many moon phases for F'lorna to come get her from the smoky coast, but she never came. Another Sand-shaper her age—who also had violet eyes—befriended her, filling the jagged hole that was clawed from her life.

Raecli's mind wandered to her mother. She had died of Smoke Sickness. She hated the smoke that obscured the Northwestern sky. The thick, sooty air concealed the Violet Moon almost every night. The air was fresher in the south, and the water cleaner. There were no friends here for her, though. Only servants she wasn't allowed to interact with. She felt lost, and her grandfather was no comfort. He forced his servants to dangle down the great stone cliffs of the waterfall from tree-bark ropes. The River could not be seen when looking directly down—only white sprays of intense water pounding the deep and rising into a dense, hazy fog. In the distance, though, the River snaked through the sandy hills like a bound rope that had been unwound and laid flat along the ground.

No one–not even her grandfather–knew where the River ended. His trusted steward, Moirel, a large man who also counseled him, suggested that the other side of the ocean was there—or the Great Expanse as her people called it. Raecli frowned. She disliked when both words from each dialect came into her mind. She had several words in her Eternal Memory from the Sand-shapers that overlapped with the River-dwellers. Even Eternal Memory was called the childhood memories by the Sand-shapers. But no matter how much her grandfather tried, he could never get rid of the River-dweller within her—with or without her horns.

14

"Raecli!" she heard her grandfather's voice. She quickly threw off the blankets and got up. She walked to the flap of the large tent that surrounded her sleeping quarters and walked outside.

"Yes, Grandfather," she said. He was talking to Moirel and some of his servants who handled short obsidian blades for digging through the stone wall. He held up his finger to her in a sign to be quiet. Then he looked back to his servants. "The obsidian is too weak. Each blade only gets us a few ounces of the auraium. We can't keep making these blades. We must find or create a denser material to cut through this stone wall."

"Lord Rencon, there are no Sand-shaper methods in all of Rodesh that offer us information on how to create a stronger substance. Obsidian is the strongest we have, but using it wears out the servants and they are cutting themselves. We were not prepared to be here so long. We must go back and analyze how we can better extract the auraium."

Raecli watched as her grandfather stared at the piles of golden stones all around them. "You are right. We must procure more help, and I know just who to ask. We need to look through my archive of cylinders and see if there is any mention of another material stronger than obsidian. We'll check the records beyond the Great Engulfing. The Lake-keepers were thought to be great warriors. They had to use weapons stronger than glass mixed with stone."

"Aren't the Lake-keepers only a myth?" Moirel asked.

"If they are written about in Sand-shaper symbols, they are not a myth. You forget my grandfather

15

and father left me one of the largest archives of cylinders in all the coastal cities. I've looked through hundreds of them and have yet to even read a tenth of what we own. Send a few of my men to Corven, the steward of my archives. He will find what I need. Have him look for any information about the Lake-keepers and gather those cylinders. Then bring them to me. I have a lot of reading to do if I'm going to create a tool to dig out the rest of this auraium."

"Yes, Lord Rencon," Moirel said.

"Start packing the auraium. I want most of it brought to my personal warehouses in the city. If any of my servants so much as take a spec of what's mine, I give authorization to have both their hands cut off. Put another pile in a trailer and have it brought with me. We are going to visit a certain landowner who may be interested in what I have to offer him."

Moirel nodded walked briskly away.

Lord Rencon finally looked toward Raecli who had been waiting. "Well, my granddaughter. How was your sleep? Still in bed, I see."

"I apologize, Grandfather. There is not much for me to do here, and I only get in the way. We are to go back home now?" she asked, hopefully.

"Not quite," he said. "I'm intending on making a deal with a powerful landowner just north of here. He owns most of the best farmlands below the coastal cities to the south marshlands. Very wealthy with grey eyes, that one. I wouldn't want to cross him, but he can be trusted. We are to visit him, and meet his—son," he finished, staring at Raecli.

She felt the heat from her cheeks rise. "Yes, Grandfather. I would like to meet new friends. I dearly miss my new ones at home."

He said nothing for a moment and continued to stare at her. "I intend that you marry this young man. His name is Lord Sabien. His father's name is Lord Tarmian."

Raecli inhaled, shocked.

"I see you have heard of him," her grandfather said amused.

"He is the landowner who supplies most of the meat and vegetation to the coastal cities," she answered. "I don't know much else about him other than we eat much of what he produces from his lands."

"His son is near eighteen years old. That is old enough to marry."

"I have not yet begun my fifteenth turn. My village does not allow us to seek relationships beyond friendship until we are sixteen turns," she said.

"That is not your village nor your people! So you need to stop acting like them and talking like them!" he yelled. "You are a Sand-shaper and daughter of the wealthiest merchant in all of Rodesh! Your mother never understood that, but you will!" He tried to calm his voice. "Nothing has been determined yet, but who can blame me for wanting to introduce my granddaughter to the wealthiest landowner's son? I have discovered Rodesh's hidden hoard of auraium. Soon I will control all of the Northwestern cities. Once I am in power in the north, I can start making my way to the southeast villages. Then the landowners will have to pay attention to me."

17

"But that is River-dweller territory," she said, trying to subdue the feeling of anguish rising.

"They are a simple, inferior race. It is time to incorporate them into real civilization. What's it to you? You have no family there."

Raecli looked down. She could sense her grandfather's volatile impulses rearing up. "My friends were my family."

Abruptly, she felt his hand grab the turban from her head and yank it off. Her horns wrenched from the pull and her neck twisted to the side.

"And those monstrosities will be extracted! We can't have you looking like a filthy River-dweller! Who will marry you then?" He threw the turban on the ground. "Get packed. We leave at dusk."

As her grandfather walked away, Raecli watched the long fabric of the turban slink along the stone ground with the swirling wind. It twisted and rolled faster and faster until it fluttered to the stone wall where the servants were building stockpiles of auraium. It got stuck behind one of the golden piles before a gust of wind whipped it around the pile. Finally, it flitted over the edge of the rocky cliff and fluttered down into the torrential waves below never to be seen again.

She walked to the edge of the waterfall and looked down. A mist of moisture surrounded her, dampening her body with a cool embrace. And the deafening roar of the water pounding the rockface engulfed her with a blanket of noise. She felt an odd sense of control. Her grandfather could try to dictate her every move, but she still had some freedom left over her life. She could jump off the cliff, and there was nothing he could do to stop her.

She wondered if Ra'ash would allow her into her Eternal Dwelling if she decided her fate. Life hadn't been a conscious choice of her own, so was it fair that she could consciously decide her death?

"Ra'ash," she whispered. "If you are here with me now, let me know. Please, send me anyone or anything to tell me to continue. Right now, death looks sweeter than life, and I'm tired of trying."

In that moment, she felt someone looking at her. She looked away from the rushing water and toward the stone cliffs where the servants were dangling from ropes and digging. There she saw a man with his bleeding hands covered in black dust from chipping his obsidian blade against the rock. He looked dirty and worn, and he wore a threadbare, filthy tunic and pants. He stared at her and slowly shook his head and waved his hand for her to back away from the cliff.

She obeyed and took several steps back. Not because he had told her too, but because he was in a worse state than she. If he could find a reason to live, she had no excuse not to at least hold on a little longer. Maybe Ra'ash was telling her to wait. Maybe hope lingered just over the horizon.

Lord Sabien crept up the porch steps of his family's expansive estate. He was thankful for the cloud cover that night. He hoped that none of the servants patrolling their lands saw him. He had no choice but to sneak out. That was the only way he could see her—Kysha, the steward's beautiful daughter. He loved her. He would take her away with him now if he had a place to go. His family was too well known. It would be impossible for them to hide in the coastal cities. Maybe the Northeastern Mountains? But what would he do there? He had nothing stored in his childhood memories except running the estate.

Kysha had learned very few skills herself. Her mother died when she was young, and her father never thought to teach her much beyond the Sand-shaper symbols. She didn't even know how to keep the steward's ledger because his father, Lord Tarmian, had banned it years ago. They were hopelessly unqualified for anything beyond their current positions—a landowner's son and a steward's daughter.

When he got to the double doors of his home, he tried to turn the knob but it was locked. But he remembered leaving it unlocked before he snuck out. A torchlight suddenly appeared on the other side of the window near the door. Then he heard a soft creak, and his father stepped out.

"Where were you, my son? With the steward's daughter again?" Lord Tarmian asked.

Sabien looked at his hands. "Father, let me explain."

"No!" his father snapped in a hushed voice. "I do not want to hear about where you have been and with whom. This needs to stop right this minute. You have one of the largest family estates to inherit, and I will not have you throw it all away for a mere servant girl.

Highborns do not marry servants. That is the way it has always been and will always be. Now, you had your fun, but this affair must end. If your mother finds out, she will force the girl out of the estate immediately. Do you want that to happen to Kysha?"

Sabien shook his head. "No, Father. Where would she go? She has nothing to offer."

"Exactly! She is good for nothing besides her pretty face and tall stature. Think about it, my son. She can add nothing to your life."

"She offers me love," Sabien countered.

"Of course she does! You're the landowner's son. Who else would a beautiful young girl choose to fall in love with? But listen to me. If you were just a farmhand, she would not love you. Her interest for you is buffered by your wealth and that is all."

Sabien said nothing. He knew any word he spoke would be disputed. His quietness seemed to calm his father.

"I am only doing what is best for you," Lord Tarmian sighed. "Now you must be ready. In a few days, a wealthy merchant will be visiting us with his granddaughter. She has violet eyes and is almost of marrying age. You know how your mother wishes for a grandchild with violet eyes. This girl may be the one to whom you are matched, so I demand that you to welcome her and get to know her. Do not treat her like you've treated the other landowners' daughters that have previously visited."

"But, Father!" Sabien began.

"No! I will not hear your complaints. If I see you with Kysha one more time, she will be sent away. Do you understand me?"

Sabien nodded his head.

"Go get some sleep. We will be inspecting the end of the harvest tomorrow."

"Yes, sir," Sabien said. He passed his father and walked into his expansive estate that felt more and more like a prison each passing day.

Chapter 3

STONE BRIDGE EXTRACTION

"I hear the waterfall," Eline said to F'lorna. "I believe it will be just beyond the clearing of trees ahead. Once we reach the rim of the forest, just sit and wait for me. Practice capturing every thought that tries to create fear in you. Don't let the Mountain Terror take root in your mind. Remember to imagine yourself safely tucked within your Achion tree at home. The Violet Moon is radiating all around you, and you hear the soft murmur of the tributary just outside of your family's cluster. You are not alone. The Indwelling rests within and around you."

23

"Yes, my aunt." F'lorna had an urge to reach to her hornless temple on the left side of her head, but instead she reached for the glass pendant around her neck. Whenever she fixated on her loss, it only caused her mind to fall into despair, which she would have to pull herself out of later. Most of the time, she felt good and confident with all that Ra'ash had allowed in her life. But when she faced hardships, her thoughts began to tell her that she was weak and incomplete. She was about to go home, and she didn't know if she would be accepted again as she was before.

Suddenly, her aunt grabbed her hand and pulled her out of her reverie. "F'lorna, I can see what you are doing," she said, sternly.

F'lorna looked at her aunt confused.

Eline exhaled. "When your thoughts go dark, it shows on your face. It's like a cloudy afternoon has landed on your grey eyes. They lose their light. And your face becomes burdened like a heavy stone sits upon it. You must capture those thoughts. They only lead to hopelessness, and you have too much to look forward to in life than to ache for what's been lost."

"I know," F'lorna said, looking away from her aunt. "Sometimes I feel good and other times I struggle. It is like the ground has swallowed up the path I was on, and now I must look for another one. But I don't know which way to go—all the paths feel uncomfortable to me. I want to go home, but I know it will not be the same."

Eline pulled F'lorna to her and wrapped her arms around her. "Those who are called to great things will never have it easy. Remember that. Rodeshians who have no trouble will never rise up because they have nothing to overcome. Every struggle that faces you is a gift from Ra'ash to become stronger and wiser."

F'lorna felt tears flow from her eyes. "I'm sorry, my aunt. At the last rise of the moon, I was totally fine and ready to go home. Maybe it is the thought of the stone bridge that causes me to doubt. My Mountain Terror is just another weakness I must carry."

Eline lifted her niece's chin. "Ra'ash has allowed you to have that sickness for a reason. You must believe it will cause you to overcome, and cause you to rise and fly. Will you do that? Will you clasp my words and bring them deep into your heart?"

F'lorna nodded. "Yes, I will."

"Good," Eline said and smiled. "We are almost there. Come and walk to that tree over there, and I will get you comfortable before I head to the stone bridge. It won't take me long. Limmian, the Spiritual Elder, told me that Sand-shapers have been spotted in their territory. They are taking much of their crops and animals to feed themselves. They carry some sort of sharp, black blade. They are doing something to the stone bridge—mining or building something—she doesn't know which."

"Should you go alone?" F'lorna asked.

Eline laughed. "They are not going to harm an old lady. Besides, I only want to see if the Marsh-landers are correct in their estimation that the Sand-shapers have traveled all this way to extract auraium. If that is true, all the elders of every village must know and be ready."

Once they got to the large Achion tree located just within the forest rim, Eline set her healing and traveling pack down. "Set your things here next to mine.

25

Stay out of sight and don't worry about me. I will be back shortly."

F'lorna nodded. She set down the traveling and healing pack she too had been carrying and sat down at the base of the tree, resting her back against the bark. "I will be fine here."

Eline walked into the clearing and absorbed the full scene of the intimidating land bridge. She had been to this very location before, but the ground shudders had changed everything. The River that once disappeared into the Desert Plains had now been exposed. It curved down the middle of the sandy hills and scurried off somewhere in the distant horizon. Just before the River fell into a massive waterfall, a thick land bridge connected the west and east shores of the River. Where they once walked through sand to get to the opposite side was now replaced with a jagged stone bridge that looked much like an aged Achion tree laid on its side.

She observed several small tents on either side of the River secured to the land just before the grassy floor made way to stone. There were two larger tents on the west side of the River furthest away from the cliffs and closer to the forest rim. Thick fabrics were draped over the many fastened wooden poles, protecting the highborn Sand-shapers dwelling within them. She could not make out the details of the fabric from so far away, but she knew they were ornate.

Sand-shapers were extremely hierarchical. A highborn family came with many servants. From what T'maya had told her and from her own travels, she knew that only a few wealthy landowners from the west farmlands and a few wealthy merchants from the coastal cities had power and prestige that dated back before the *Great Engulfing*. The rest of the Sand-shapers were servants. As of late, however, many servants were unhappy with their lifestyle and living conditions. They wanted to leave the farmlands and coastal cities in favor of the Northeastern Mountains or even the River-dwellers' villages. This caused the families in power to reign in more control. The so-called servants were more like slaves now—unable to leave and create their own destiny independent of the wealthy few. Eline thought of Weston and the other Marsh-landers and sent voiceless words for their protection. *May Ra'ash keep them secluded and lost to the world of Rodesh.*

Eline noticed a young hornless Sand-shaper walking up to her. His skin had been tanned brown from the Heat Source. His clothes were covered in black dust, and his face and hands were smudged with dark pasty grime. She saw dirty bandages and instinctively knew that they had soaked up blood many moons ago.

"You do not belong here, old River-dweller," he said loudly.

"I offer you my apology of healing," she began. She needed to speak up, so she could be heard over the roar of the waterfall. "I am a Healing Elder," she shouted. "I see that your hands need tending."

He looked at his hands and thought for a moment. "Wait here," he stated and walked off.

Eline took the moment while he was gone to further inspect the scene. Sure enough, she saw piles of the yellow stones Merriton had worn around his neck. They were extracting auraium—and lots of it from what she could see. All the piles were on the opposite side of the River close to the large tents. She looked toward the overhanging cliffs on either side of the waterfall. There were long ropes wrapped around boulders and protrusions in the stone earth that were then thrown on either side of the falling River. *Dangerous work*, she thought. She tried to imagine how the servants were performing their task—dangling from ropes on either side of a torrential waterfall using the black blades they held to dig the auraium out from the rocky grip of Rodesh itself.

She shook her head. Not safe at all. She was glad F'lorna was not inspecting this intimidating view. Unfriendly land, indeed.

She spied the hornless Sand-shaper returning with an older one. She noted his hands were not bandaged, and his clothes appeared freshly washed.

"I am told that you are a healer," he said, gruffly when he approached her.

"Yes," she hesitated, wondering if she should have used another excuse to get close. "I saw that his hands needed tending, so I offered my services as required by my Adoration."

"Adoration?" he asked. "Never mind. We require a healer. We are leaving these lands when the sun sets and returning to the coast. We have need of your services. We will pay you for your work."

"How many of your people need of healing?"

"Almost all of the servants need tending. The land is different down here—harder. We can't cut through this stone so easily. And we don't know the landscape, so we can't find any of the medicinal plants we recognize. Some of their blisters are swollen and many of their cuts are burning like flames. I cannot risk going back while they are untreated lest we lose some on our long travel home."

"Why did you not bring a healer?" she asked unsatisfied with the state of the servants.

"We did not know we would be staying so long, but unexpected conditions changed our plans."

Eline kept her eyes on the Sand-shaper. She did not want him to think she noticed the auraium. If he saw her as a threat, he might not let her go freely. "My medicine bag is just back there in the forest. I will go fetch it. But I will not be able to make it over that land bridge," she said pointing. "Your servants will have to come here if they want me to tend to their wounds. I will need a fire, fresh cloths and many large bowls of freshwater."

"Only do what needs to be done to get them home. We have a schedule to keep," he said. "We can tend to them more once we arrive home."

The Sand-shaper left her. She turned and began her trek back to the forest where F'lorna waited. She could use F'lorna's help, but she worried about her Mountain Terrors striking her. It was best just to have her wait. She felt an innate need to hide F'lorna. She didn't want the Sand-shapers to know that her niece was there. One extra night wouldn't delay their travels too much. They would begin their journey back to Right River Hook before the Heat Source rose in the morning. Then she would tell every Village Elder that the Sand-shapers would be back. The auraium they had extracted so far was merely a taste of what was to come.

Lemmeck smoothly pulled the stems, allowing the yellow roots to pop out of the ground. He had gotten better at harvesting the roots once Le'ana showed him how to properly pull them without causing so much soil to fly into his face from the force. He smiled and shook his head. His twin brothers had found reason to leave before the Heat Source awoke that morning. He had a suspicion that they knew Le'ana was asking for help with the last of the harvest. Lemmeck didn't mind. He looked at Sage pulling roots alongside him. Friends helped each other. Besides, he knew that Le'ana would offer him some of the vegetables once they were done. That wasn't the reason why he agreed to help, but it was a benefit.

"Le'ana, you know that I love you, which is the only reason I stick my hands into the dirt for you," Sage said. Her burgundy hair gleamed in the light, and her light green eyes seemed to glow as perspiration glistened off her umber cheeks.

Le'ana stood and wiped sweat from her forehead with the back of her hand. Her scarlet hair was tied back and her speckled, pale skin had a hint of pink all over. "This is not dirt. It's well-tilled soil. Not all of us get to sing for our Adoration. Besides, I would rather be in the dirt than on stage with everyone looking at me. No thank you."

Sage smiled in thought. "I feel alive on stage, singing the *Songs of the Prophets* and *Chants of Jeyshen*. Watching the villagers fall into worship before Ra'ash gives me such a feeling of purpose. I'm so relieved Elder Trenton didn't get his way. The Shoam-sha has been part of our way of life since the very beginning of Rodesh. If we lost it, we also would have to do away with the Dancing and Singing Adorations. Who has ever heard of such a thing?"

Lemmeck felt anger rise inside of him. Any time someone mentioned the Fishing Elder's name, resentment bombarded his emotions. Elder Trenton was the reason F'lorna had to leave for a full moon phase right when he began revealing his feelings toward her. It didn't matter now. F'lorna would be back at Right River Hook soon, and Elder Trenton realized he didn't have as much power as he thought he had—though, several families still agree with him.

"I love how you three work together so well," Elder Jaquarn said, as he walked onto Le'ana's land with his wife, Elder T'maya.

"Spiritual Elder, my father is not here. He is with the other Planting Elders preserving the rest of our harvest for winter," Le'ana said, walking up to F'lorna's parents.

"That is quite alright. I've come here to speak to you three," Jaquarn said. "F'lorna should arrive any rise now, and T'maya thought it would be a wonderful idea to prepare a celebratory dinner for F'lorna and a few of her friends."

"I'll be making several of F'lorna's favorite dishes," T'maya added. "I want her to know how much she has been missed."

Lemmeck noted that F'lorna's parents were not celebrating with the entire village at the Village Achion cluster. Probably a good idea, but it was still indicative of the tension that still existed between their family and the rest of Right River Hook.

"We wanted to invite Ralona also. We know that she and F'lorna became close as they gathered the sinews at the River this summer," Jaquarn said. "Would one of you extend our invitation to her?"

Lemmeck looked to Sage and Le'ana. They were both quiet, so he decided to simply offer the truth. "Her parents have not allowed her to visit with us since F'lorna left."

"I have not seen any misgivings in her father," Jaquarn said.

"That may be, Elder Jaquarn," Lemmeck said, "but she is still banned from seeing us beyond village meetings and the Shoam-sha."

"There is no sense fretting over it," T'maya said too quickly. "F'lorna will feel completely honored with the presence of the three of you. And, Lemmeck, please do invite your brothers."

"Yes, Elder T'maya," he said.

"We'll let you three get back to harvesting. I sense the cooler weather will be coming our way soon," Jaquarn said. He turned to leave but instead walked briskly to where Lemmeck was pulling roots.

"I wanted to talk with you briefly about the pendant you made F'lorna," he said in a hushed voice. "It is very beautiful, and I see you are wearing a similar one."

Lemmeck looked down. The cylinder pendant he had made with the mane of a White Diamond Stag enclosed in the melted glass dangled from a sinew around his neck. "Yes, is this gift acceptable to you?"

"The fact that you have given her a gift is completely acceptable to me. I'm honored by you and your family. It's just I worry about the gift itself. It is a Sand-shaper cylinder, and they have been banned from Right River Hook. Although I don't completely agree with the decision, we must be willing to enforce what has been decided to keep the peace."

"Even if the enforcement of such a rule shuns the ones you love?" Lemmeck asked.

"It does not shun—only tries to ignore, I think."

Lemmeck could tell that Jaquarn had been struggling with his thoughts about the course Right River Hook was on. A direction that did not include a Sand-shaper wife and a daughter born of both worlds. He could see the concern in Jaquarn's eyes and the weight of someone who cared deeply about his village and family.

"I understand your love for this village and your desire to keep the peace. However, I gave F'lorna this necklace to express that I care for her—all of her, including the Sand-shaper in her who writes symbols and who wants her mother to have the *Divine Oracle*. I wear this pendant as a dividing line to others. They can either accept me with it or reject me. Either way, I will not allow a desire for peace and fitting in to supersede my feelings for F'lorna."

"Are you insinuating that I do not care about my family?" Jaquarn asked, trying to conceal his irritation.

"Not at all, Elder Jaquarn. I know you care for them deeply, but I fear that Right River Hook does not.

And I am not willing to keep the peace for their indifference to continue."

Elder Jaquarn straightened. "And you think F'lorna would say the same thing?"

Lemmeck shrugged. "I don't know about her feelings in regards to the pendant I have made her, but I know her feelings towards her mother. She will continue to side with T'maya, and that will cause Right River Hook to push her farther away."

Jaquarn sighed and looked to T'maya who was now helping Le'ana pull the yellow roots from the soil. Her dark hair fell around her shoulders, and she laughed when she flung soil into her face after pulling the root too hard. "Lemmeck, you see how the soil is violently dispersed if the root is pulled out too quickly?"

"Yes, I see that," Lemmeck said.

"That's what I fear for my daughter and my wife. I don't want them to be pulled too quickly because I can't control the effects."

"I understand," Lemmeck said. "But they are stronger than you think, and only Ra'ash has complete control."

Chapter 4

FOREST HIDING

F'lorna heard her aunt's footsteps coming through the dried grasses beyond the forest. Although she wouldn't look toward the sound, she knew the pattern of her aunt's walk from traveling by her side for a moon phase. She noted the roar of the waterfall in the distance, so she kept her ears attentive to the sounds of the forest – shaking leaves, chirping birds and the rustling of forest critters. Her aunt had not taken as long as she thought. She had just begun examining how the particles of the air came to life within the light of the Heat Source streaking through the shadows of the forest. But when she heard movement, she quickly got up and decided to ready their bags for their departure home. Eline would want to leave right away with the information she had uncovered.

"No, you can put those down," her aunt said as she entered the tree line. "We won't be leaving yet."

"What happened?" F'lorna asked, trying to mask her disappointment.

"One of the Sand-shapers asked me what I was doing there, and I explained to him that I was a Healing Elder and I wanted to look at his wounded hands. He got someone in charge who has asked me to tend to the whole lot of them."

"Are there many of them?"

Eline sighed and nodded. "Yes. I didn't want to refuse them. I was afraid that they might think I was sneaking around gathering information—which I was."

"I can help. If it's basic wound care, I know what to do."

"I thought about it, but I would have to bring them here and expose you. I think it's best that you stay hidden in the forest and wait. An old lady like me is nothing to bother with. You have grey eyes, and I know that those are a sign of prestige with the Sand-shapers. They'll be curious about you and ask who you are. I'd rather they not know you are here."

F'lorna reached to her left temple. "I only have one horn. They may think I'm them—" F'lorna stopped. "Which I am half Sand-shaper. I never really thought of it like that. Now my missing horn matches who I am—mixed."

Eline leaned toward F'lorna. "River-dweller, Marsh-lander, Sand-shaper…we are all Children of Ra'ash. We are all different, but we are all Rodeshian. You are unique, and that is a good thing. Don't forget that."

"Yes, Aunt," F'lorna said.

Eline bent down and grabbed both medicine packs. "I will take both bags. I'll probably run out of all my supplies that we've gathered. Those Sand-shapers are digging into the rockface on either side of the waterfall. Dangerous. They are using black knives. I don't know what the material is, but it's cutting their hands."

"Do they have auraium?" F'lorna asked.

"Loads of it. From what I can see, they've only tapped the surface of the rockface. There may be much more. Sand-shapers excel at building. The bridge they built to connect the Northwestern Coast to the Northeastern Mountains just before the River splinters into the Four Horns is massive and wonderous. I've only seen it at a distance from the lower part of the mountain, but, let me tell you, it makes the tiny bridge we built at North River Hook look simple in comparison."

F'lorna had the urge to look toward the land bridge, but resisted. "Do you think they will build a bridge here?"

Eline nodded. "I can almost guarantee it. They were not prepared this time. They came here simply to inspect the land bridge and see if the rumors of auraium were true. But even unprepared they have extracted much. They will be back ready to build a bridge and whatever else they need to create to mine the deep rockface. I fear they may establish their presence here permanently, and bring many Sand-shapers with them to work."

"But they can't do that. There is no room for them here. All the livable land has been taken by villages and the animals who make the territory their home. With that many workers, the land around the River will not sustain them. Nothing grows there. They won't be able to fit." F'lorna felt fear rising her in chest. Sand-shapers had no home in River-dweller territory. She stared at her aunt waiting for a reply of solace, but her aunt gave none. Her expression became even more solemn.

"You are right. They don't fit, but they will take the room they need. They will confiscate our lands, and when that is not enough, they will enslave our people. River-dwellers have but two choices: we can hide or we can fight," Eline said, matter-of-factly.

"But we haven't fought wars since before the *Great Engulfing.* We don't have weapons. The Lake-keepers were the warriors, and they are all gone. How can we defend ourselves?" F'lorna thought of Lemmeck. "We have hunters."

"Thankfully, all the villages have Hunting Adoration. It is a crucial Adoration to the livelihood of our people. We must warn the Elders and let them prepare, starting with the southern villages. They are the closest to the land bridge. Though, all the villages must be prepared because the Sand-shapers travel the full

38

length of the River to return to the coast. At any time they can enter a village along the way."

F'lorna's head felt dizzy. She could barely comprehend what her aunt was telling her. An image of Rae'cli's grandfather coming into her Achion cluster at night and stealing her birth friend came into her mind. He had easily infiltrated their village and taken what he wanted.

"I know these are difficult words to hear, F'lorna. But you are a Novice Elder now, and I will need your help to notify all the villages. Now, I best hurry and get back to the land bridge. Stay here and out of sight. Don't look for me. The scene over there is extremely unfriendly. Stay here and focus your thought on the forest. Remember how I taught you to capture the images that try to make their way into your mind?"

"Yes," F'lorna whispered. "Please hurry. I don't want to be alone here."

"I will go as fast as I can," she said and smiled. She leaned toward F'lorna and wrapped her niece into her arms. "Not to worry, my dear niece. They have to leave before the Heat Source descends the Upper Realm. I won't be gone long. You just stay hidden, and no harm will come to you."

Raecli walked along the thin tree line away from the sound of the roaring waterfall and the chipping away of rock. The constant noise of her grandfather shouting near her sleeping quarters and the clinking of the auraium began to grate on her. The hum of the forest beckoned her to enjoy the cool, fall morning. Her grandfather warned her that this area to the west of the River was dangerous marshlands, but from what she could see, the ground was dry now that autumn was upon them.

The land she now walked was slightly different from her childhood home of Right River Hook, but she still heard the tweets of forest birds and the low rushing of wind blowing through thick grasses. The aroma of the forest cloaked her with childhood memories, and for a moment she could imagine her life was as it should be. The noises were so different from the lapping waves and city noises of the Northwestern Coast. They were softer and slower here but just as profound—maybe even more so.

She spied movement up ahead and wondered what forest animal was scurrying through the thick, marshy floor. When she saw little horns on a young boy, she stopped. She didn't remember any River-dwellers being so far south on the west side of the River. The young boy smiled and giggled, and he kept looking back like he was looking at something following him. Raecli looked behind the boy and watched as a young fear-stricken mother quietly ran after the boy. She had no horns and was dressed in the basic outfit of a Sand-shaper servant. The mother finally caught up with the boy and snatched him up in her arms. She gently covered his mouth and whispered something in his ear.

The mother turned and her mouth fell open when she saw Raecli watching her. The mother did not move and waited for her reaction. Raecli hadn't realized people were living in the marshlands, especially Sand-shapers.

She stared at the young mother until she understood that she had to do something. She smiled and waved at the woman to go back into the marshlands. The woman placed her hand slowly over her mouth and bowed several times. Raecli nodded and again waved for her to go back into the marshlands. Finally, the young mother wrapped the boy close against her chest and made her way into the thicket.

Raecli instantly began walking back to main part of the River where her sleeping quarters were located. She couldn't explain it, but her grandfather could not know that Sand-shapers were living in the marshlands. Raecli recognized the look in the Sand-shaper's eyes. It was the same look her mother had when she began showing signs of Smoke Sickness—a look of fear that something could be lost.

"Raecli! I need you here now!"

Raecli felt her hands become cold even though her brisk walked had warmed them. She instinctively drew her hand to her forehead and rubbed her horns. She knew why her grandfather wanted them to be extracted. He wanted her to be presentable for the landowner's son. Her grandfather once doted on her, but now his façade of tenderness faded like the last rays of the Heat Source or sun, as the Sand-shapers say. But what could she do? After many moon phases of planning to escape, she never did leave. Instead, she created friendships to fill the void of everything she lost.

"Raecli!" Another demand rang out. She knew now that her grandfather was in no mood for her to disobey.

"Coming, Grandfather. I was just taking a walk." She ran into the clearing and the noise of the waterfall engulfed her once more. Her grandfather stood outside of her sleeping quarters waiting impatiently. She noticed that he tried to contain the irritation that permeated his aged face.

"Fate has brought you luck today, my granddaughter," he began. "There is a healer on the other side of the bridge. She will have medicines to numb your pain when Moirel extracts your horns. Then she can bandaged you, so you will be almost completely healed by the time we get to Lord Tarmian's lands."

Raecli had an urge to run, but she knew it would be no use. Her grandfather's men would chase her down and capture her. If she truly had wanted to leave, she should have done it the night they had passed the lands of Left River Hook. But even then, she knew her grandfather would attack any villagers who harbored her. He would never rest until she was found. And if she didn't obey his whims, life would be miserable for her. Maybe it was better that she marry the landowner's son. She would be away from her grandfather's control. She would be mistress of her own lands, but it came at the sacrifice of her horns, the last remaining piece of her wonderful childhood with her mother and F'lorna. She ached for her best birth friend. The Smoke Sickness that had taken her mother had also stolen her childhood from her. The coastal cities were filled with plumes of smoke. Going to the farmlands would be better for her. Hopefully, she could escape her mother's fate. And maybe—someday—she could find F'lorna again.

"Yes, Grandfather. I am ready."

Instantly, her grandfather's face relaxed and was replaced with a serene expression that came so easily when people obeyed and circumstances were going his way. "Good. You will be free from those bondages trapped to your head and the myths of Ra'ash and His dying Son. I will have Moirel take you over the land bridge. It is very slick, so watch your every step."

"Yes, Grandfather," Raecli nodded. She waited while her grandfather found his chief servant. She looked toward the great land bridge. It would be so easy to slip over the edge and fall into the deep, ending her constant struggle to stay happy. Her list of things to look forward to was running out. If the landowner's son was as horrible as her grandfather, she would return here and dive into her eternal dwelling.

"Ra'ash," she whispered. "Are You still with me? Do You see me? Don't be angry with me."

She waited to hear voiceless words back, but only the droning of the waterfall surrounded her.

Chapter 5

COLLISION OF PATHS

Raecli carefully walked behind Moirel. She didn't like that she had to hold his hands, but the stone ground was uneven and slippery from the ever-present mist surrounding the land bridge. The roar of the waterfall was thunderous around them. It reminded her of the night that Rodesh shook. She had been entertaining her new friends for dinner—one of her favorite things to do. Her grandfather had many servants, and they would serve luxurious meals and put on entertaining shows when guests came over. Her grandfather condoned these extravagant dining experiences because her friends were also members of highborn families. Most of them had violet eyes like herself, but none of them were as wealthy as she.

They were in the middle of dining when the ground and walls of her coastal mansion began convulsing. Much of her home was made with glass, and the crashing sound of shattering glass tore through the air. Several servants were badly wounded. Luckily, she and her guests were seated on oversized, stuffed fabric bags around the low, long table. None of them were badly wounded beyond a few cuts and imbedded slivers of glass.

The ground shudders destroyed much of the Northwestern Coastal cities. Many of her grandfather's factories had been completely decimated or—at the least—in need of much repair. Quite a few of them needed to be completely demolished and rebuilt. Raecli wondered if that was why her grandfather was so eager to travel south down the River to see if the rumors about auraium were true. Had he lost so much that he was desperate to recoup his losses? Raecli knew that Right River Hook probably wasn't as affected by the ground shudders as the Sand-shaper cities. River-dwellers live simply and they did not shape glass. She had wondered if F'lorna worried about her that night. Or had she already been forgotten?

"Watch your step!" Moirel shouted.

Raecli hadn't been paying attention to her steps and her right foot came so close to the edge that her knees buckled slightly. She quickly regained her footing and refocused on the immediate path before her. She could see the end to the land bridge just ahead. There were more piles of auraium on the east side of the waterfall that they were taking across the land bridge. She didn't know how they would carry it all back to the coast. There was so much. Hopefully, it was enough for her grandfather to rebuild. Maybe he wouldn't have to come back after all. His presence in the south lands would eventually be noticed by the River-dwellers if it hadn't already. They would not want the Sand-shapers here for long, but she wondered if they would do anything about it. River-dwellers valued peace above wealth.

"We are here," Moirel said, letting go of her hands. "Sit by the fire over there."

She looked toward where he was pointing. Several servants were sitting around the fire with their injured hands resting on their laps. They looked tired and depressed. She was glad she was not one of them, but she too was facing pain and sacrifice. Her horns would be extracted. She couldn't imagine anything more painful. As she walked to the fire, one of the servants sitting on a large boulder got up and motioned for her to sit. She sat down and tried not to look at anyone in the face.

Suddenly, she heard Moirel's raised voice. "You will do as I say!"

"No, I will have no part of it. Extracting horns is a monstrous procedure, and I will not do it!"

Raecli looked behind her. She saw the back of an old woman. She had horns, so she must be a healer from a local village.

"I do not expect you to extract them!" he shouted. "How would a River-dweller know the proper way to extract those bondages from her head? I only need medicine to help with the pain. And when I am done, I simply need you to bandage the area, so she doesn't get an infection. It will be done whether you agree to help or not. But I do not want to go back to my master and tell him that his granddaughter had to experience it without medicinal aid. And if you refuse to bandage her wounds and something happens to her on the way back north, he will hold you personally responsible. Look, I'm telling you in all honesty. You do not want to cross Lord Rencon. He always gets what he wants—either the easy way or the hard way. Her horns will be extracted this very moment."

Raecli watched the old woman's shoulders drop in resignation. She couldn't hear what she murmured, but she leaned down to one of the bags she had brought and started rummaging through it. She found what she was looking for and handed it to Moirel. "Have her put these dried herbs in hot tea. Let them seep until they are soft and the water turns a yellowish-brown. Then have her drink it all. She will still feel the procedure, but the pain will be dulled."

Raecli's hand rushed up to her horns. She would no longer be a River-dweller. She didn't know what she feared most. The physical pain or emotional pain of losing them. There was nothing she could do. There was nowhere she could go. She had no family other than her grandfather. She closed her eyes when she felt tears slide down their edges. She knew the servants around her were watching her. She did not want them to see her breakdown. She knew too well how the servants talked about the highborn families like they were a form of entertainment.

"Everyone!" Moirel yelled. "Leave us. Go down to the River and wash the grime off your bodies. We will be leaving soon." He stopped. "Where are you going?"

"I'll wait in the forest. I'll be back when it's done," the old woman replied.

"Don't go far or I'll send my servants after you. They will find you."

"I understand," she said.

Raecli heard the servants around her leaving the fire. They began walking back down toward the River. Raecli opened her eyes. As she did, she saw the old woman pass by her. She was looking straight ahead, but in a brief moment she looked her way and their eyes locked.

"Elder Eline," Raecli whispered.

Eline instantly stopped. "Raecli?"

"There is no need to talk with her, old healer. I'll call you when I'm done."

Raecli looked to Moirel. He was fetching water from a large, stone basin. He poured the water into a smaller glass bowl. Then he took the slender glass shovel and scooped up several small stones that were heated by the fire. He poured the stones in the glass bowl with water.

Eline was about to say something, but her face became resolute, and she turned and continued walking away.

Raecli's heart began to pound rapidly and she looked toward the forest where Elder Eline was walking. Could F'lorna be in there? Or at the farming village that was not far away? If Eline was traveling this far south, F'lorna might be with her since she was a Novice Elder now. It made sense that F'lorna would learn healing along with her Adoration of Dance. Dance alone would limit what she could give back to the community.

"Here," Moirel said gruffly, handing her the glass bowl. "The water is hot so be careful. Give the herbs a moment longer to seep."

Raecli wanted to continue looking for her friend, so she quickly grabbed a bowl and stared at the browning liquid.

"I will have to use great force. I will be twisting your horns and then pulling them out. You will hear a crack before I pull. When your grandfather comes, he will be holding your head from moving. I can do it very quickly, but you must be very still."

The breath left her body and she felt more tears streaming down her face. She couldn't hold back her fear any longer.

"Now drink the medicine. It will help relax you."

Raecli brought the bowl to her lips. Her hands were shaking and the drops began to spill down the sides of the bowl. The liquid was very hot, but she took big sips. Eline had seen her and walked away. There was nowhere for her to go. She looked toward the forest rim again. Eline was gone—hidden in the trees. She saw no one else there. F'lorna had probably not come with her or else she would have seen her by now. She looked toward the land bridge. Her grandfather was carefully making his way down the stone ledge with a servant leading him. She continued to drink the hot liquid. She didn't know if she should drink the herbs, but she allowed them to slip into her mouth and down her throat. She wanted to go numb. She didn't want to feel anymore. She thought of the landowner's son, Sabien. Maybe he would be different. Maybe her horns were really forms of bondage, like her grandfather said, instead of signs of honor.

She drained the bowl of liquid just as her grandfather walked into her view. "This will be painful, but the freedom you will have once those bondages are gone is worth the momentary discomfort. Moirel is strong and quick. He will have them out in a moment. Then we will have that healer come over here and bandage your wounds, and you can rest in the traveling case as we begin to make our way to Lord Tarmian's lands."

Raecli set the bowl down calmly. "Yes, Grandfather."

F'lorna listened as her aunt's footsteps came closer. She heard much movement on the other side of her tree like the Sand-shapers were leaving, but she dared not look. She felt her resolve wane, and it was getting more difficult to control her thoughts. The Heat Source had already begun its descent and the Violet Moon would be rising over the hills soon. She did not want to sit and hide anymore. She was ready to return to her Achion cluster. She missed her parents and her friends.

Eline finally walked into the forest and F'lorna could tell something was very wrong. She stood up.

"What is it, my aunt? Why do you look concerned, no sad? Or are you scared?" F'lorna asked. She had never seen such a mixture of emotions on her aunt's face before. Not even the night of the ground shudders when her mother had fainted did Eline look as worried as she did now.

"You must go, F'lorna. Right away! Go back to the village and go straight to Elder Limmian. Tell her that I have been asked to help the Sand-shapers at the land bridge for the night, and I will return before the Violet Moon retreats in the morning."

"Aunt Eline, what is wrong. I see something grave troubles you. Are the Sand-shapers keeping you? I will not let them take you. We can both leave right now." F'lorna grabbed her aunt's hand and began to pull her deeper into the forest.

"No!" Eline shouted. "I'm sorry, F'lorna. I can't explain it now, but you must hurry. Leave! Run away from here before it's too late!"

"You are scaring me. I don't want to leave you. Tell me what's wrong!"

Suddenly, a familiar scream cut through the forest.

F'lorna's head instantly turned to the sound of the voice. "Raecli!"

She felt her legs begin to move drawn by the sound of her best birth friend in pain. "Raecli! Raecli!"

"F'lorna, no!" Her aunt yelled. "Your Mountain Terror!"

F'lorna used her arms to propel her forward as her legs kicked long strides. She could see her now. An old man was holding her head, and another, larger man had his hand on her horn. Blood spilled out from the empty socket on the other side of her forehead.

"Let her go!" F'lorna yelled, as her long legs deftly ran up the stone cliff. She saw the land bridge in the distance, and she felt her head begin to spin. "No! No! Ra'ash help me!"

"F'lorna!" she heard Raecli yell just before another piercing scream echoed off the stone cliffs and fell into the roar of the waterfall. F'lorna ran faster. Her feet barely touched the ground, and she felt as if her body were almost flying. She was almost to her friend who had passed out from the pain. She would grab her hand this time and never let go. They would have to drag her with them all the way back to the coastal cities.

"Take her! And get her over the land bridge now," the old man said, letting Raecli's head droop to the side as blood continued to pour out both sockets.

The bigger man grabbed Raecli and threw her over his shoulders.

"F'lorna, stop!" she heard her aunt say from behind her. "Don't go any further!"

F'lorna didn't listen. She saw Raecli's hand swaying over the back of the large Sand-shaper. If she could just grab her hand, everything would be okay. Everything would go back to the way it should be.

F'lorna saw the land bridge coming closer and her legs began to give out. She willed them to keep running, but they wobbled violently. She fell to her knees and began to crawl desperately over the hard ground. She looked up just in time to see Raecli's hand disappear in the mist surrounding the land bridge.

"Stop her!" she heard the old man shout. She knew who he was now. The grandfather who had ripped her life away from her. She continued to crawl as anger filled her body. She would not let him steal Raecli again. She crawled faster, but her vision began to blur. The roar of the waterfall taunted her. The sharp edges of the rocky floor tore into her hands and knees. She closed her eyes. The ground under her hands felt wet. Water began to seep into her pants. She continued crawling, keeping her eyes squeezed shut. A misty atmosphere engulfed her and the growl of the waterfall was now deafening. She must be on the land bridge now. She tried to imagine she was crawling on the soft floor of the forest, but the crashing rumble mocked the image.

She thought of Raecli's lifeless hand dangling. She would grab it. She needed to grab her hand and never let go. She reached out trying to find the tender, warm hand of her friend. But she only felt air. Where was it? It was right there in front of her. She reached out again. She felt something tug her and she went limp. Her mind slept as her body plummeted down the ravenous waterfall. And she dreamed that she was back at South Village, floating on the wooden raft along the soft current of the circular tributary. Around and around she floated until, finally, she woke up asleep.

Chapter 6

THE FISHERMAN

Morgo loved his life. His wife, Voddie, just had their second son, Paxton. Their son, Range, was two years old and overflowing with energy. He had inherited his father's small but thriving fishing business. His family was secure and comfortable. Did he mention his wife was the most sought after maiden in all of East Basin? With her red tendrils and her milky white skin, she had been a favorite of their village. Her dark eyes had a hint of scarlet that reflected the sun. She had chosen him, and his family paid a dear price for her—

one of their best fishing boats and a complete set of fine rods. But she was more valuable than all the boats of Domus Lake.

He smiled and looked at the pile of fish in his little boat. His workers were running his three larger boats that day, so he took the little one out to catch his wife's favorite fish—Sukio. It was the hardest fish to find and usually lingered near the warmer water closer to the desert. He had to row into Highland Cliff territory to find them, which took him all morning. He didn't worry about the swordsmen interrupting his work, though. They were miners and traded their metals for fish and produce. They knew nothing of fishing. Although, much of that might change if the Chieftains from Highland Cliffs and East Basin merge. He wondered if the constant warring from all the Chieftain families would finally stop. Would having one strong leader promote peace?

Morgo shook his head. Not even the Befores could anticipate the Chieftain's actions, especially Lothar bar Haven. His extreme volatility was incited due to his inability to produce an heir. Lothar had the largest spread of lands, all the metals at his disposal and a wall filled with Goliathan heads, but he did not have a family—only a discarded line of wives. That's why Morgo liked to keep things small and hidden. He would keep his family safe and happy by staying out of the way. He would pay his twenty percent tax gladly to whichever chieftain controlled East Basin, and right now that was Darmin bar Holthen family. They could take their portion as long as they left his family alone.

He felt a cool breeze ripple over his boat. The winds had shifted and cooled. Autumn had already begun. Fishing would slow down as the days grew colder, but he would have enough dried meat to sell through the winter months at a much higher price. Salted fish was a difficult and expensive process, but Lake-keepers loved this delicacy. He enjoyed winter most. He could sleep in through the morning, play with his kids and spend hours walking Atlatl Forest with his wife. She was not only beautiful but intelligent, as well. She questioned life and its purpose. Things he never contemplated but enjoyed listening about. She would also make up songs and sing them. She had over a hundred traditional Lake-keeper songs in her youth memories, but she added songs daily—songs about things she could see, touch and smell and even taste. He enjoyed sitting by the fire at nights, drinking his root ale while listening to her recite old songs and new ones.

Though his lands were small and he only owned one pier in the lake and a few boats, he was a rich man, indeed. He looked down at his pile of fish again. He had only half a dozen of the Sukio fish. He wanted to get a few more, so his wife could invite over her family for dinner and make her favorite recipe. Her brothers were healthy eaters. He needed at least eight fish, but ten would be best. He reeled in the lure he had been using. Time to switch to live bait. He looked up. The sun was right overhead. He had about an hour to fish, and then he would have to begin rowing home. He'd get home just as Voddie was finishing dinner. She would worry if he returned late.

He put the small baitfish on the metal hook. The metal was sharp. He traded much of his fish to purchase the raw metal to make his reels, hooks and knives. His ancestors once used bone, which could not contend with the durability and usability of the metal. He still owned several ivory hooks and knives passed down to him from his great-grandfather, though. They were not in use; rather, they rested on a soft cloth in a small wooden chest his father had made—a wedding gift over three years ago.

Morgo whipped the thin line made up of carefully processed and stretched animal intestines and it buzzed across the air and into the water near the cliffs. The crashing waves upon the rocky shore produced a melodic sound that he loved. Maybe it wouldn't be so bad if the Highland Cliffs and the East Basin territories united. He wouldn't mind having some land where the forest met up with the cliffs. No one lived on the borders since the lands were always under dispute, but if the two territories merged, he could pay for some lands. He had plenty of coins stashed from both Chieftain Lothar and Chieftain Darmin. A merger would make both coins valuable beyond their worth in metal. And if the merged territories conquered all of the Lake-keepers, his coins would be valuable to everyone. Now, he knew his life couldn't get much better. Either way, the tide swayed, he couldn't lose.

In the distance, he heard the screech of a scavenger bird. He looked toward the cliffs. Sure enough, a few scavengers were flying and more perched in the cliffs. There must be a dead animal on the shore. He reeled in his bait. He couldn't pass up the opportunity to harvest some bone, intestines and fresh meat if possible. Although bone wasn't used for fishing, it was still valuable for making jewelry and other non-essential items. If he gathered enough, he could have a headpiece created for his wife. One of his best fishermen kept on him about not spoiling his wife—the beauty of East Basin—more with gifts.

He set the rod down on the others and grabbed his oars. He began paddling to the shore. He looked up and down the waterline just to make sure he was still alone. He saw none of the swordsmen from the Highland Cliffs and continued to paddle toward the two circling scavengers. He saw something crumpled on the shore. It didn't look like an animal. Maybe a blanket that washed ashore. But, no, it was too thick to be simply a blanket. Maybe a net had tangled several items together and washed up. There seemed to be some orangey seagrass caught on it. He would gather the seagrass as well. It would taste nicely sautéed with the fish. He squinted trying to gather more details when his breath caught in his throat. It wasn't seagrass but hair. Long hair the color of auraium.

He quickly looked around again to make sure no one was watching him. He was still alone. He felt an impulse to just turn his boat around and leave, but he knew he couldn't withhold information from his wife. She would never forgive him if he didn't check to see if the girl was alive. He sighed and continued rowing toward the shore faster. He needed to move quickly. He would check if her breath continued. If it had left her, he would leave. If there was breath—well, he would worry about that when he got there.

He deftly got the boat onshore and hopped out. A scavenger had proceeded to dive down on the girl and he waved his arms and shooed it away. She must have just washed ashore if the scavengers had only recently noticed her. He ran up to the girl and kneeled in the sand. She laid on her side, but he couldn't see her face. Her long hair was everywhere. He noticed that she only had one horn. Not a good sign. He moved the hair from her face and rolled her onto her back. He noted the dried blood around her remaining horn. It had been hit and cracks were going through it. She would lose it eventually. If she lived, he would take the bulbs from it and replant them. That's only if she had survived whatever happened to her.

He placed his hand just over her mouth. He jerked back when he felt warm, moist air coming from her lips. He couldn't believe it. She lived. Wherever she came from and whatever happened to her, she had survived. Her clothes were different. He had never seen anything like them. She was a foreigner but from where? A small tribe he had never heard about? There were still families who lived completely separated from territories around Domus Lake. They were woodsmen. But how would she make it so far north without being seen?

He sat back on his heels. He would have to take her home. This might cause trouble, though. Just when his life had been perfect, the Befores aimed an arrow at his plans. But what was attached to that arrow? A gift or a curse? Suddenly, he heard a whispered moan. He leaned back over the young girl. She was very tall, like the Highland Cliff people. If they were her people, he needed to know if this was purposely done or an accident. If she had been discarded on purpose, he could be condemned for saving her. If she had been discarded by accident, he could be a hero for saving her. It all depended on who she was.

She moaned again and her eyelids flickered. Finally, her eyes opened. He fell back in shock. Her eyes—they were colorless. How could that be? She laid there with her eyes wide saying nothing. He leaned toward her and her pupils dilated. Yes, they had absolutely no color, like the stones found on the lake bottom.

"Can you get up?" he asked.

She only stared at him. The Lake-keepers had only one language. And as far as the traditional songs go, all of Rodesh had only one language even before the Shaking. If she didn't answer him, maybe she didn't know his language. She was definitely not from here. He scanned the horizon and looked to the river flowing up the desert. Could she be from a land beyond the desert?

"Where are you from? What's your name?"

Before he could get an answer from her, her eyes closed and her face fell to the side. She was lying on top of a thick set of branches that he didn't recognize. He wondered if she had floated on them down the river to the shores of the Highland Cliffs. He looked to the edge of the horizon where the river dumped into the lake. His people had always assumed there was nothing out there but endless sand and a river that never ended.

He heard yelling and looked toward the cliffs. He was too close to the Chieftain Lothar's fortress. He didn't want trouble, and if they found him here with this girl, they might accuse him of something he didn't do.

60

He knew that Voddie would want him to protect the girl, so he gently picked her up. He held the back of her head up against his shoulder. Once he carried her to his boat, he laid her on the blanket he kept for his son when he went fishing with him.

After he checked to make sure she was safe and comfortable, he pushed the boat onto the lake. He rowed as hard as he could to get some distance between him and the shore. When he saw the swordsmen walk down the stone-cut steps of the cliffs leading to the fortress, he grabbed his fishing rod and pretended to fish. They didn't seem to notice him. They grabbed the bundle of branches and took them back up the steps.

Morgo felt his heart pumping in this chest. He didn't know if it was from rowing the boat or seeing the swordsmen carry off the strange branches washed up on their shores. But he realized that if he hadn't have intervened, the girl would be getting carried up those steps right now. He didn't know if he had changed her course for good or for bad, but if he had a daughter, he would not want her at the Highland Cliffs Fortress. It was cursed by the Befores.

Chapter 7

BUDDING HORNS

The young girl blinked. Her forehead throbbed just above the temples. She instantly drew her hands to where the pulsing pain was coming from, and she felt two bony knobs coming out from her head.

"Don't you worry, my sweet," a kind voice said above her. "Right when Morgo brought you home, we took out your remaining horn and quickly planted two of your bulbs. I worried about your left horn growing back.

That scar had already been healed. I'm sorry I had to recut you, but I knew if you were like any young lady, the momentary pain was worth getting your horn back. Plus, you were asleep, which made it easier on my part. And look at you now! They are budding beautifully! The second set of horns always grow back much quicker in adults, so I'm guessing yours will be completely back by winter's end. I'll have to bind them for you, of course, so they don't grow straight up. I wouldn't want you looking like those savage woodsmen with their spindly horns, now would I?'

The girl blinked again and stared at the woman. "Savage woodsmen," she repeated.

"Oh my! You do speak. Thank the Befores! I was so worried." The woman leaned forward. "And my husband was right. Your eyes have no color at all, not one single shade of the moon. I've never seen such a thing. Colorless eyes. You know, Morgo and I can't figure out where you come from. You are tall like the Highland Cliff people. Your round face and auburn hair even favor them. But we've asked around, and no one has said a word about a missing girl. And believe me, they would talk about you. I know that I'm considered attractive for the East Basin people, but you! You are simply exquisite! So let me ask you a few questions. How old are you? I'm guessing about fifteen or sixteen."

"Fifteen?" the girl said.

"Is that a question, dear, or an answer?" Voddie giggled. "Where are you from? You can't be born of the woodsmen because the horn you had before we pulled it out was not sticking straight up. But you can't be from around here because of your eyes." Voddie leaned in closer. "Morgo thinks that you are from beyond the desert. Wouldn't that be something? After the Shake, our people believed we were the only survivors, but Rodesh used to be so big. How could it all end so quickly?"

The girl blinked again. "Rodesh?"

Voddie stood straight and crossed her arms. "You know, I have heard of this happening before. After a fall, some people lose their memories for a while, but they eventually get them back again. But I've even heard of rare stories where people never regain their memories. It's like their youth memories are damaged beyond repair. And, of course, we only get one set of them when we are born. So they sit there all day unable to talk or to say anything. They don't remember their childhood or family and friends. So sad. I'm glad that's not you. Obviously, you are absorbing what I'm saying. But I know that your youth memories should be finished by now. You are too old to have them still available to learn. However, you are repeating my words. Maybe what I'm saying is opening your damaged youth memories bit by bit, like a chest slowly being opened. That is exactly what I will do. My husband knows just how much I enjoy talking. I will just keep chatting away until your youth memories snap open again!"

"Mama," a young voice said.

The young girl looked to see a little boy walking through an opening from another smaller room.

"Come here, Range. I want you to meet…um, we don't know her name yet."

The little boy walked up to his mother and reached up his arms. She grabbed him under the arms and placed the boy on her right hip.

"What should we call her until she remembers her name, Range?"

"Pretty," he said in a giggly voice.

"Yes, she is pretty, but that is not a name. Let me think. It has to be something not common because she is truly a unique young lady. Wow, this is difficult, but if your little brother were a girl, I would have named her Amorfia. Isn't it beautiful? It comes from a song before the Shaking, and it means pretty. I guess that's what we will call her. Can you say it, Range?"

"Amorfia!" the little boy repeated excitedly.

"You are such a smart boy, and you talk so much more than other boys your age. Probably because I've chatted to you ever since you were a baby when your dad was off fishing. Well, probably even when you were in my belly. Yes, Amorfia is perfect." Voddie looked toward the young girl. "Can you say, Amorfia?"

"Amorfia," the girl repeated.

Voddie set the boy down back on the ground. "Here let me try this." She gently touched the girl's shoulder. "Amorfia." Then she touched her chest. "Voddie." Finally, she pointed to the boy. "Range."

The young girl smiled.

"Oh, look! You are smiling. You understand!"

"Range," she said pointing to the boy. "Voddie," she said pointing to the mom. "Amorfia," she said pointing to herself.

"Perfect!" Voddie squealed. "I must confess, I do believe I am the best mother in all of the East Basin. Probably out of all the Lake-keepers if I were truthful. You must understand, I'm not bragging. I'm simply sure of who I am. I am gentle, yet stern. I am loving, yet I set high standards. I'm pleasant to be with and I care for my family. I'm good to my husband. A woman can tell these things, now can't we? I see his contented face even when I'm talking too much or I get caught up in one of my songs that I burn dinner a bit. He doesn't mind. That is why I chose him, you see. Richer boys wanted to marry me, but I thought to myself: *Voddie, it is better to be happy and comfortable than wealthy and miserable.*

Those Chieftains are always warring and fighting for more and more. They waste away their whole lives, and for what? The prime example is Chieftain Lothar bar Haven. He is probably the wealthiest of all Lake-keepers but he is miserably unhappy with no family to show for it all. So sad, really. I wouldn't dine with him for all the Goliathan meat he would serve. The happiest people are the people who are thankful for what they have—that is what my Morgo has taught me."

A soft cry sounded from the room that the young boy had exited from. "Oh, my Paxton is awake now. I love him with all my being, but babies take a lot of work. I can't wait until he can crawl a bit on his own. Oh well, a few more months or so. Let me go get him. He'll be wanting to eat," Voddie said. "I'll be right back, and then I'll cook us my favorite fish, Sukio! Range, now keep talking with Amorfia. See if she'll answer some of your questions. We are trying to get her to remember. Her youth memories have been hurt a little, but they will come back alive just as her horns have begun to bud.

"So no one is missing a young girl?" Voddie asked again.

Morgo stared at his beautiful wife. She sat on the large cushion next to him in front of the fireplace. She had already put the boys to bed, done the final housekeeping and now she was ready for the nightly talk from the village. Morgo couldn't help but smile. She had even poured him a tankard of his nightly ale. He knew she wanted to talk.

"Like I said, not a peep has been said about any missing girl. The only news I gathered was that Dalia bar Haven is looking for an adoptive daughter to marry Chieftain Darmin's son, so they can merge the Highland Cliffs with East Basin."

"They wouldn't want to take our Amorfia, would they?"

Morgo shook his head. "No, they are looking for a younger girl who still has her youth memories available. Amorfia, as you have named her, is a few years passed that point. Plus, she's already on her second pair of horns, and her memory has been damaged. There is no way that Chieftain Lothar will want such a damaged, no name girl. Where is the girl?" he asked, looking around.

"Oh, she's sleeping on a pallet I made in the boys' room," Voddie said, taking a sip of her ale.

Morgo looked toward the room. "Do you think that it is wise?" he asked.

"A mother knows these things," Voddie assured him. "She's been with us for almost a week and awake for four of those days. She had been nothing but a help to me. She loves playing with Range, and you know how much energy he takes. And she is so tender with Paxton. She would hold him for hours if I would let her. It is tempting, to let her care for them all day, but I want to be the main caregiver in this house. Aye, she is a nice help though, especially with Paxton still nursing. She plays with Range, so I can feed Paxton without worry."

Morgo smiled at his wife. He loved her honesty. She hid nothing from him, which helped him open up from his normally reserved stance. "Has she learned more words?"

"Oh goodness me!" Voddie said, getting up to fetch more ale. "She has already begun to string words together. I think her youth memories are coming back to life, but she still doesn't remember anything from before you found her. Oh, and how pretty is she? If I were a jealous woman and you had a wandering eye, I would be concerned. But since I'm not and you don't, I can say in full confidence, she is one of the prettiest young ladies I have ever seen."

"Aye, she is pretty," Morgo agreed. He grabbed his wife's hand after she had finished refilling his ale. "But you are a priceless gem that no man could rip from my fingers."

Voddie blushed and squeezed his hand. "Aye, don't I know it, which is why I married you." She let him hold her hand for a moment longer before placing the pitcher back and returning to her seat.

"What if no one claims Amorfia? What then?" Voddie asked, trying not to sound overly concerned.

Morgo leaned back into his chair. "I wanted to speak with you about that," he said, slowly. "The girl is close to marrying age, and I don't doubt that there will

68

be plenty of fisherman from East basin who would want her as a wife. But, it all depends on her memory or if someone finally comes to claim her," he said. "So I think if we just keep things as they are with her helping you at home and with the boys, and as long as you think she will adjust well into our family, she could stay with us until something changes—on a provisional basis."

"Oh, you do love me!" Voddie exclaimed, setting her mug down. She crawled into his lap and draped her arms around his neck. "Do you think you can have my brothers build an additional room off the left side of the house? They are needing some work before winter comes, and this would give the young girl some privacy. I know she's already fallen in love with the boys, but she'll be needing her own space if she is to stay with us. And then when we marry her off, maybe I can finally have a daughter of my own."

"What did I do to deserve a gem like you?" he asked softly before kissing her.

"I don't know," she whispered with her eyes closed. But I think the Befores are pleased with us."

Chapter 8

TRUTH OF DYING

T'maya stood on the water's edge and stared at the bridge half expecting her daughter to walk over it at any moment. She was due back anytime, but she found herself becoming more and more anxious. She wouldn't let herself fall into fear. Eline was taking good care of her, and Blaklin had heard from some travelers visiting Left River Hook from the south that they had seen F'lorna and Eline and they were doing fine. Still, she couldn't shake a feeling that something was not right.

"T'maya, your staring will not bring our daughter back faster," Jaquarn said, as he walked up behind her.

"I know," T'maya whispered. "But I can't help feeling that they should be here by now."

"I've been on many travels with my sister. She knows everyone and almost everything. If anything were to happen, Eline would know what to do."

T'maya exhaled. "But you forget your sister is very old. She is old enough to be F'lorna's grandmother. And I know she is healthy for her age, but she does walk slower than she once did and she is absentminded at times."

"Yes, but you forget my wife that our daughter is strong and resilient. I am convinced that she could overcome almost anything. Ra'ash has given her a warrior spirit."

"I know you are right. I just miss her. I want her home. Everything has calmed down here. Trenton has agreed to stop trying to get rid of the Shoam-sha. The Sand-shaper cylinders are no longer coming down the River. Even Zelara has asked when we were expecting F'lorna home. I know that Lemmeck has several times found reason to travel into our Achion cluster. We need her here. I love you, Jaquarn, but things are so silent without her. I'm not ready to have her out of our cluster yet."

71

Jaquarn took his wife into his arms. "Me too. I'm not ready to be without her. That's why I know she'll make it back to us. What is that crackling sound?"

T'maya looked away with embarrassment. "I'm sorry. It's the *Chant of Acceptance* that F'lorna wrote for me with the Sand-shaper symbols. I started carrying it with me. I know I can't memorize it, but having it near me helps me to feel better. I know that at any moment I can take it out and read it."

Jaquarn stared at the tunic pocket that held the folded parchment. "How often do you read it?"

"Several times between the rise and descent of the Heat Source," she admitted. "It is a personal experience for me. I can listen for voiceless words from Ra'ash without someone with me. Please, don't misunderstand me. I love when you sing the *Sacred Songs* to me, but when I read the symbols, it's a different experience. It's like all of me—my life as a Sand-shaper and now as a River-dweller—can feel the Indwelling."

Jaquarn stood beside T'maya and stared at the bridge with her. "Will you ask F'lorna to write you some more? I know that she has already suggested that she would."

"I don't know. Half of me is so hungry for more of the *Divine Oracle*, but the other half wants F'lorna home and safe. I don't want any of the Elders, especially Elder Trenton, to have a reason to banish her for good. One moon phase is enough for her to be away from us."

"I believe it is truly not up to us," Jaquarn said, hesitantly. "I've been offering many voiceless words about whether F'lorna should create the Sand-shaper symbols. They've always been viewed so negatively by

72

the River-dwellers like they are an evil trying to erase the *Divine Oracle*. But I now see that they can be used for good."

T'maya thought. "I've heard of River-dwellers closer to the mountains who have both the *Divine Oracle* and the Sand-shaper symbols memorized. Usually, they learned it as a youngling from a Sand-shaper friend who wanted to share what they were learning. The symbols truly don't take up much memory. It is memorizing all of the Sand-shaper methods that occupy all the space."

"I agree, but fear of them has rooted itself so deeply into the River-dwellers' tradition. Remember when I brought you to this very cluster to meet my mother and father. They were not happy at first that we were to be joined."

"I remember," T'maya said. "Your parents were so old and set in their ways. Eline instantly liked me, though, and I remember her speaking with your parents about our union. They finally came to accept me. When your mother died, she even told me that she had grown quite fond of me."

"You did take care of her during her final moon phases on Rodesh. And you learned how to make her favorite dish. I do believe it was the food that did it for her. She loved you from that point on."

"I was glad to care for them. I wasn't able to deal with the passing of my own mother. I ran away from the pain when I left the Northeastern Mountains, but tending to their needs gave me the peace that I had been needing. I'm only sorry that F'lorna never met them."

73

"Yes, that grieves me, as well. But she'll meet them in our Eternal Dwelling. Plus, Eline was so much like them both, and F'lorna is very close to her."

They both stopped when they heard the yell. It was Jornan, Blaklin's husband, running over the bridge. He looked winded like he had run all the way from Left River Hook. He continued to run quickly into their Achion cluster. When he finally caught up with them, he leaned his hands on his knees and began to breathe heavily.

"What is it? Is something wrong with Blaklin? Did you need us to get Sage?" Jaquarn asked, worried.

Jornan shook his head no and continued to suck in air. "Just—just give me a moment," he said between breaths.

"Jornan, did you run over here from Left River Hook?" T'maya asked.

He nodded his head. "Yes, and you are needed right away. Eline is sick. She is with Blaklin at our home. She wants you both to come right away."

"What about F'lorna? Is she there too?" T'maya asked.

He shook his head, and T'maya felt as if a boulder had landed on her stomach. "Why? Where is she?"

"You need to go right away. Eline is very sick. We don't think she'll make it much longer," Jornan said.

"Come, T'maya. There is no time to ask questions. We must get to my sister immediately," Jaquarn said, grabbing her hand.

"Leave without me. Lemmeck has already gone. I saw him on the way here. Blaklin insisted that I get

Sage and Le'ana. We will be right behind you," he said. Then he stood up, took a deep breath and dashed back into the forest toward Le'ana's family land.

T'maya allowed Jaquarn to drag her forward. She brought her right hand to the pocket that held her piece of the Divine Oracle. "Ra'ash, protect my daughter!"

"Where is my brother?" Eline asked again. She felt her Eternal Dwelling pulling her. She had pushed herself too hard trying to return. She had never traveled so fast, and at her old age, it truly was a miracle she made it. Seven moon rises from the land bridge to Left River Hook. She wanted to make it back to her family's Achion cluster, but her body gave out. Thankfully, Blaklin had been there to catch her fall. Jornan had pulled out their fiber mattress from their Achion hole and laid it on the ground for her. The temperature had cooled and the breeze lured her to sleep. Her body was so tired from hard travel. It would be so easy to close her eyes and drift off.

Blaklin's dark, beautiful face filled with concern as she leaned over to where Eline rested. "Elder Eline, remember what you told me? Please don't fall asleep. You must stay away to speak to your brother. Jornan is a fast runner. I'm sure he has already made it to Right River Hook. We are just waiting for Elder Jaquarn and T'maya to make it here. I know they are running as fast as they can."

Eline tried to shake her wooziness. She had no fear in the brilliant ecstasy she was feeling. It was like hands of peace were wanting to cradle her. She needed to resist, but the temptation to just let go was so alluring. She needed to talk to her brother before she passed. He needed to know what happened to F'lorna, and he needed to know the truth about who he was.

Blaklin got up and came back with a wet, thick section of fabric. "The water has finally warmed. Let me wipe some of this sweat. I can't believe you traveled so far, so fast. I will repeat your story to the younglings who I'm training."

Eline smiled. "Ah, yes. The Storyteller. You have the best stories. I wish Right River Hook would have been more opened to your Adoration, but they can be sticklers about such matters. Don't let anyone tell you that your gift is unworthy. We all need to hear stories of heroism. Stories that will break your heart and renew your faith. "

Blaklin continued to dab the sweat—although a bit slower. "That is what Jornan says. I get discouraged because many of my songs are about simple life and simple people. Sometimes I would rather tell their stories than stories of the great prophets all the time. Though, I like those stories very much."

"Ra'ash has given you a passion, so protect and grow it. And we do need to hear stories of our time. How do you think we got the stories of old? Simple Rodeshians telling stories about the heroes in their time. We are all children of Ra'ash. And like any good Father, He enjoys listening to the exploits of His children. He revels in our overcoming."

Blaklin grabbed Eline's aged hand. "Thank you. I believe Ra'ash has sent you to me."

Eline's face became serious. "I must tell you something. I am leaving now. Please, do not repeat what I'm telling you to anyone but only to my brother and his wife. You must repeat it over and over again, so you do not forget it. I've held the secret for so long for the benefit of our way of life, and I would have forgotten it if I didn't have Jaquarn's face to always remind me. But now he must know. F'lorna's life depends on it."

Blaklin leaned closer to Eline's aged face. "I will repeat the story to him."

Eline swallowed and nodded. "Good, now listen closely."

Chapter 9

THREE CRIES OF RODESH

"Blaklin," Jaquarn said sternly, "if this is a story that you have made up, it is not funny nor appropriate. I have just lost my sister." He felt his knees begin to buckle. The forest around him began to tilt and sway.

T'maya instantly steadied her husband. "Jaquarn, we must find out about F'lorna. Please, listen to her."

Blaklin's lower lip began to tremble, but she stood her ground. "Eline said you would question me, and she wanted you to know that you will always be her brother, but even more like a son to her. She knew right away when she delivered you that Ra'ash had gifted you to her, but she was not joined, so she could not claim you. But she brought you home, and she and your mother left to a northern village for a while until the time was right to bring you to your family's Achion cluster."

Jaquarn looked at the mattress on the forest floor where his sister's body laid. Her face was in complete peace. She had always been like a mother-figure to him. She had energy that his aged mother always lacked—or who he thought was his mother. He tried to set those feelings aside for the moment. He could tell that Blaklin was struggling with what she had to say next.

"Where is F'lorna?" he asked.

Blaklin's expression grimaced with pain and tears began to fall down her cheeks. "I must tell you the first part of the story. Then I can explain about F'lorna. I have to recite it exactly as your sister said. I just need you to listen. This is very difficult for me, but if I don't repeat it now word for word, I will lose her story."

Jaquarn looked around the Achion cluster. Lemmeck and F'lorna's friends had gone to the Village Achion cluster to wait while Blaklin spoke his sister's final words. He only wished that he could have run faster, but from what Blaklin said, even if he had run at Jornan's pace, he wouldn't have made it. Ra'ash had willed it so; therefore, he needed to accept Blaklin's account and listen. "Please continue."

Blaklin closed her eyes. "Eline was traveling south over onefold ago. She was foraging for medicinal plants that grew only where the River meets up with the Desert Plains. She was getting a drink of water from the River, and spied a cavern deep under the waves. She decided to swim to it since it seemed rather odd and out of place. As she swam close, she noticed another cavern to the left under where the Desert Plains met up with the River. This cavern had water lapping up it like she could walk into it. She swam to it instead. Once she got there, she crawled into the cavern and was able to take a breath."

Blaklin opened her eyes and continued. "She carefully walked down the lightless cave as it followed along the River's rim. She wanted to find the end, but she could see that it went on for what seemed forever. She tripped over a tiny plant, and plucked its leaves and placed them into her tunic pocket. As she was feeling around for more of these little plants, she felt something like an animal. She jerked back, but the animal did not move. She began to feel the animal and realized it was a body. The body still felt warm, but there was no breath on the lips. When she felt around more, she found that the body was pregnant—very pregnant—and the baby squirmed within. She moved toward the head of the body, so she could pick it up, but she heard a low snort from something close by. Then feathery tendrils embraced her arm, like soft roots that were alive. It startled her at first, but she dare not move. It wrapped itself around her wrist, and instantly she felt peace and love and a need to care for the woman.

The feathery vines let go. And the animal snorted one last time. Eline went back to the head of the body and grabbed under her arms, carefully holding her head and torso and dragging her legs toward the opening of the cave. Some of the light from the Heat Source filtered through the water and she could see the end of the cave in the distance. When she finally got the body to the light, she knew she needed to extract the baby. But the knife she brought with her was only for cutting plants. She looked upon the woman and found some sort of dagger around a belt that she wore over her dress. The dagger had a sliver blade that reflected the light—nothing she had ever seen before and would ever see again.

She cut the belly of the woman and brought the baby out. His cry echoed through the caverns. She cut off a large piece of the woman's skirt and wrapped the baby in it. She did not want to leave the body there, so she pulled it out from the cave and into the River. The body disappeared in the waves and finally got swept up in the current that leads under the Desert Plains. She swaddled the baby and walked several steps back into the cave. There she jabbed the dagger deep within the rocky floor. She felt that for some reason she needed to mark the cave where the baby had been born.

She held the baby and quickly swam back to the shore. Once she got on land and knew that he was okay, she inspected the leaves that she had pulled from the small plant growing in the cave. It was an Achion sapling—never to grow much more than an arm's length because of the lack of light. Finally, she brought the baby back to Right River Hook, avoiding all other villages save one in which she purchased a Gida that had just weaned her young. She milked the Gida daily as she traveled and fed the baby. The baby survived and became Jaquarn, the River-dweller and Spiritual Elder of Right River Hook." Blaklin finished.

"But why? Why didn't she tell me that I was found and that my real mother had died?"

Blaklin blinked several times as the tears continued to flow. "Because she believes that—that the Lake-keepers live beyond the Desert Plains. She believes that your mother was a Lake-keeper, but she didn't want to spread the news and disrupt the peace of the villages. If Ra'ash wanted the Lake-keepers exposed, He would do it. She would not unlock the past until the future was ready."

"Blaklin, what does this all have to do with F'lorna?" T'maya asked.

Blaklin looked away quickly. "I don't know if I can continue. I'm forgetting her words now."

"Please, don't forget," Jaquarn said. "We need to know what happened."

Blaklin nodded. "Eline started fading when she talked about this last part, but what I gathered was that she and F'lorna went to the land bridge. There were Sand-shapers there digging in the cliffs. They were collecting yellows stones—she called auraium—or something like that. The Sand-shapers were leaving, but they would be back. They would all come back to get more. They would move into our lands and possibly use River-dwellers to mine the stone."

"What Merriton said was right," Jaquarn said. "The Sand-shapers have found it and they want it."

"So is F'lorna with them?" T'maya asked. "Did they take her because of her grey eyes?"

Blaklin closed her eyes and continued. "F'lorna hid in the forest while Eline inspected. But Raecli was there," she said in a hushed voice. "And they were extracting her horns and F'lorna heard the scream. And she ran to the land bridge to get Raecli."

"Oh no!" T'maya exclaimed, bringing her hand to her mouth. "Her Mountain Terror!"

Blaklin began to cry uncontrollably and she collapsed to her knees. "She fell over the edge. She fell down the waterfall. But Eline insists that she survived. She said Ra'ash Himself told her to not lose hope, but to offer up voiceless words for her protection. She is alive where the Lake-keepers have gone—beyond the Desert Plains!"

"No! No! My daughter! My F'lorna!" T'maya also fell to her knees and grabbed the grassy floor with her hands and fed the ground her tears. "My girl! My baby girl!"

Jaquarn felt his soul had ripped into pieces. His daughter was gone. A fall from that land bridge—how could she survive? He had seen Weston's drawing of it. The water roared from such a deep drop. And his birth mother, if she traveled from beyond the Desert Plains and had not survived, how could F'lorna? The land was too harsh around the River's edge and the rest of the vast region was desert. Was that arid land even passable? And even after her fall, someone would still have to find her. "No, no," he said dully. He looked back to his sister's lifeless form. "She should have never gone so far south. This is all my fault. I sent F'lorna off to her death. No! No!" he yelled louder. "My F'lorna! Please, Ra'ash! Please, take me! I will gladly go! Take me, not my girl. Not my F'lorna!"

Jaquarn overwhelmed with grief fell to his knees and wept with his wife and the Storyteller. Three cries spilled out from the forest and entered into the Village Achion clusters alerting all to their pain. Three cries poured out and fell into the current of the tributary flowing toward the main River. Three cries lifted to the Upper Realm and mingled with the violet rays of the moon. Three cries rang out from a River-dweller, a Sand-shaper and a Lake-keeper—a phenomenon that has not occurred since the *Great Engulfing*.

Lemmeck paced the ground, walking from one Achion tree to the other, back and forth, thinking over everything that F'lorna's father told him. His hair was tightly braided, and he had grown at least two finger lengths in the phase of the moon that F'lorna had been gone. Sage, Le'ana and the twins, Dashion and Rashion, sat around the hearth in Le'ana's family Achion cluster.

"Where is Ralona?" Le'ana asked.

Lemmeck stopped. "Her parents won't let her meet with us. Ever since F'lorna was banished for a moon phase, her parents have tightened the cords on where she can go."

"Yes, but the length of the cord goes anywhere except to us," Sage said. "Her parents are scared of Elder Trenton, and so they have decided to agree with him."

"They don't agree with him," Le'ana interjected. "They simply don't want to fight with him. They would rather have peace than to stand by what is right and make a ruckus."

Lemmeck turned to Sage. "Did your sister say anything else about what F'lorna's aunt said? Elder Jaquarn is hiding something from me. He has only told me about F'lorna falling off the land bridge, but I know Eline told Blaklin something more that really affected him. He doesn't simply mourn. It's like everything has been altered in his eyes."

Sage shook her head. "I know there is more to the story, but she won't say. She said it's not up to her to tell us right now. But she said to offer voiceless words to Ra'ash for F'lorna's safety and for Elder Jaquarn."

"How does Eline know that F'lorna still lives?" Lemmeck asked, holding back tears that threatened to expose his heartache. "She passed out before she fell. There was no way she could fight for her survival. It was left all up to circumstance."

"She said that Ra'ash told her that F'lorna would still live," Sage said.

"Could that be a dying aunt's wish?" Dashion said, staring at his twin. "We talked to Weston about the land bridge. He said that the drop of the waterfall was several tree lengths down and that the force of the water was so hard that the sprays leapt up from the River and filled the air with mist."

"Nothing is impossible," Rashion countered, though his tone contradicted his words. "Eline's Indwelling is strong. If Ra'ash told her F'lorna was still alive, we must believe her."

"I had a dream about her a few moon rises ago," Le'ana said tentatively. "But I don't know what it means. I fear it is not good."

Lemmeck walked to Le'ana and knelt by her. "What did you see?"

Le'ana closed her eyes. "I saw F'lorna flying from the Desert Plains and over the land bridge on a large animal of some sort."

"What animal? Like a large bird?"

Le'ana shook her heads. "No," she whispered. "I think it was a Swarve."

"A Swarve?" Sage asked shocked. "Like the one Jeyshen will ride when He returns to Rodesh?"

Le'ana nodded and began to cry. "And I don't know what it means. Does it mean that she is already in her Eternal Dwelling place? Or is Ra'ash going to help her come back home? I don't know, but it scares me. I dreamed in full color, and the Swarve had golden fur that clung to F'lorna. Together, they almost looked like one."

Dashion walked over to Le'ana and knelt next to Lemmeck. "Was Eline in the dream?"

Le'ana thought. "No, she wasn't there."

"Then it couldn't have been her Eternal Dwelling place because we know for sure Eline is resting there now. Do you know what I think?"

"What?" the friends asked simultaneously.

"I think the Swarve symbolizes that the power of Jeyshen is carrying F'lorna. She may have been asleep when she fell off the land bridge, but she rode on the back of Jeyshen."

"I agree," Lemmeck said, as he stood. Elder Jaquarn is leaving tomorrow to search for his daughter. T'maya is going with him and staying at South Village, which is near the land bridge. I have already told him that I will join him. I invite any of you to join us, but please do not feel pressured. Most villagers would think this is a hopeless journey, but we refuse to believe that Ra'ash has taken F'lorna so early."

The twins both shouted. "We will go with you!"

"My father will need some convincing, but the crops have already been harvested and the cooler months are here. I'm sure he will let me go at least to South Village for the winter," Le'ana said.

"My parents have already decided to move in with Blaklin and Jornan at Left River Hook, so I'm currently homeless. I will join T'maya at South Village."

"That only leaves one more…" Lemmeck's voice trailed off. His mind thought of the Marsh-lander, Weston, the one who taught F'lorna the symbols. Did he deserve to know what happened to her? There was no time to find him.

"Weston!" Sage said. "We must let him know. How will we notify him of what's going on? None of us write Sand-shaper symbols. Even if he sends his falcon here, we won't be able to communicate with him unless T'maya stays. But she won't if she knows that she could be close to the land bridge where F'lorna will return."

The friends sat silently for several seconds before they heard movement coming from behind Le'ana's parents' large Achion tree.

"I will write him," Zelara said, as she walked into view.

Lemmeck's mouth dropped open. "You were listening to us?" he asked, looking around for Elder Trenton.

"Don't worry. My father is not here," she assured.

Lemmeck walked to her. "Why should we trust you? You might be gathering information to get us all banished from the village."

She looked hurt by his words but quickly covered her feelings. "Because I know the Sand-shaper symbols."

"Aren't you the one who told everyone that F'lorna was writing them? You're the reason she got banished," Lemmeck said, raising his voice.

"No, my father walked in on us. I was reading what she had written. She gave her mother one of the small *Chants of Jeyshen*. I never thought the symbols could be used for good. I was so ashamed that they were in my Eternal Memory. When I was very young and we lived close to the Northeastern Mountains, I had a friend who wrote them on the ground with a stick and pronounced each one to me. She wasn't a Sand-shaper, but she had cousins who were, and they taught them to her. I learned them quickly, and then the symbols were stuck. I heard my father complaining about the abomination of the symbols one night, and so I instantly stopped playing with her. She had tainted my mind. But F'lorna—she told me that the symbols came from the *Divine Oracle*. They are the Images of Jeyshen and the sounds of His Chants.

"We don't know if the falcon will come. Or even how to get him to stay if he flies by," Lemmeck said.

"I will get a swatch of leather from Vauntan. She and I and Ralona have become close friends because of everything that has happened. Our parents too are becoming stricter, and they walk in fear. They only let us visit each other's clusters and no one else."

"I thought you three were conspiring against F'lorna. I never realized you would try to help her," Sage admitted.

"I understand your mistrust, but I can tell you that F'lorna has given me freedom from guilt and shame that I've carried for almost ten turns of the moon. I will always be indebted to her, and I want to do anything to help—even in this small way," Zelara said.

Sage stood up and walked to Zelara. She placed her hand on her shoulder. "I offer you my apology of healing for every single negative word I spoke about you—and there were a lot them."

Zelara smiled. "I offer you mine, as well. I did speak a lot of ugly words too. They helped me deal with the ugliness inside."

Sage hugged Zelara and then went to sit back down next to the hearth fire.

Zelara continued. "I will wrap the leather around the branch of F'lorna's Achion tree like I saw she had done before she left. Then Ralona, Vauntan and I will take turns checking her cluster while you all are gone. If a note comes from the falcon, I will read it and respond with the dye and pine needles that F'lorna used to make the symbols so small. Vauntan knows how to make the dye. She is the one who showed F'lorna."

"Ra'ash is with us," Lemmeck said, stepping into the middle of the friends. "Do you see how we are all working together? It is like the time we went to the River to harvest sinews. It has prepared us for this moment. I feel the Indwelling moving His purpose within our plans."

The friends nodded in agreement.

"No matter what happens, we will stick together. We will fight and overcome every obstacle. If F'lorna has survived falling down the waterfall, we too can survive any difficulty that comes our way. We must believe that the victory has already been won. The power of Jeyshen is on our side!"

Chapter 10

THE LANDOWNER'S SON

Raecli did has her grandfather ordered and stayed in the traveling case. The wounds over her temples still ached, and they weren't healing properly. She felt feverish and weak. She no longer had an appetite, but her grandfather forced her to eat. She had seen F'lorna emerging from the forest and flying to her like a bird of prey. She was there and had heard her cry. Why did she have to faint before she could hug her best birth friend? The pain was unbearable even with the herbs. She asked her grandfather many questions, but he grew weary from her questioning and finally shut the

91

conversation down for good. However, Moirel finally told her what really happened. She knew from the look in his eyes that he felt remorse for causing her pain.

He said that the healer hid F'lorna in the forest because she had Mountain Terror.

F'lorna had Mountain Terror? Raecli thought. *How could we know? We never left Right River Hook until that night Grandfather took me away.*

Raecli moved her head slightly on the overstuffed pillow, still not accustomed to her horns being gone. Her mind turned back to F'lorna. She had risked coming to her when she heard her scream. All this time she waited for F'lorna to rescue her, and she finally did, dying in the process. Raecli felt tears slip from her eyes. Much to her grandfather's disgruntlement, she couldn't stop them from overflowing. F'lorna had heard her cries and ran to her. She thought of the deep drop into the roaring waterfall. She envied F'lorna's death.

If she hadn't have fainted, she would have jumped into the waterfall after F'lorna, and they could both finally be together. Instead, she was stuck with her grandfather, and now she was about to meet the landowner's son. She would not try to impress him. She had already lost everything, and she did not care to forge any more relationships. There was nothing to live for anymore. Not even her friends in the coastal cities could replace what had been taken from her. Even though F'lorna was far away, it had given her a sense of solace that she was still at Right River Hook living the life that she would never have. Now F'lorna was gone, and all of Rodesh seemed hopeless and numb.

The curtain of the traveling case was drawn, and she could see Moirel motioning for her. She slowly got up and scooted toward the opening. Moirel easily scooped her up and stood her legs on the ground. Before her was an aged Sand-shaper she knew to be Lord Tarmian and his son, Sabien. They had dark hair like many of the Sand-shapers and no horns. It was too dark to see their eyes, which was fine by her. If they were grey like F'lorna's she didn't want to see them.

"Moirel, now go see to my auraium," her grandfather said.

After Moirel left, the landowner approached her.

"By all that is decent, Rencon. Your granddaughter is sick! Where is her nurse? Where is her maid?"

For the first time, Raecli saw her grandfather squirm.

"Ah, we had an incident down at the new land bridge," he said. "A healer was supposed to help us extract Raecli's horns, but she refused."

Raecli knew her grandfather was not telling the full truth. There was more to the story than a simple refusal, but she kept quiet.

"And you trust a River-dweller with the health and well-being of your granddaughter and only heir. Shocking. Look at the state she's in! Sabien, go get your mother. Tell her to call on Marva and that new maid and bring them all to the front room."

"Yes, Father," Sabien said, bowing slightly.

Raecli watched him walk back up the porch steps. He had a nice voice, but she had no more trust for anyone. As her stare followed him to the front door, her eyes opened wide. Their dwelling was massive. She arched her neck to gain the full perspective, and the wooden structure was several tree lengths wide and at least two high. There were stone basins with small fires hanging from the side of the house, and larger basins with bigger fires lining the perimeter. She thought her grandfather's dwelling was big, but this one made his home look like an Achion hole.

"Bring the girl up, and we'll see if we can make her appearance less ghastly," Lord Tarmian said gruffly. "But as of now, things aren't looking good for what you are planning for our two families. I don't care how much auraium you brought us. I will not let my family lineage be tainted by a sickly River-dweller turned Sand-shaper. Does she even have the Sand-shaper symbols in her childhood memories?"

"Yes, I assure you. I got her just in time. We were able to teach her not only the forty-four symbols, but also much of our family's history and many of our prized Sand-shaper methods. She will be an asset. And what she does not know, I have kept safely in cylinders in our family's storehouse."

"They did not break with the earthquakes?" Lord Tarmian asked, skeptically.

"They were each wrapped in thick fabric and placed in boxes filled with the dried grasses from the shoreline. Only a few of them cracked, but we rescued those, recopied them and placed them in new cylinders."

"At least you thought ahead on that point. So many Sand-shapers lost all their family's cylinders because of the quakes. Most of ours are safe, but I'm sure you have quite a few more than we since you and your family are merchants. I prefer the simpler life—farming and herding. Not much to build except fences, gates, windmills and that sort of thing."

"We have parchments from before the *Great Engulfing.*"

Raecli noticed that this news pleased Lord Tarmian. "Now that would be something to read. I've always enjoyed Rodeshian history, which is why I buy old cylinders when I can, but there are few landowners with historic Sand-shaping parchments, and I've only heard of a rare few from before the *Great Engulfing.* You merchants seem to have them all."

"I have quite a few. Probably more than most. My great-grandfather was an avid collector."

"That is good to know," he said, turning to Raecli. "Now let me get a better look at this granddaughter of yours," Lord Tarmian said and walked to where Raecli was silently standing. "It's a good thing you pulled her horns out when you did. Wouldn't want my son's first image of her to be as a River-dweller. The scars look even, but they are infected. We'll have to remedy that right away. He grabbed her chin firmly but without hurting her. "Yes, she has the violet eyes. They match our current moon. I do like them on her. They go nicely with her dark hair." He dropped his hand and walked back to her grandfather. "Bring her up, we'll tend to her needs. Maybe in a few days, she'll look more presentable."

"Ah, yes. Thank you," her grandfather said. "Moirel will bring the auraium to you when it arrives. He is waiting on the perimeter of your land. We have brought you quite a heavy load, and understandably, they are delayed. But you will have my granddaughter's dowry by the morning."

"Good, good. I look forward to seeing it," Lord Tarmian said.

Raecli's grandfather motioned for her to follow him, and she obeyed. She watched the two older Sandsshapers walk up the steps in front of her toward another new life that she would have to accept and navigate. As they entered the giant double door, she couldn't help but long to be falling with F'lorna. She wanted the waterfall to engulf her and shut away the pain and heartache for good.

Once Raecli entered the large double doors, two older women and one around her age were there to meet her. One older woman wore a layered, intricate robe rimmed with a thin strip of fur. She had to be the lady of the house. Her silver hair was long and thick, flowing across her shoulders and down her back. The other older woman and the younger one wore the simple tunic dresses of the servants. They were the housemaids. The older maid also had silver hair, but she wore hers wrapped in a tight knot at the back of her neck. The young maid had dark brown hair that she also wore in a knot. She noticed that Sabien was nowhere to be seen.

"How appalling!" the lady of the house said. "Just look how sickly she is. And this is the first impression I get of my supposed future daughter-in-law?"

"Not to worry, Lady Rosarian," the older maid said. She walked over to Raecli and gently grabbed her head, moving her forehead down. "This is a simple fix.

Give me a few days, and she'll be her beautiful self once more."

"I should hope so," Lady Rosarian retorted. "And to think this petty thing is to marry my son."

"Now, Rosi. You remember what I said. No judgments until we give it a few days—maybe a week to see what Sabien says. He has shown that his tastes differs from yours. It is his happiness that we are after, not our own."

"He is my only son," she sniffed. "But you are right. I will give Sabien room to decide. He has been picky and refused so many of the bright grey-eyed girls I have brought to him."

Lord Tarmian turned to the older maid. "Marva, take the girl and the new maid to their living quarters. I don't want to see even a glimpse of the girl until she is doing better, do you understand me? And if my father starts nosing about like he always does, insist that he go back to his room where he belongs."

"Yes, sir," she said with a curtsy. "Come now, Lainie. We have some work to do."

Raecli saw the younger girl come up to her and take her by the elbow.

"Follow me, Lady Raecli. I will show you to your room. Then we will wash you up and get you some treats for you to eat," she said smiling.

Raecli looked back at her grandfather and he simply waved her away. She couldn't help but feeling like that's exactly what he was doing with her here—waving her away.

Lord Rencon took the torch from Moirel. "You can leave us now. Make sure my men wash up and clean their wounds. Let them have the day off tomorrow. I don't want any more of my servants getting sick but keep them away from the farmhands. They might start scheming together. And did you send someone to notify my archive's steward, Corven? He needs to begin the search through my family's cylinders."

"Yes, my lord. He will find the cylinders about the Lake-keepers from before the Great Engulfing and send them to you when they are found," Moirel said.

"I trust no one but him. In fact, have Corven himself bring them to me. He knows how to read the old dialects better than I do."

"But, sir. He is weak and lame in the feet. He won't be able to walk the distance."

"Just send my traveling case to fetch him. He's of highborn birth—though lame. He grew up riding in traveling cases before his father disowned him after the accident. He might enjoy the ride for memory's sake."

Moirel nodded and walked to the doors of the small storehouse. As he exited, he shut the doors behind him.

Lord Rencon brought the torch closer to the pile of auraium that his servants had brought. "You see, Lord Tarmian, there was nothing to worry about. My men were right behind us with the auraium—my gift to you. They are not so prone to betraying their master as you fear."

"And that is all raw auraium?" Lord Tarmian asked, disbelieving.

"Every single stone. And there is more. That is why I have come to you. There is so much more than I can harvest all by myself; but, of course, I would rather other merchants not take the overflow. But you and I, we are not competitors. I need you to supply the food and meat to the coastal cities, and you need to buy the goods we create to bring down here. It is a perfect balance."

Lord Tarmian brought his torch closer to the pile and crouched to get a better look. "And you say the earthquakes caused the river to be exposed in the desert surrounding it? That's preposterous!"

"If I hadn't seen it with my two eyes, I wouldn't have believed it either. An expansive rockface with a land bridge is there now with a waterfall that falls into the lower location of the river. And that rockface is riddled with auraium. We don't have much time. I left a few men to guard it, but they could be overrun."

Lord Tarmian stood and began laughing. "By who? Those River-dwellers? They don't care about auraium and they definitely don't fight."

"But haven't some of your servants defected to their lands? They could create trouble for us in the future."

"I have had my people search for those confounded families, but to no avail. Either they have spontaneously grown their horns or those River-dwellers are excellent at hiding them. Either way, they are gone, and I know it has caused unrest with my servants. I'm having to guard their sleeping quarters every night. It is a troublesome matter."

"Maybe if I send a few of my servants to look for them? They won't be as sympathetic as your servants who might be prone not to investigate thoroughly. My servants don't have any connections with the traitors, so their judgment won't be clouded by emotion. They do enjoy pleasing me, and I have a few in mind who would be up for the challenge. I may even offer them a piece of auraium as their prize to energize their search a bit."

"Would you do that?" Lord Tarmian asked. "If I could just find one of them, I know my steward could get the information out of him, and we can finally know the whereabouts of the others. Your steward, Moirel, seems like a cunning, intimidating man."

"Yes, he is. He is the one I was planning to lead the expedition. I would be honored to help your cause. A servant is a servant no matter if they are from the farmlands or the coastal cities, and they must be kept in line at all cost to prevent an uprising." He paused and thought. "I assume now is as good a time as any to bring up my granddaughter, Raecli. She is a beauty is she not? Much like her mother was."

"From what I can see, she appears pretty enough—though I can get a better look in a few days when she's cleaned up and feeling better. However, she is rather petite," Lord Tarmian said.

Lord Rencon bristled. "Her size is very adequate. Just because we don't have the tall stature of many of you landowners, doesn't make us any less distinguished. Her hair is dark like the midnight sky and her eyes as violet as the moon. She is dutiful and obedient. What landowner would not want her as his wife? I've already had several inquiries from other merchants."

"I am not trying to belittle your granddaughter's beauty. It seems that my son has a liking for tall ladies, so I was hoping perhaps she might suit that fancy of his. But not to worry. He knows he must take a wife who will profit our estate and family legacy, and I do believe your granddaughter is the one to do just that." When Lord Tarmian finished speaking, he pointed the torch back at the pile of golden rocks that glimmered in the firelight.

Chapter 11

MEMORIES BORN

Amorfia listened as Voddie sang another one of her created songs. Her sweet, soprano voice streamed into the open air from the other side of the small window in her room. She loved to sing while she nursed Paxton, and Amorfia loved to listen. This was one of her favorite songs about a tormented cliff chieftain and his eight wives who could not bear him a single son or daughter. One by one, he banished the women until he was left alone in his giant fortress with only the heads of his conquest mounted on his stone walls to greet him.

When the song ended, Amorfia couldn't help but feel sorry for the poor chieftain.

She looked to Range playing with several smoothed sticks and a long piece of sinew that she made for him. The game was to make as many different shapes with the sticks and sinew as possible. She was impressed with him so far. He had already created five different designs and had no intentions of stopping there. He enjoyed the little game that she had made up for him, and it kept his attention for some time. With him distracted, she could sit on the grass and listen to Voddie sing.

When she had awoken several weeks ago, she didn't know where she was. Everything seemed strange and she couldn't remember anything beyond that moment. She didn't even have the words to express what she was thinking. It was frightening, like being shut up in one of the barrels she sees Morgo buying to fill with his fresh fish. Then Voddie began talking. At first, her words sounded like mumbles, but after a few days, the words started making more sense. Now she had many words to explain herself. She didn't feel scared anymore, but she still felt like her life before meeting Voddie had been shut up in a barrel. She didn't know if she would ever get her memories back. She noticed that Voddie's singing had stopped.

"Amorfia, my sweet," Voddie said from the front door. "Paxton has been fed, and he's wide awake ready to enjoy the cool, late afternoon."

"Is he feeling better then?" Amorfia asked. "I heard him crying late last night."

"Aye, he had me up all night with his dreaded sniffles. But yes, he seems quite alright now that he has slept the morning and afternoon away. I am so tired, though. Would you mind watching the boys just for a bit, so I can get some sleep before starting supper? I don't want Morgo to come home to a grumpy, tired wife. I do so enjoy my evenings with him."

Amorfia smiled. "Yes, of course, Voddie. No need to even ask. That will please me so much. I enjoy holding Paxton. He's so cute without his little horns."

Voddie walked up to Amorfia and gently handed her the baby. He squealed when he saw Amorfia. "His horns won't break the skin for several more weeks now. Even then, the first set of horns grow so very slowly. Tilt your head down, so I can inspect yours."

Amorfia tilted her head. Voddie had placed a horn brace on her head to prevent the horns from growing straight up. After moving her head from side to side, she let go.

"I must say that I have done well by you. First, I plant the bulbs in the perfect position and now they are growing out so perfectly. I am very pleased, indeed."

"Thank you, Voddie. I am glad they will not look like the woodsmen that you speak of."

"And you know that I've kept your other two bulbs?"

"My other two?"

"I must have forgotten to mention it. Each horn has four bulbs. I planted two of them and dried the other two. They are perfectly dormant now. Of course, I hope nothing else happens to you. You've been through enough, but there is nothing wrong with being prepared.

I'll have Morgo find you a little box to store them in.
Keep them dry and in the shade, and they will preserve
longer."

"Thank you, Voddie."

"I'm off to bed. Range, Mommy is going to take
a nap," she said, looking at her firstborn still playing
with the sticks and sinew.

He didn't look up. "I busy," he said, simply.

"Aye, let me not bother the builder," Voddie
teased and looked back to Amorfia. "I believe he takes
after my side of the family. We are builders. Didn't my
brothers do a fine job on your room? I know it is small,
but they built it in only three days."

"I love my space. The size suits me. I would
prefer it over the biggest cliff fortress."

"You remember my song?" Voddie asked,
genuinely pleased. "I made it up just before my youth
memories finished. That poor, old chieftain. So sad."

"Is he still alive?"

"Aye, and still miserable. He's been alone since I
was about your age. Let me see, we think you're around
fifteen or sixteen. My youth memories stayed available
until I was way into my fourteenth year. Quite rare for a
Lake-keeper, but it was good they stayed open. I
memorized all of my ancestors' songs by then, so I
decided to make up my own based on what was
happening in the East Basin and the Highland Cliffs at
the time. I have more than two dozen songs that I created
myself. I will pass them on to my daughter when I have
her."

"I would like to hear them all," Amorfia said. "I
believe I have only heard—let me count." She spread out

her fingers and began counting them. Then she stopped, closed her hands into fist and then spread her fingers once more continuing to count. "Yes, I have only heard eighteen of them. I am missing four more."

Voddie's smiled faded. "How can you possibly keep track of my songs?"

Amorfia cocked her head to the side. "Because you sing them all the time. I have lost count of your ancestral songs, but I'm sure I have heard several dozens of them if not more. But my favorite are the ones you have created. I can hear the difference in the language you use."

"Ah, Amorfia. Which song is about my great-great grand aunt who saved her baby from the forest leopards?"

"Oh! I love that ancestral song! Her name was Listal the Brave. She helped her husband fishing's business by throwing the fish into barrels. Her aim got so good that when forest leopards entered her lands during a cold winter to eat her baby, she threw rocks right at their heads. They all ran away except for the one she mortally wounded. She took that one and skinned him. She used its fur to keep her baby warm during the rest of winter, and she wore his teeth as a necklace. Isn't that right, Paxton?" she asked, rubbing her nose against the baby's cheek causing him to giggle. "Those filthy leopards could not take her baby."

Amorfia looked up. "Voddie, you must get some sleep. Your cheeks are pale."

Voddie slowly sat down next to her. "Amorfia, do you remember the details of all my songs?"

Amorfia nodded. "Yes, and I adore them all. Your Great Uncle Shardon. His design was used for the Temple of the Sages in Atlatl Forest. How wonderful to create a design with so many little rooms. Kind of like the ones your brothers built me. They each had their own space to meditate on the information they were given. Why? Is that wrong? I know that I'm not your daughter, but I can't help but love your stories. It's like they fill up a blank room in my mind and my heart. They offer me a sense of who I am. I am Amorfia, one who plays with children, listens to songs and wonders about the lands around her. Voddie, did I make you cry? I'm sorry. I didn't mean to."

"No, you have done nothing wrong," Voddie said, quickly wiping her eyes. "I'm just tired. Let me rest for a bit, and I'll feel better. I promise."

Amorfia bounced Paxton on her knee. "Yes, you will feel much better. I will play with this hornless guy. And, Range," she said, turning toward the toddler on the ground. "Have you created a new shape for me yet?"

Range held up his new design and smiled. "You like it, Morfie?" he asked.

"Aye, that I do. And I love it when you call me *Morfie*. Now I have two names instead of none," she said, as she turned her gaze back to Paxton. She didn't notice Voddie staring at her for a moment longer before wiping her cheeks again and returning to the house.

Morgo sat comfortably on their overstuffed cushions directly in front of the fireplace. The house was spotless as usual and the kids were asleep, including Amorfia who enjoyed her room now. Voddie's brothers built the structure quickly yet securely. Not even a snowstorm would tear it from the house. He noticed that Voddie's younger brother, Boru, was making eyes at Amorfia while he was here. She, of course, was oblivious to his advances. Even though the evening was much like every evening, Voddie was not her normal jovial self. He could feel the worry radiating off of her. Her transparency left little room for guessing how she felt. She continued to busy herself in the kitchen, placing the last clean dishes on the drying rack. Normally, she would simply rinse them and leave the washing for the morning, but tonight she insisted on making her home pristine.

"You are tired, Voddie," he said, quietly. "Come join me by the fireplace. Did you not find time to rest while I was fishing? You know all you have to do is ask Amorfia to watch the boys. She enjoys playing with them so much," Morgo said, picking up his tankard from the floor and cupping the cool metal in his hands. Metal tankards were a luxury, but this one was a gift from Voddie's brothers. He knew the metal would be better used for hooks and reels and such, but this was one of those indulgences he enjoyed. He savored this evening routine with his wife—a tankard of root ale, sitting by the fireplace and talking about the happenings of the family and village after working hard all day.

Voddie finally walked back into the main room and dried her hands on her skirt. She poured a mug of root ale into her stone mug and sat down next to him on her cushion. Her fiery eyes had dark circles under them and her expression was weighed down with worry.

"What is it, my love? I see you carry concern?"

"It's about Amorfia," she finally said. "I think her youth memories are opened, but they are not filled with her past memories. Instead, they are empty and thirsty for information."

"But that can't be, Voddie. Amorfia is too old to have her youth memories still absorbing information," Morgo said after sipping his ale. He tried to sound confident, but he had his suspicions after a lengthy conversation with Amorfia about boats and fishing. It seemed she had been listening to his words about work and remembering them. "It's just not possible that a new set of youth memories would be born within her. Who has ever heard of such a thing?"

"You remember what you said when you found her? You think she comes from beyond the desert. Maybe the folks there have youth memories that stay open longer," she pressed. "Or maybe they have two sets of youth memories. Or maybe like our horns, if one is damaged, another one can be planted."

"Are you sure she's memorizing everything, like for good? Things that shouldn't be memorized without the youth memories?" Morgo asked. Before they jumped to conclusions, he needed to know if she were truly memorizing things that weren't simply part of her daily life.

"Today, I realized that she has many of my songs memorized—word for word. So I recited the songs she hadn't heard—all of them—right in a row without stopping. I sang them without passion but only to perform them. When I was done, she easily recited each one back to me. She now knows every single song stored up in my youth memories."

"Did she sing them or recite them?" he asked, intrigued.

"I only asked her to recite them. I've never heard her sing. I don't know if she can sing or if she thinks that singing is only for me to do. Do you see how I may be limiting her? Do you remember what I cooked the first night after she woke up?"

Morgo thought. "No, I can't say that I do."

"She does. It was my favorite recipe for Sukio fish. She told me every ingredient I used and how much. I remember her watching me, but I didn't realize that she was memorizing it all. She's like Range, curious about everything. The only difference is that she has the mind of a young adult. She is learning so much so quickly. I fear she will become bored here with us. I can't keep filling that empty space in her mind. It's endless. I'm no good for her anymore!" Voddie burst into tears.

"That is not true, Voddie. She needs someone to care for her," Morgo said, reaching for his wife's cheeks and wiping away the tears. He loved how her red waves framed her face like silky, scarlet ribbons. "You love her and that is exactly what she needs right now. Can't we just keep things as they are, and see where they go?"

"How can I? I care for Amorfia. She's like a sister or even a daughter to me. I want what's best for her. There's a gift inside of her. I don't know. Maybe it's her colorless eyes, but she is definitely different and very special. I sense something beautiful locked away deep within her. I don't know what it is and I can't explain it, but it wants out. What if she's destined to be more than a mother and wife? What if songs will be sung about her? What if she was truly sent to us by the Befores to make some kind of change for all Lake-keepers?"

"Now what is wrong with being a mother and wife?" Morgo asked, becoming agitated.

"Nothing at all. I love what I do. It's where I belong, but Amorfia—her way may not be like mine. Who am I to limit her? And that thing inside of her—I want to know what it is. When I talk with her, it is there, and this strange feeling of longing nags at me."

"Now, Voddie. You are not a jealous woman."

"No, I'm not jealous of her. I'm jealous of what's inside of her, locked up and wanting to get out. Do you understand? There is some power in her...I sense it."

"What do you want me to do?"

Voddie set down her stone tankard and leaned toward her husband. "Go talk to the sages. They will know what to do. There might not be a precedence for Amorfia's condition, but the wealth of all the Lake-keepers knowledge is with them. They can communicate with one another and find the best path for her."

Morgo placed his tankard on the floor next to him and reached for his wife's hand. "I know you love this girl, and you enjoy her company every day. Are you sure you want to do this?"

Voddie looked away allowing the tears to continue to flow. "No, I don't want her to leave. I want her to stay with me and marry someone from East Basin and live just down the way from us. That is what I truly want."

"Then why don't you just let things be as they are?"

Voddie looked back at her husband. "Because I ask myself what a mother would do if her daughter's mind had been gifted so profoundly. Would I keep her hidden to satisfy my selfish desires? Or would I let her go, so she can be true to her full potential? Maybe the sages will say that her mind is nothing special—that this is all a misunderstanding or an exaggeration. But maybe they will say she has a gift that needs to be let out and cultivated. Who am I to decide?"

"Aye, Voddie. Who are we to decide?" Morgo leaned back into his cushion and thought. "I will take Amorfia with me to visit the sages in the morning. We'll go to their south sanctuary in Atlatl Forest, the one your great uncle designed. We'll see what they have to say about her."

Footsteps sounded behind them and Morgo looked back to see Amorfia crying. She had been listening to their conversation. Always listening and learning.

"Please, don't make me leave you. I'll stop memorizing things. I promise I will. I don't want to leave Range and Paxton. I don't want to leave my room. Can I please stay? I want everything to stay as it is."

Voddie instantly got up and walked to the young girl and took her in her arms. "Don't think for a moment that we don't love you. You are our Morfie. I want more than anything for you to stay with us. But I must trust my motherly instinct on this one. And no matter what, things never stay the same. Paxton and Range will grow up, and they'll start families of their own. Time always

112

changes life, do you understand that? No matter what we do, time transforms the world around us." Voddie looked up at the young girl who was much taller than she. "Just go with Morgo in the morning and see what the sages have to say. Don't hold anything back. Be true to who you are. They might not want you. You are much older than the sages who begin their training. If so, you will simply come back home. But if they sense a gift in you—the one I know is there—they will want to cultivate it. But not to worry, all sages come home several times a year. We will always have your room available for you. Either way, your home is with us. Do you understand? Your life started here?"

Amorfia nodded. "Yes, Voddie. I do understand. You have been so good to me and have taught me so much. I just fear I will lose you, but if you say I won't, then I trust you. I will go to the sages and see if any of them are wiser than you. I do doubt it."

"Aye, a mother's heart is very wise, indeed," Voddie agreed. "But let's see if the sages can add to it."

Chapter 12

NEWS AT THE MARKET

Amorfia followed behind Morgo taking in all the sights of the lake village. The air was humid and chilly, but Voddie had given her a cape made from the coarse threads of a Lana tree. It scratched a little around her neck, but it did keep out the cold. She held a small pack with one set of clothes and a few other items that Voddie had given her—a couple of small loaves of grain bread, a sack of salted nuts and dried berries and the two bulbs she had left from her horn tucked away into a small, wooden box. The horn itself had to be thrown away because it shattered when it was pulled out. Voddie said it was a wonder that it was still anchored into her forehead from the cracks it had received from whatever happened to her.

Amorfia felt the horns on her forehead. They were growing. They were now longer than Range's horns. Voddie taught her how to secure the brace, so they would grow down. She would adjust it every few days to keep up with their growth.

"Look over there, Morfie. Those are my boats just setting out. This will be one of our last runs before the winter sets in. My men are looking forward to their time off," Morgo said, pointing in the direction of the East Basin. "And that is Domus Lake. There used to be five lakes in all, but they vanished after the Shaking. All we have left is this lake. Many, many Lake-keepers died. The ground swallowed them up. We think the Befores were unhappy with our constant warring, so they destroyed most of our lands."

"I hear you and Voddie talk about the Befores. Who are they?"

"I really shouldn't be the one telling you about spiritual matters. The sages know much more than I do, but I will tell you that they walked Rodesh before us, but in another way. They didn't have skin like us and they had no need to eat or drink or even sleep. They had no bodies that would grow old and die—they were eternal. And the history is unclear but the Befores attacked their leader, Rash. And there was a war between the Rash and his enemy, Vorn," he looked up at the fading moon. "You see that hole in the moon?"

Amorfia looked up. "Yes."

"That happened during their war. The Befores have this energy that can cause tremendous damage. That is why we think the Befores caused the Shaking and made us lose all of our lakes but this one."

"Why was Vorn against Rash?" Amorfia asked, captivated by the story.

"It didn't begin that way. Vorn was Rash's most trusted friend. But Vorn became envious of Rash's power and wanted to be the supreme leader, so he got others to follow him—and they started the war. So now the Befores are split into two groups. Some Befores send you arrows with gifts. While others send you arrows with curses. Many Lake-keepers want nothing to do with them. Others simply ignore them. The sages try to distinguish between the gifts and the curses sent from the Befores."

"Is that what the sages will teach me how to do?" Amorfia asked.

"Yes, along with the information and stories they will impart to you. But, remember, the Befores are not like us, and we can't truly anticipate them."

Amorfia paused. "Will the sages see me as a gift or a curse?"

"I can't say what they will think of you, but always know that Voddie and I see you as a gift. And you are welcome back home anytime."

Amorfia nodded and smiled. They continued to walk, and she took the chance to look around. She had this moment to experience the village, and she didn't want to miss anything. She spotted many people up ahead grouping around wooden tables with items on them. "What is that ahead?"

"That is the village market of East Basin. It is open every day except the end-day. I'll show you where my stand is. My first captain's wife monitors it three days a week, and my second captain's wife monitor's it the other three days. Vexi should be there today. I will introduce you to her."

More people crowded together on the well-worn paths. Lake birds flew overhead vying for bits of unchecked food that fell to the ground. A little girl running from her older brother darted across the way. All the women and girls wore the same sort of cape that Voddie had given her, but many of the men did not dress for the cold. She wondered if it was a sign of weakness for them. The water scents that blew in from the lake mixed in with scents of baking bread and roasting nuts. There were also aromas of meats turning on spits over fires and bubbling berries being cooked on stone stoves. Amorfia sniffed the air searching for the smell that was new to her. "What is that sweet smell?"

Morgo sniffed the air. "Berries?"

Amorfia shook her head. "No, it is sweeter."

"Oh, that is honey. It is very rare. Only the woodsmen know where to get it, but they don't bring it to us very often. Someone must have traded winter clothes for a jar or two. Those nomads will come in just before winter and get what they need to last during the long months of cold."

"What do they do with the honey?"

"Oh, they put it in their tea or melt it over their dried nuts to sweeten them. Sometimes, they'll mix it with their jams to make them even sweeter. I've even heard of a loin chop brushed with a mixture of honey and spices to sweeten the meat, but that's for the chieftain's and their families. We normal folks get by just fine without it."

"I wonder how it tastes," she said sniffing again. "It smells delightful."

"The one thing we simple folks used to have before the Shaking was sap from an ancient tree. Atlatl Forest doesn't have them. Those are only pines," he said, motioning to the trees speckling the hills to the north. "Those trees are great for building. Their wood is sturdy and pliable, but they never grow very big. However, these ancient trees grew tall enough to touch the sky and wide enough that people could live in them."

Amorfia cocked her head. "People lived in trees?"

"That's what the legends say. These great big trees that grew near the streams that broke away from the main part of the river were the homes of the people. And the trees would produce a sap that our ancestors used to sweeten foods. You'll learn all about them from the sages. Each sage carries a portion of our history. Usually, they pass down their information from one set of youth memories to the next. But I think you might surprise them. I don't doubt your youth memories can hold more than a dozen of theirs."

"I am very curious," Amorfia admitted.

Morgo patted the young girl on the back. "Aye, my Voddie did know what was best for you. She could sense your need to learn, and she knew she wasn't enough. It is good that we seek the sages. Ah—there is Vexi, haggling over prices, I'm sure."

Morgo walked up to a large stand with several barrels of fish behind it and small wooden container on the table. "How is it going this morning now, Vexi. You selling my fresh fish to the people wanting to salt them down for the cold months?"

"Aye, that I am. But this bloke here wants to pay half the prices for one of these barrels. I'm offering him two of the smaller containers, but he won't have it."

Morgo looked at the older man. "I know you. You are an innkeeper from South Basin? Is the ale business not going well for you? Everyone suddenly stopped having a pint to drink?"

"No, not at all. It was Chieftain Darmin's son, Rathtar. He came into my tavern a few nights ago—him with several of his buddies and local girls. There had to be at least twenty of them. They drank all my ale and destroyed all my guest quarters. Rathtar kept promising me that he would pay me before he left in the morning. But they drank every barrel of ale I had and ate all my food—even the food that was stored for my family. Then he left in the morning without paying a cent. He didn't leave a single coin, not even for my two daughters who served them all night long."

The man wrung his hands together. "Now all my food and ale are gone. I can still rent my rooms, but with winter coming and no food, I don't know how I will provide for my family. Many of our neighbors have given us what they could spare, but I still need meat to keep my grandchildren fed. I came to your stand because

119

I know you to be a fair man, and your wife is known for her good heart."

"Did you not go to the Chieftain's fortress in East Basin and take it up with him in the wooden halls?"

"I did, and Chieftain Darmin sent word that his son would pay, but he never did."

Amorfia stared at the old man. She knew he was telling the truth. She saw the desperation in his eyes. She waited to see what Morgo would do with the new information.

"Aye, I heard that Rathtar was a sketchy fellow. Look, you know I can't be giving away my fish for free or else I would have every man walking through hard times begging from me. I got my family and my workers' families to provide for, but—" he thought for a moment. "I have several barrels of fresh fish that I've been needing to salt and dry. I'll give you one of the barrels if you help me for the next few days getting the work done."

The man's face lit up. "I got my sons-in-law with me. They're right over there," he said, pointing to two young men lingering down the path a ways. "Together, we will have the work done by tomorrow. My uncle on my mother's side was a fisherman. I would help him dry fish when I was a young lad. And don't worry about us. We brought food and we can sleep outside. Just may need wood for a fire, is all."

Morgo said nothing for a moment and eyed Amorfia. "No, we have a guest room you all can use. My wife won't mind one bit making you all dinner as long as you can fill her ears with stories from South Basin."

The older man's smile widened. "I will ask the Befores to send you a gift for helping me and my family. We are indebted to you."

"I still have something I need to see to. Why don't you and your boys meet me at my pier when the sun is directly above in the sky? That should give me enough time to finish what I need to do."

"That sounds fine by me," the man said.

Amorfia watched as the older man walked back to the two younger men waiting for him. She had been sad to leave her room behind, but it gave her comfort to know that it would be used to help people like that.

"I hope you don't mind, Morfie. I fear the temperature is about to drop, and I didn't want them to become ill if I can prevent it."

"I don't mind at all," she said. "It makes me happy that my room will not be empty."

Morgo nodded and then turned his attention to the woman running his stand. "Vexi, this here is Amorfia or, Morfie, is how Range likes to call her."

The woman stared at Amorfia to the point that she became uncomfortable.

"Oh my goodness. Your eyes have absolutely no color in them whatsoever. They look like the lake on a cloudy day." She turned to Morgo. "And they say that you found her near the cliffs?"

"Yes, but she's doing fine now. I'm taking her to the sages to see if they can make sense of it all."

Vexi nodded her head with approval. "They will know what to do with the girl." She turned back to look at her. "I can see why Voddie's little brother, Boru, is so enamored with you," she giggled. "You are a pretty one.

Be careful of those sages. They are a smart group, but some of them can fall over the edge of the pier, if you know what I'm saying. Don't let any of them lead you to where you don't want to go."

Amorfia nodded.

Morgo looked at the sun coming up over the lake. "We need to hurry. We still have a ways to walk," he said, turning to Vexi. "If you see one of your girls, can you send her to Voddie to let her know we will have three guest tonight? She doesn't like it when I forget to warn her of guests ahead of time."

Vexi nodded. "Of course, I will. My eldest is supposed to take over, so I can have lunch. I will go to Voddie myself and let her know what's going on. Don't you worry about a thing."

"Aye, thank you. I trust you'll fill her in with the news about what our chieftain's son has done in South Basin."

"That is the first thing I'll be telling her," Vexi said with a tone of contempt.

Chapter 13

TEMPLE OF THE SAGES

Amorfia walked up the steep incline. They left the village a while ago and entered Atlatl Forest. She had seen the temple in the distance on the incline, and she was already impressed by Voddie's great uncle's design. The middle building had several long pointed roofs with plumes of smoke puffing out. She knew this to be the main temple area. Then the larger structure had several rows of thinner buildings stretched out on either side. These were the living quarters of the sages. She noticed a short, wide building behind the main temple, which was fenced inside several acres of land.

"What is behind the temple?" she asked Morgo who was several feet in front of her.

He stopped and looked. "That is the Swarve stables," he said and continued walking.

"Voddie has a few songs about them. What are they exactly?"

"They are an animal that the sages and the wealthy ride. They are faster than we are, and they can carry a lot of weight for long distances. All the temples and fortresses have them. They only live around five years or so. They were once believed to be able to fly, but they have these tiny wings that dangle at their sides—if you can call them wings."

"What do they look like?" she asked.

"I am sure you'll see them soon, but they are beastly animals with kind eyes. They eat moss and grasses, but they hate the needles that grow on pine trees. Their coloring varies from brown to bronze to gold. There can also be red ones, but no one has seen ones of those since before the Shaking."

"Can I touch one?" Amorfia asked.

"Yes, but make sure not to touch a new hatchling. It has to be weaned from its longing first."

"What is its longing?"

"Their fur is like a cross between a feather and soft vines that are each alive. When they are born, their fur tries to clasp onto someone. Each wisp reaches out in longing to connect. If they do connect, their feelings of wellness and peace will merge with that person. If they don't grab hold of someone during their longing, they usually will never connect with another."

"Why wouldn't someone want to connect with them?"

"They don't live very long, so you would have to continually reconnect with a new one every four or five years. Plus, once a Swarve connects, it will not allow anyone else to ride on its back unless the connected person is with them. This is difficult for the Chieftains especially those who expect servants to take care of them. It has become customary to cover each new hatchling with a thick paste made up of melted lake grasses and some other ingredients. Once the paste wears off, the Swarve is usually weaned from the longing."

"But one of Voddie's songs speaks about the Chieftain's mother of the Highland Cliffs. Why did she have a personal Swarve?" Amorfia asked.

"I think she was sickly, but I don't remember with what. Voddie would know. Sickly children of the wealthy are always given a Swarve. It helps them to feel better. The Swarve attaches to them and gives them a healing of sorts that lasts many days. Every time the children feel sick again, they allow the Swarve to attach once more."

Amorfia nodded and continued to walk several steps in silence before deciding to ask what was really on her mind. "When I met Vexi, she said that Voddie's brother, Boru, was enamored with me. What does that mean?" Amorfia asked. "Does he see me like a sister?"

She noticed that Morgo shrugged his shoulders like he did when he didn't want to discuss something. "That'd be a better conversation between you and Voddie. Best wait on that question until you come and visit us."

"Alright," Amorfia said.

"There are the steps to the Temple of the Sages. I haven't been here since before my youth memories stopped. You see that large, golden disk? You must take the padded hammer next to it and strike it."

Amorfia walked over to the disk. "I strike this?"

"I would, but I'm just a fishermen. They may not venture out for me, but they will come out for you, I believe. Just strike the disk with strength. Don't be intimidated."

"Okay, I will do as you say." Amorfia grabbed the hammer that rested on the ledge of the fence and faced the shimmering disk that dangled from two thick sinews. She gripped the bone handle and struck the densely padded head directly on the center of the disk, making a loud whacking sound. The clamor sounded like a crashing melody, and the vibration of the disk continued to announce that it had been struck to all who would listen. She set the hammer back down and waited next to Morgo.

"Okay," he whispered through barely moving lips. "They are most definitely looking at you. Wait patiently until someone comes down. You will know the prestige of the sage by their clothing. The more color and the more design, the higher ranked the sage. The plainer and duller the clothes, the lower-ranked the sage."

126

Amorfia waited. She could feel others looking at her. It was the opposite feeling of her home with Voddie. Strangers who did not know her were contemplating her value. She wondered what she must look like. A tall, full-grown girl with horns barely bigger than a two-year-old. She wanted to adjust the cape around her neck, but she wouldn't give the onlookers the satisfaction of seeing her discomfort. She continued to wait as the shadows of the trees shifted around her. She noticed that Morgo began fidgeting and looking toward the sky. She gave him the questioning look that she had learned from Voddie.

"We may have to leave," he whispered. "The sun is almost above us. As of now, I will have to run back to the village to meet the innkeeper in time at the pier."

"They haven't come out yet. I don't want to leave until a sage at least comes up to me and tells me that I am unwanted or else Voddie may still want me to return."

"Aye, but I have to go. And if I leave you here without knowing that you will be taken care of, at least for the night, Voddie will not forgive me."

"I know the way home. I can manage."

"This is the first time you've ever left to the village market, let alone the Temple of the Sages. You cannot be left alone. You have no idea what someone would try to do if they found you alone. Not everyone is like Voddie and me."

"What do you want me to do?" she asked. She couldn't explain it, but she would not give up. She would at least get one of them out of the door. She wanted to see who they were. Her curiosity needed to know.

"You need to show them who you are. Impress them somehow with what you are good at," he said, looking back at the sun.

"I'm only good at learning," she said.

"Then mimic something that you've learned that impresses you," he said.

Amorfia thought for a moment and then closed her eyes and inhaled slowly. She allowed the song of Voddie's Great Uncle Shardon, who designed the Temple of the Sages, to fill her memory. Then she opened her mouth and began to sing. At first, she sang like Voddie, but the pitch was too high. Then she lowered the tone a bit and her voice poured out like sun's rays streaming through the clouds. The song was short, but she savored every lyric. She had almost as much pleasure listening to her own voice sing the words as she did Voddie's. The beauty of the story and the creativity of the builder almost made her voice crack with emotion, but she sang strongly until the very end.

As she finished the final word, she enjoyed the echo of it as it flowed like water across the temple lands and over the horizon. Something deep within her awakened with joy like she recognized a long lost friend. Even if the sages rejected her now, she would be satisfied. She opened her eyes and she looked toward Morgo. He gaped in awe at her.

"What?" she asked.

Suddenly, the large wooden doors at the entrance of the temple opened. A woman with white, flowing hair walked out. Her tapered gown was sewn in an intricate design with long, cream-colored feathers rimming the neckline. The robe around her dress shimmered golden like the sun and dragged several feet behind her.

Morgo instantly fell to his knees. "It is the Supreme Sage herself," he whispered and bowed down.

Amorfia didn't know what to do. She didn't want to bow down or else she would miss beholding the descent of such a sage. She stared at the woman, captivated by her aging beauty and dominating presence. Amorfia noticed several other plainly dressed sages following behind the one with white hair. The sage came directly up to Amorfia.

"How do you know that song? We have never heard it before; though, we do know several stories about the builder, Shardon, of whom you speak. We owe him a great debt for building our temple to last as long has it has."

Morgo stood up next to Amorfia. "Shardon is my wife's great uncle. Her mother would tell her stories about him, so my wife created that song herself."

"And your wife, has she written songs for the sages at the Highland Cliffs' temple or the chieftains?" the Supreme Sage asked perplexed.

"Ah, no. She only creates them for herself and our family. She is a wife and a mother is all. I am a fisherman from East Basin," he said.

"Your wife is the grandniece of Shardon?"

He nodded. "On her mother's side."

The Supreme Sage reached into one of the folds inside of her robe and brought out a small woven sack filled with coins. "Give this to her from the Temple of the Sages in the Atlatl Forest. We are grateful for her family's services to us, and our debt of longevity has now been fulfilled."

Morgo looked scared to touch the small sack, but he finally reached forward to take it since the Supreme Sage continued to hold it out.

She looked back at Amorfia. "We have stories saved in our memories of those with colorless eyes, but one has not been seen since the Shaking. Who are you and where do you come from?"

It was Amorfia's turn to feel scared. "My name is Amorfia," she began.

"Who gave you that name?"

Amorfia looked at Morgo and back at the sage. "Voddie did, but Range calls me Morfie."

"And where do you come from, Morfie?" she asked.

"Morgo found me on the shore next to the Highland Cliffs near where the river flows through the desert."

"Is that why you are on your second set of horns? They are your second, are they not?"

Amorfia looked down. "I don't know. The last thing I remember is waking up with Voddie talking to me in her home."

The Supreme Sage looked at Morgo. "And how long has that been?"

"Around a month now."

"And why have you brought her to us?"

"My wife and I, we believe that her youth memories are still available to learn."

"That is outlandish," the Supreme Sage scoffed. "She is too old."

"Yes, we agree with that, but it's just that she's memorized all of my wife's ancestral songs and the songs she created when she was young. She can repeat them word for word."

The Supreme Sage looked back to Amorfia. "How many songs have you memorized?"

"One hundred and sixty-seven," she whispered.

"And you still want to learn more?"

Amorfia nodded. "Yes, Voddie says my curiosity is unquenchable. She fears that I need more than what she can offer me. She did not want me to leave our home and come here, but she also did not want to limit my potential. That is what she said."

"And what do you say?" the Supreme Sage asked.

"I did not want to leave at first, but—"

"But what?"

"I feel that I must find something, something very important. And my mind keeps searching for it, gathering and gathering information until the day it discovers the truth."

The Supreme Sage placed her hands on her hips and grinned knowingly. "Yes, the voracious need to know what is truth. That is the signifier of a true sage, and very few of us have it," she said. "So Morfie from the shore who has been given new horns and a new set of youth memories are you a gift or a curse to us from the Befores?"

Amorfia no longer had to consider her answer. "I don't know about the Befores, but I am most assuredly a gift."

Chapter 14

THE EARLY NOTE

Weston's fingers stroked the papyrus plants. He would have to harvest them soon. The temperatures were dropping, and they would not survive the cold. He probably planted too many stalks, overzealous about his communications with F'lorna. He wanted to make more parchment, and he only had a few precious sheets left. Though, he now realized that he had enough papyrus to communicate with her for a lifetime. He hoped that wouldn't be the case. He didn't want to simply write to her. He wanted to be with her.

He looked around his small piece of marshland. If the landowners knew how lush the land was down here, they would take it from the Marsh-landers. Once the shrubs and other grasses were cleared, the land became fertile soil for planting almost anything. The landowners never let their lands rest, and their plants were becoming dull and tasteless. But their farms had to feed the densely populated coastal cities. He would never move to the Northwestern Coast with their factories pouring smoke into the air. The fresh water ocean was becoming unclean. The water that flowed from the coast down through the Four Horns and into the main river was affecting the northern region lands.

He heard Banthem's wings pumping the air above him. He was returning home from a hunt. The falcon looked full and satisfied—ready for a nap. He landed on the worn leather swatch strapped to one of the few large limbs of the marsh tree. These trees weren't as thick and full of shade as Achion trees, but they allowed him to string his hammock from one to another for sleeping, which was enough for him. He didn't have to sleep within a tree; though, he had enjoyed it when he stayed at the visitors' Achion clusters during his travels through the River-dweller territories.

"So my brother," he heard Merriton's voice say from behind him. "While the rest of us are harvesting our grains, berries and vegetables, you are harvesting your parchment plants. I see your heart is in it, but how about your stomach?"

Weston smiled and turned. "I planted some Ibimi and Arborio plants. I even planted a nut sapling; though, it will be some time before it yields anything. Besides, your wife dotes on me. She will always spare a place for me on your land for a meal. And look! You have brought me, my nephew."

Merriton held a young boy on his hip. "Nice way to change the subject," he laughed. "Yes, Ruvarren wanted to show his favorite uncle his horns. They seem to have grown a finger width overnight." He set his son on the ground, and the youngling toddled to Weston.

Weston bent down to snatch up the boy. "And look how well he is walking now. I'm so impressed. The boy grinned and bent his head forward to show Weston his horns. "They are looking very good." He turned to Merriton. "When he gets older, you will have to put on that horn binding thing that Lemmeck gave you. Do you remember what to do?"

"It looked simple enough. I showed my wife, and she said she would handle it. I doubt I would have the patience. It seems easier just to pull them out, but much more painful. But I am glad that Ruvarren is beginning a new way of life for us Marsh-landers. We now have several new babies who will keep their horns." He paused. "So no more notes from F'lorna, I see," he said, pointing to Banthem whose head was tucked into his back feathers. A sign that he was fast asleep.

"No. The last note I received, she told me she was returning to Right River Hook. I was thinking about sending just one more note. She can just ignore Banthem if she thought it was too risky. I only want to make sure she made it back okay. Also, maybe things have loosened up over there and that irritable, old elder—what was his name?"

"Trenton," Merriton replied.

"Yes, him. Maybe he's decided just to leave things alone and let River-dwellers and Marsh-landers live their lives."

His nephew started to wiggle in his arms. "You want to swing on my hammock?"

The boy nodded.

Weston let him down, and the youngling toddled over to the hammock and struggled to get on. Weston was just about to help him when Merriton shook his head.

"He can do it. Just give him a moment."

Finally, the boy swung his legs over and rolled onto his back. As he laid, the wind gently rocked him side to side.

"I don't know," Merriton began. "If she said not to write for a—how do they say it? A moon raise? What's a month? I can never remember."

"My dear brother, you will never remember their calendar language and neither will I. It's not in our childhood memories."

"It's interesting, though, that we could use their words when we were traveling through their villages and speaking with their people. But now I can't remember any of it."

"That's because it was right there in front of us being used and spoken. Easy to remember when you just heard it. By the time we met F'lorna and her friends in the forest, we sounded like them. But now, they are not with us, and we are back to being Marsh-landers again."

"So how do you communicate with her without getting confused?"

"I am glad you asked, Brother. I have found a wait to cheat. Wait here, and I will show you." Weston walked over to a large wooden crate next to one of his trees. It was filled with glass cylinders.

"You gathered all of those cylinders from the marsh after the ground shakes?"

"Yes, and they are all mine. I've found some useful information in them, too. I heard many merchants lost most of their precious heirloom cylinders. I even have a few of those," he winked. The shakes really affected the north territories."

"Don't forget. They were strong down here. We just have less to lose. Those coastal cities are designed to break."

"Ah! Here it is." Weston took out a parchment and read. "A *rise* is a day. A *phase* is a month. A *turn* is a year. A *cycle* is the seven years of a single colored moon, which now we are beginning the second year of the Violet Moon. Onefold is forty-two years—all the six-colored moons and their seven years. And Twofold is eighty-four years—all the moon cycles twice."

"It sounds too complicated to me," Merriton shrugged. "And what was their sun?"

Weston looked down at the parchment and continued reading. "The Heat Source is the Sun. The Upper Realm is the sky. The Great Expanse is the ocean. I think that was it—oh, and they greet each other by extending their hand and squeezing the other person's shoulder. You remember that?" he asked, looking up from the parchment.

"I do remember liking their greeting. It seemed very personable to me," Merriton said.

"I think their entire dialect is beautiful. They are a people who live by the rise and descent of the moons."

"It is F'lorna you like, which is why you think that calendar system and complicated usage of words is beautiful," Merriton teased.

"She does have those gorgeous grey eyes. I would have never thought I would like anyone with those colored eyes. They have been nothing but cruel to me all my life," Weston said, rolling up the parchment and placing it back into the cylinder.

"You were friends with Lord Sabien at one time," Merriton countered.

"Do not call him Lord!" Weston demanded.

"Sorry, it is the name that comes out first from my childhood memories."

"We were friends until his father told me that I was a bad influence on him, and then banished me from ever seeing him again. His mother thought me useful while he was young, so I could keep her rambunctious son entertained and out of her way. But when he grew up, she no longer needed my services."

"No sense brooding over the past. Lady Rosarian and Lord Tarmian are no longer a threat to us. We have our own village, the Marshland Village. And we have escaped their rule," Merriton said.

"Not before their steward put his mark across your face," Weston said, feeling the anger permeate his hands.

Merriton rubbed his cheek where his face was split in two with an obsidian blade as an example to all the farmworkers. Then, he looked at his son who had fallen asleep on the hammock. "Small price to pay for freedom. It is what caused me to realize that life as a Sand-shaper would never get better, only worse."

Weston walked to his brother. "But what if the auraium brings the Sand-shapers south? What if they find us and take our land? We introduced ourselves to as many River-dweller villages as we could during our travels and warned them about the auraium. But they are a peaceful people. They know nothing of fighting and risking their lives. I think of F'lorna's father. Would he really kill someone to protect his family? He cares too much about what people think and about keeping the peace."

"You forget, my brother. I was much like Jaquarn. I tried to keep the peace between us and the landowners until I realized that my family's well-being depended on me fighting back. He loves his daughter. I believe he would fight for her if that's what it took."

"In her note to me, F'lorna said she was just about to go to the land bridge with her aunt. I wonder if they saw anything suspicious. I should write to her," Weston said. He went to the leather pouch that held the last of his parchment. "I'm glad she showed me that new way of writing the symbols. Much easier than using smokestone, which is good because I was running out of that too. It can only be harvested in the mountains, and there aren't any of those down here."

"But didn't she tell you not to answer her back for at least a month?" Merrion asked.

Weston smiled. "Actually, she said two moon phases, which is two months, but I believe I've suddenly forgotten what a moon phase is, and I don't have time to look it up."

Chapter 15

GREY-EYED GRANDFATHER

Raecli swept her glossy dark, hair behind her ears and stared at her translucent image in the large framed looking glass on her bedroom wall. It had been over a week since her horns were taken from her, and she still wasn't used to seeing herself without them.

Her head felt light like the weight of her existence was stripped from her. She wore a deep berry-colored dress that had so much extra fabric, Raecli feared she would trip over it.

"You look so beautiful, Lady Raecli, and your wounds from your horn extraction are all healed up. Still a bit tender, though, so don't beat your head on anything," Lainie said. "Can't believe you had them taken out at fifteen years old. Can't even imagine the pain."

An image of F'lorna falling over the massive waterfall instantly came to Raecli's mind. She didn't want the maid to see her cry, so she tried to distract Lainie's train of thought. "You really don't have to call me Lady. I believe I am younger than you are."

"I know, Lady Raecli. You said as much yesterday and the day before. But I like to stay on the good side of Lady Rosarian, so I won't be calling her guests nothing but Lord and Lady, and there's nothing can change that. I like working in the main house. It sure beats working under the sun all day in the fields. And they are having to rush now because the weather is cooling down faster this year. When they're done with the fields, they'll be up in the storerooms preserving the vegetables, fruits and nuts and getting them ready to ship. I would much rather be here with you, in this here spacious, elegant room, than over there with them. Now sit down, so I can finish braiding your hair." Lainie moved to the vanity chair and patted the embellished back cushion.

"Is that where you were before this?" Raecli asked, sitting down.

"Oh, no! You have to be trained as a child to be a housemaid or else you won't know what's expected of you. I used to work in the steward's home. That's Lord Tarmian's right-hand man. His name is Mr. Barton, and I do believe he is more cantankerous than Lord Tarmian himself," Lainie stopped abruptly and leaned down to look at Raecli. "I hope you don't mind me saying so. I know that they might become your future family and all. If I have offended you, I will stop this instant."

Raecli was accustomed to servant gossip. She rather enjoyed listening to her servants at home complain about her grandfather. It made her feel better that someone could vent their frustrations since she had to keep hers hidden. "You are not bothering me one bit. I would like to know who this family is before I decide on anything."

"See, I knew you would think that way. The housemaids always tell their ladies the newest gossip. It's just how information is passed on. I used to do that for the steward's daughter, Kysha, until they moved me over here after Miss Marva's daughter got married."

"Where is her daughter now? Why is she no longer here?"

"She married a farmworker. Housemaids can no longer marry, so she had to go to the fields to be with her husband."

"That's a shame," Raecli said. "Why wouldn't they just let her stay here?"

Lainie looked around and leaned in discreetly and whispered in a low voice. "On account Lady Rosarian doesn't want any babies in this house but her grandchildren. She said that the servants only cause problems. She wants her grandchildren to have no influence whatsoever from servant children their age."

"But she doesn't even have a single grandchild yet?" Raecli said, incredulously.

Lainie straightened. "Well, that's why you are here, isn't it?"

Raecli's eyes opened wide. "I'm not even fifteen turns yet!"

"Turns? Is that how River-dwellers say years?"

Raecli bit her lip. "Yes. I sometimes fall back into my old way of talking."

"That's understandable. You lived as a River-dweller for most of your life. But now you live here, and you look old enough to me to have babies. I'm just thankful that I don't want any. I don't want a husband. I don't want a family. Let me just stay in this fine house and take care of you Ladies. I am perfectly happy here. And when you do marry Lord Sabien, I will be honored to serve you and give you all the servant gossip. Now turn around and let me see the front. I want to make sure no hairs pulled out while I was braiding." Lainie stared at Raecli's face. "You have the prettiest eyes. They match the color of the moon."

Raecli studied Lainie's face. She had deep brown eyes that seemed to be filled with many lifetimes. Her chestnut hair was pulled back into a knot. "I think your eyes are very beautiful. They have strands of honey in them."

Lainie looked surprised and instantly blushed. "I'm just a housemaid, but I do appreciate you noticing the golden hue of my eyes. Most people miss it. Well now, you are all done and look very presentable! Did you want to take a walk in the outer courtyards? You haven't seen them yet, and they are quite lovely. I wouldn't mind taking a few spins around the fruiting trees to see if there is any fruit that has fallen for us to eat. You might even see Lord Sabien. He does love walking his mongrels."

Raecli hesitated. "What does Lord Sabien think about marriage? It seems every time I enter a room, he is always leaving."

"The heart dictates for a time, but reason will come to its senses. Don't you worry about him, he'll come around. Just keep being beautiful and sweet, and he'll notice you soon enough."

Raecli didn't understand what she meant, but she guessed that Lord Sabien might be overcoming a broken heart.

"Follow me. I want to show off my handiwork to the house—let them see what I can do when given a prized Lady as yourself," Lainie said, taking Raecli's hand and gently pulling her up. She began to lead her to the door. "You were a dreadful sight when you first arrived on our doorstep, but now I must say you are prettier than Lady Rosarian ever was."

The two left the room and walked the stately hall adorned with ornate cloth wallpaper and dotted with slim, glass torches which stayed flameless until the sun went down. Framed glass windows along the top of the corridor were pushed open and their frames held up with rods. The chilly breeze mixed with the scents of harvest flooded in. As they began their descent down the stairs, Raecli heard the commanding voice of Lady Rosarian in the kitchen.

"What do you mean they have not processed the sweet canes yet? You need them to make our dinner tonight. Sap and honey will not do for my grandmother's cocoa cake recipe. Send one of your girls to go to the storehouse and have her bring a stack of sweet canes back and process them yourself. Or are you too good to be a farmhand?"

When Raecli got to the foot of the stairs, she tried to continue through the backdoor, but Lainie held her back. "Wait until she's finished. She likes an audience. Besides, I want to present you," she whispered.

"No, Lady Rosarian. I would never assume to be more than your servant. I will get it taken care of right away," the cook said.

"Good. I want tonight's meal to be especially grand. I'm having a few thin slices of auraium cut, and I want you to lay them on the cake perfectly as the directions instruct. That is how the cake is supposed to be served, and I'm glad we are finally able to taste my grandmother's recipe as it should be. And here," she reached into one of the folds her elegant, crimson dress. "This is the cylinder that holds my grandmother's recipe. Be sure nothing happens to it and no one peeks at the symbols except for you. I wouldn't want someone trying to copy it down."

The cook gasped. "No, Lady Rosarian. You know that we would never do such a thing. That is against the rules!"

"I know what the rules are, but after recent events, we must not get careless about enforcing them." She turned dramatically, making her dress swish, and sauntered her way to Raecli and Lainie.

145

"Oh my, so sorry you had to see that, but I must lead with a strong arm in this house." She took a moment to inspect Raecli. "How stunning you are, my dear. You look like a completely different young lady than the one they dropped on my doorstep several days ago. And how ravishing that dress looks on you. When I found out you had violet eyes, I had my personal seamstress create a violet dress but with the color even more saturated than the moon. It is a little long, but we will remedy that for you in the morning. I do hope it will suit you fine for the evening, though. I have been planning every detail."

"It is perfect," Raecli assured.

"Oh good! Did you know that my grandmother— the one whose divine cocoa cake we will be enjoying for desert this evening—also had violet eyes. My mother did hope that that mine might be violet, but, alas, they are grey. But hopefully, my grandchild will remedy that longing of hers after all," she said and paused again, studying Raecli's face. "Yes, I do believe that is quite possible now!"

Raecli didn't know what to say, so she stayed silent.

Lady Rosarian looked at Lainie and her tone became immediately less sweet. "Where are you taking her? I hope not into the cold. The weather has quite shifted this morning."

Lainie curtsey. "My Lady, Raecli has not seen the courtyards yet, and I did see Lord Sabien walking his mongrels. I thought maybe just a quick walk around the grounds would liven Lady Raecli's spirits. She's been cooped up inside for days, and Miss Marva says she is fit enough to run to the River and back. I thought she could work up a small appetite by taking a stroll to better enjoy this evening's dinner. I will monitor her and take her in if I sense any weariness."

Lady Rosarian gave a quick smirk but quickly covered it with a smile. "How impressive you speak, Lainie. And how persuasive are your words."

"Yes, my Lady. I do believe being raised in Mr. Barton's home has taught me to speak wisely."

"I guess that is a good quality to have. Do be careful, and bring her in the moment she becomes the slightest fatigued. I have much to do, so I will leave you two at it." And with her last word, Lady Rosarian swept back through the kitchen toward the front of the house.

Lainie led Raecli out the back door and down the path toward the courtyard. As they walked, she looked around to make sure no one as listening. "Lady Rosarian loves you! She has not only planned out her dinner, but she has also planned out your wedding, babies and entire future."

Raecli didn't know what to think. It felt good to have a mother-figure to like her—even if she was a bit theatrical. It filled an emptiness in her heart that had been there since her mother died. But Lainie was right. Lady Rosarian would plan every aspect of her life. Would it be any different than living with her grandfather? She would have to meet Lord Sabien before she could answer that question, but he never stayed near her long enough for them to speak.

"Oh, look! There is Lord Dexarian. He is Lord Sabien's grandfather. He is a quiet, gentle old man. You will really like him. He's not like the other Lords and Ladies. He spent so much time abroad, visiting different villages and exploring all of Rodesh! He has a very sympathetic heart to the servants. His son, Lord Tarmian, gets quite upset with him. Let me introduce you."

Lainie led Raecli slowly to the wooden bench he was resting on that faced the courtyard. "We can walk faster than this," Raecli insisted.

"No, I wouldn't want you to catch a cold. You heard what Lady Rosarian said. She would most definitely blame me. There is no need to rush. He's not going anywhere. I can see he is lost in his thoughts, dreaming about all the places he's seen and the people he has met."

When they finally arrived at the bench, the pair waited for Lord Dexarian to notice them. When he did nothing, Lainie cleared her throat loudly. Finally, he looked up, and Raecli could see his kind, grey eyes filled with memories.

"Lord Dexarian, I want to introduce you to Lady Raecli. She is the merchant's granddaughter. He's the merchant from the coastal cities who found the auraium in the south lands."

Raecli was surprised at her candor, but the aged man didn't seem to care. He merely patted the bench for Raecli to sit down. She looked at Lainie to make sure it was okay.

"You'll love chatting with Lord Dexarian. He has many adventures to tell. His wife and son had to run the house and business while he was gone, which didn't make them too happy. But they did love his stories when he returned. *Tell us another one*, they would say. Or, at least, that's what Miss Marva tells me. She was a child and her mother the lady's maid at the time, so all his stories are caught up in her childhood memories. But I do believe they sound better coming from Lord Dexarian himself."

Raecli was surprised that Lainie spoke so easily in front of Lord Dexarian, but she assumed that he had a more casual relationship with the servants. She pushed her dress in at the sides and sat down next to the aged Lord.

"You stay right here until I get back. I will see if any fruit has fallen from the trees. I won't be long," Lainie said and scurried off.

"So what story do you want to hear?" the aged man said.

Raecli thought for a moment. "My mother once lived in the Northeastern Mountains for a time. She has told me a few stories about how beautiful and clear it is there. I would love a story about your travels there."

The old man's faced filled with emotion from a memory. "How about I tell you my favorite story. You will be the first person to hear it. Not my wife nor my son nor my grandson have heard this one, but I will give it to you. You might not remember it after a while since it is not information that's locked deep within, but you will enjoy hearing it none-the-less."

Raecli was excited. She hadn't heard a story in some time. "I would very much enjoy hearing it."

The aged man looked off to the distance. "When I was a young man, much the age my son is now, I got bored with running the business. I wondered what it was all about. Was I just another landowner in a line of landowners living one moment and dying the next? So I decided to explore all of Rodesh. First, I started in the coastal cities, and I was not impressed with them. They were busier than I preferred and preoccupied with creating, selling and burning. So I wandered to the Northeastern Mountains, and there I met a beautiful young woman who shaped small glass beads for a living."

The man paused lost in a memory, so Raecli waited patiently. Finally, he looked at her and continued.

"I fell in love with the young worker. She gave me a sense of renewed purpose. I would have stayed with her, but there was no place for me among her people. I had no talent other than to be a landowner. I could not take her with me to my home. My wife and son would not approve. When I discovered she was with child, though, I left. I could not bear the thought of the child growing up as a landowner's illegitimate child—a mix of highborn and servant is unacceptable. It would be better for her to grow up in the mountains where life was simple. Many years ago, I did look for my love, but she had died. I found out that she had given birth to a girl— one with grey eyes. When I tried to find her, she had left the mountain villages to go south."

Raecli sat stunned. If she heard him right, she just might be sitting next to F'lorna's grandfather. The information darted into her Eternal Memory and attached itself to the memories of her childhood friend never to be forgotten.

"I see that you are speechless," the old man quipped. "But I am too old to care. My only regret is that I did not go back to find my love before she died. I wish I could have told her how dear she was to me. And I would have liked to meet my daughter before she disappeared. She is out there somewhere—probably with children of her own."

Chapter 16

THE SILVER DAGGER

R alona picked up the pace through the woods, her
curly, dark hair bounced across her shoulders. Her
mother would wonder where she had gone if she
was late for the village dinner. She forgot to check
F'lorna's Achion tree the rise before, and Zelara was

upset with her. If the falcon had been unattended overnight, he could have been seen by the villagers. The parchment with Sand-shaper symbols that Zelara wrote had been in her tunic pouch for many rises, feeling like a burning ember about to burst into flames at any moment. If anyone caught her, she too would be banished like F'lorna. But compared to Zelara and Vauntan, her parents were the least strict, which wasn't saying much. Now that Elder Jaquarn and T'maya left with Le'ana, Sage and Lemmeck and his brothers to find F'lorna, the entire village was in an uproar. Elder Trenton rekindled his plan to end the Shoam-sha, but most of the Elders wanted to find a new Spiritual Leader. She doubted they could find someone who would want to live in their village with all the internal struggles they've been having. Plus, Elder Jaquarn demanded that his lands be left alone. He would be back once he found his daughter.

Truth be told, she didn't want to stay in Right River Hook anymore. Sage's parents moved in with Blaklin and her family, and Lemmeck's parents are now giving their meat offerings to Left River Hook. All the nice families were leaving, and she was stuck here. At least, she had Vauntan and Zelara. When Zelara tried to make friends with her after F'lorna was banished, she refused. Their Achion clusters were close to each other, but she didn't care. But when Zelara told her the secret that she knew the Sand-shaper symbols and F'lorna helped her overcome the guilt she lived with, she changed her mind. Zelara was a very loyal friend— although a bit bossy at times.

Ralona finally heard the rumble of the River. She was close to F'lorna's cluster. She slowed her pace and began listening to the forest noises, wondering if she could hear the falcon breathing in the dark. She saw the Large Achion trees where F'lorna and her parents slept and she began to walk quietly. She was almost more scared to see Banthem than not see him. She moved passed the cooking hearth and walked to F'lorna's tree. She looked straight up where Zelara had placed the swatch of leather that Vauntan made with scraps of animal hide.

The Violet Moon was covered with a fall fog that occurred often when the colder air pushed away the warm. The weather was changing just as drastically as the village. All she saw was darkness. Nothing moved. Relieved, she took a step back and was about to turn when two beady, white eyes turned and looked down at her.

Surprised, she whispered, "Banthem, is that you?" The beady eyes just stared at her. Ralona tried to focus on the silhouette to make out if it was indeed Banthem. Finally, she saw the wooden band around its ankle and a light-colored, rolled sheet of parchment. "That's it!" she exclaimed in a hush voice. "Now I need to climb up. But how? Doesn't Zelara realize I am one of the shortest of all our birth friends?"

She went to F'lorna's Achion hole and brought her right foot onto the bottom lip of the opening. Then she hugged the tree with both arms and lunged her other foot up. She reached for the branch to the right of her head, and grabbed it with both hands. Her jump off the hole shook the branches of the tree, and she looked up to see if Banthem was still there. He waited patiently.

"Thank you, Banthem, for waiting for me," she

whispered, gratefully as she dangled from the branch. "Now if I can just get my legs up there, I can scoot to where you are."

She swung her right leg over the branch and then the left. "All I need to do now is get myself over the branch instead of under," she said. She pulled her body up with her arms and sat on the branch. "I made it! Thank you, Banthem. I appreciate you waiting for me. Now please do not peck me when I take your parchments." She inched closer to the falcon and reached over tentatively to retrieve the parchment he brought. He simply stared at her, and she slipped it out of the band. She tucked it in a pouch on her tunic belt. Then she reached into her tunic pocket and pulled out the rolled parchment Zelara gave her. It was wrinkled by now, but it would have to do. She rerolled it and pushed it inside the band connected to Banthem's leg. "That wasn't as difficult as I imagined," she admitted. "Now go fly away before someone sees you."

Ralona scooted away from the falcon and grabbed the branch allowing her feet to dangle. Then she dropped, rolling onto the soft mossy floor. She looked toward Banthem. He had not left. "Fly away, Banthem. Go to Weston. He needs to read the note Zelara wrote." She waved, but the falcon didn't move. She might have missed something. What was it? "I forgot your snack. Oh, Ra'ash! How could I forget to put a piece of dried meat into my pocket? Wait here, Banthem. I'll be right back."

Ralona turned and ran to Le'ana's land, which was next to F'lorna's. When Le'ana told her parents she was leaving to help find F'lorna, they were surprised but they understood. They let her go as long as she promised to stay in South Village with T'maya. Since they were sympathizers with F'lorna disappearance, they wouldn't mind if she took a piece of dried meat in the pursuit of finding her.

When she finally returned to Banthem, he spun his head instantly to look at her. The fog had dissipated a bit allowing some of the rays from Violet Moon to shine down, and she could see him more clearly. She was out of breath and needed to hurry, but she wanted to make sure he knew again just how much she appreciated him waiting. "I will give voiceless words for your travels back to the marshlands. I am honored that you would wait for me while I found you a treat." She felt silly talking to an animal, but she didn't want to take the chance of offending him. "Here is your treat." She aimed and threw the piece of dried meat, totally missing her aim. He instantly lifted off the tree, swooped down to grab it before it hit the ground and flew away.

"How beautiful! How amazing would it feel to fly like that?" she asked, as she watched him soar over the tops of the tall Achion trees. When he had disappeared into the night, she turned and headed to the Village Achion cluster.

Jaquarn waited while the twins inspected the land ahead. The weather had turned, and he wore his animal pelt around him. He looked to the right of him. T'maya's eyes scanned the landscape—never resting, always looking for her daughter. He knew they were close to South Village—the village near the land bridge. He had visited it when he trained with his sister—no, not his sister. He shook his head. Yes, Eline may not be blood, but she was his sister—the one who helped raise and train him. She was more than simply his sister. She saved his life before it had even begun. He thought of the woman dying alone in the cavern. Something was with her—an animal he had never heard of before.

His biological mother sacrificed her life to bring him to the River-dwellers, and he would not accept that his daughter would die the same fate. His lineage would not end with him. F'lorna was always meant to carry the torch of his family. Maybe if he hadn't been so stubborn, insisting that they stay at Right River Hook when his wife obviously didn't fit in, this wouldn't have happened. His daughter may have even carried the stigma a bit, having the same color eyes as the Sand-shapers. Lemmeck was right. There was a dividing line between people who would accept his family and people who wouldn't, and peace could not be made in the middle.

How could he have been so blind? Why did he want to stay in a village that did not embrace those he loved? Because he always believed they would eventually see how he saw, through the eyes of Ra'ash. But they didn't. They could only see through eyes of fear and tradition. He told his village that they would return, but now that they had been away from the village for these several days, he had second thoughts. He saw his wife flourishing during their travels. She walked more confidently in the freedom from the whispers and slights of others. He realized now that subtle actions and secret mutters of the villagers had weighed his wife down over the years.

"What do you see?" Lemmeck yelled across the field. The twins were now retreating from the edge of the forest that was just up ahead. Dashion motioned for them to come.

"Do you think they see South Village?" Le'ana asked, as her scarlet hair blew in the chilly breeze. "I am tired of walking, and though it is cool outside, the Heat Source has brought out more speckles on my skin than during the harvest."

"Not to mention you are the shortest one here," Sage said, giggling. "You must walk twice the speed to keep up with us." Sage's entire body was hidden under a thick over-tunic, but her burgundy hair flowed down the tunic like soft vines. Her umber cheekbones were highlighted with perspiration from their walk and her light green eyes gleamed from the brightness of the Heat Source.

"Dashion wants us to come. I believe my brothers have found South Village or, at least, the direction to it."

Jaquarn followed behind Lemmeck. Although he was many times older than the Novice Elder, Jaquarn let him lead. He was a good leader and listened to the advice of others and relied on their talents. Jaquarn wished to have visited Lemmeck's father more, but they lived a distance away from the village, and he was a silent, stoic fellow. He did raise three fine young men. Lemmeck and the twins were all skilled hunters and could survive anywhere. Jaquarn noticed the slight crack

in Lemmeck's horn from when F'lorna glued the broken
piece back on with the Sand-shaper method. It had
stayed intact. She saved his horn but lost her own. His
daughter had already been through so much, and now
she must endure more.

He looked at T'maya by his side, still scanning
the land as they walked. She insisted that F'lorna lived.
Le'ana told them all the dream she had of F'lorna flying
on a Swarve over the land bridge. It could be a symbol
of life or death—or even renewed life. He didn't know
which the dream symbolized.

Unexpectedly, six River-dwellers came out of the
other side of the forest with spears in their hands. They
crouched low and held their spears ready to throw. The
twins and Lemmeck each grabbed their bows and aimed
toward the speared men.

"Wait!" Jaquarn called out holding up his hands.
"We are from Right River Hook! My sister, Eline, and
my daughter were here several moon rises ago. Eline
was a Healing Elder. We are here to find my daughter!"

A seventh River-dweller, a woman with dark skin
like Sage and silver hair that was tied in a knot in the
back, walked out of the forest. She held no spear and
motioned to the others to bring theirs down. She walked
toward the group with long strides. "Is this your wife?
The one who once was a Sand-shaper from the
mountains?"

T'maya spoked up. "Yes, I am the mother of
F'lorna who came to visit you."

"My name is Limmian, and I am the Spiritual
Elder of South Village. I am sorry to bring out spears.
We are normally a peaceful people. But the Sand-

shapers near the land bridge have been stealing our harvest, and they just recently attacked one of our Novice Elders. Healing Elder Eline warned us about them before she journeyed back to Right River Hook. I didn't listen to her then, but I am now. She said they will be back, and we must defend ourselves. I am sorry about your loss. One of our young Storytellers has created a song in F'lorna's honor. We have given voiceless words for your family."

Jaquarn nodded. "Thank you, Spiritual Elder Limmian, but we believe our daughter is still alive."

Limmian shook her head. "You have not seen the height of the land bridge yet or the force of its waters. Even if she did survive the fall, there is nothing beyond the River but Desert Plains that go on forever."

Jaquarn looked at his wife and then to the others. By then, Dashion and Rashion had retraced their steps back to them. He had decided to never tell anyone about his true identity, but now that Right River Hook was a memory behind him, he felt like he could be honest about what may lie beyond the Desert Plains. He couldn't explain it, but he had an urgency that all the River-dwellers knew that their neighbors, the Lake-keepers, still existed. "We have reason to believe that the Lake-keepers still exist beyond the Desert Plains—that the Great Engulfing did not swallow them all up as we believed."

Limmian stood motionless for several moments. Jaquarn knew she was thinking that he must be confused or ill, but she didn't want to hurt a tender man's feelings who had just lost his daughter.

160

Finally, she spoke. "That would answer my many questions."

Jaquarn stared. "You believe me?"

"Yes. There have been changes in our waters and our lands. We have seen insects that we have never seen before, and fish that are new. I thought that there had to be something on the other side of the River beyond the Desert Plains. But I wasn't fully convinced until I found something interesting." She pulled out a shiny dagger from her tunic pocket. "This blade. I have never seen this material before. It gleams in the sun and it can cut through anything without breaking."

Jaquarn walked forward and gaped at the knife. "My mother's dagger," he whispered in awe. "Where did you find it?"

"Your mother?" she asked. "I found it after the ground shudders. As I inspected the new land bridge, its reflection burned my eyes."

"Please!" Jaquarn cried. "Show me where you found it. It might be our only way to find our daughter!"

Chapter 17

UNQUENCHABLE MEMORY

"That's enough," Amorfia cried out. "I don't want to hear another sage speak. It hurts!" She sat on the wooden floor of the main temple sanctuary with her head leaning forward into her hands. She wore a simple tunic shirt and pants of the new sages. Her horns had grown to about half their initial length. Her chest hurt. Her head hurt. She couldn't hear one more story or her insides would burst open.

The Supreme Sage hovered over her. She wore another elegant gown with the cream feathers that signified her elevated rank. Her focus for the last week had been exclusively centered on Amorfia, the gift from the Befores. "Are you telling me that your youth memories can't store anymore? Are they finished?"

"No, they're still available. I feel them searching, but nothing I have heard satisfies them. They seek but don't hear what they need." Amorfia looked up. "Please Supreme Sage. Let me have a rest. I want to walk outside and visit the Swarves. I need to be outside in the crisp air and walk among the trees. The softness of the Atlatl Forest soothes me."

The Supreme Sage straightened and looked around to the many sages in her company. "Not one of you has what Morfie's youth memories need. Not one of you! Do you see them searching for truth? Do you sense their yearning? Darton, come here!"

One of the older sages came to her and bowed. His tunic was more ornate than the younger sages but not nearly as extravagant as hers. "Yes, Supreme Sage."

"Go to the Temple of the Highland Cliffs. Talk to the Supreme Sage there and send me more sages—sages who have information we lack. Tell him that we will send sages back to him in kind," she said looking around. "Those of you with your youth memories still available, meet me here in the morning. You will be gaining new stories from the Highland Cliffs."

There were gasps all around.

"I know what you are thinking, but it is time we begin to share our knowledge. Morfie is the gift from the Befores after years of silence, they are sending us one whose eyes have no color to guide us to truth. There is something they are trying to tell us, and her youth memories search for it. It will not shut until the truth has been found! The rest of you, be prepared to travel to the Highland Cliffs in the morning. You will tell your stories there. Do you daily chores for today and tomorrow. You are dismissed!" Her voiced echoed off the towering walls of the sanctuary.

The band of sages got up from the floor. "Go, Darton, and don't come back without new sages."

"Yes, Supreme Sage," he said and bowed. He instantly turned and retreated out of the temple doors.

The Supreme Sage sighed. She walked around Amorfia's form still lingering on the floor. Her wooden throne waited on a humble platform in the middle of the sanctuary. The throne itself was not humble. It had been chiseled with designs that matched much of the ornate robes she wore. She sat on the gaudy chair and stared at Amorfia. "Get up, Morfie. The other sages are gone."

Amorfia wiped her tears. She did not want the Supreme Sage to mock her distress. Amorfia had been hopeful the first few days in the temple that after hearing the sages, her memory would be unlocked, but none of the words spoken satisfied the burning curiosity inside of her. She felt her memory there inside of her, but it was trapped and unable to come to the surface, like it had been buried in the belly of Rodesh itself.

Amorfia slowly got up.

"Come here, Morfie. I'm not going to bite you. I am on your side. I understand now that you were sent to me by the Befores. They are trying to show me something, but I need you to cooperate with me. What else can I do?"

Amorfia stood and walked to where the Supreme Sage was sitting. "I don't know if the stories I am learning are helping me or if they are blocking what's already inside. I listen and hope that a ray of light will penetrate the darkness within my youth memories. But the youth memories I have now feel bottomless like an endless drop and the light only gets swallowed up. I feel like what I'm searching for is already in there, but I only need to see it."

The Supreme Sage scoffed. "You say that your memories feel endless, yet then you say they feel full. How can that be, Morfie? They cannot be both!"

Amorfia nodded. "I know, Supreme Sage, but that is exactly how it feels, like they are both available and hidden."

The Supreme Sage stared at Amorfia for several moments lost in the battle within her mind. "Very well, go visit the Swarves. Go walk the forest. Go rest your mind, but tomorrow be ready. You will listen to the sages from the Highland Cliffs."

Amorfia bowed. "Yes, Supreme Sage. I will do as you wish."

Amorfia quickly turned and walked quietly to the front of the temple. She could feel the Supreme Sage staring at her, so she wanted to get out as soon as she could. Once she finally closed the doors behind her, she closed her eyes and inhaled a deep breath of relief. When she opened her eyes, she spied the golden disk that she had hammered what felt like a lifetime ago. She wondered if it would have been better to stay content with Voddie or would her curiosity eventually have brought her here? She turned to the right and walked the long porch that wrapped around the main temple. She would visit the Swarves first. Then she would walk the forest.

The cool breeze felt good on her skin. She should wear her cape, but she didn't want to return to her room. Her room at the temple was very similar to the one that Voddie's brothers had made her, but it was less appealing because its surroundings had no joy. Her room at Voddie's home brought her the fun of a toddler and the sweetness of a baby. She could listen to Voddie's continuous stream of words without ever getting a headache. And sometimes, she would watch Voddie and Morgo sip their root ale and talk in front of the fireplace. She didn't have to hear their whispered words to know that tenderness and affirmation was being shared. She could sense it. She wondered how it felt to be so completely loved by someone.

At the temple, the sages kept secrets and competed with one another. They were isolated, like individual stories that would not relate to one another. Amorfia had heard them all, and she knew that the stories of the sages were not distinct. They all overlapped into the history of their people. Amorfia had heard the full scope of their stories, each being like a thread in one of the Supreme Sage's ornate robes. But the sages did not unify, so instead of a grand design, they were mere threads scattered on the floor.

She heard the soft growls of the Swarves as she made her way behind the temple. She could smell them too. Their odor wasn't necessarily bad, just strong. And their breath—Amorfia hated to admit it, but when she first went up to a Swarve and petted its face, she wrinkled her nose and coughed when it breathed on her. But the sweetness of the Swarve made up for the smelly odor they breathed out, so she gladly endured.

She saw the bronze one first. He was eating on the troughs of grasses that the sages continually tended for them to eat. He looked up. His long, wispy fur floated in the wind. Although their fur looked soft, the individual strands had veins running through them that were strong yet pliable. When the Swarve saw her, it lifted its large, flat face. It tried to flap the useless wings dangling at its side, but they only wiggled. He was taller than she, but only by an arm's length. It was about her length wide and two of her length long. Bronze fur covered its entire body.

She learned from Morgo that when a Swarve was a hatchling, its fur could move, and the strands searched for something to connect to. If the fur did not find another, they would lose their ability to move, becoming lifeless. The sages layered a thick resin all over the hatchling's body, to prevent the fur from connecting with anyone. Amorfia did not like the tradition, and she wondered what it would feel like for the Swarves' fur to embrace her back as she stroked their soft fluffs. She also didn't like that the sages did not give the Swarves names. They explained that Swarves didn't live long enough to warrant that honor.

"Bronzie," she called. He ambled to her. He was one of three bronze Swarves. There were also about a dozen brown ones. There were no gold ones, but she heard that those were only for the chieftains and other wealthy Lake-keepers.

Bronzie came to her and brought his large, moist nose to her. His mouthed opened slightly as he excitedly nuzzled her hand. Amorfia wrinkled her nose and laughed. "Bronzie, your breath is extra potent today. I can tell you have just finished your lunch. Go to the pool and have your fill of water to wash the grasses down." She pushed his nose and laughed some more. His wings wiggled, and he turned toward the pool near the back of the fenced in land. She waited for the other Swarves to come to her, but she knew that most had eaten their lunch and were taking their midday nap. Maybe she would take a walk and return after they had rested a bit. She would slip into her room and grab her cape before anyone noticed, so she could take her long walk through Atlatl Forest.

After she left her room, she grabbed the edge of the cape and wrapped it around her neck, connecting the clasp in place. Then she stepped off the wraparound porch and made her way into the forest. The chill of the air had grown colder even though the sun was high in the sky. She thought of Morgo. He was probably done fishing for the season and enjoying salted fish with his wife and boys. She missed Range's energy and Paxton's giggles. Even if she could never return, she was thankful she had that short moment with them and to see what family life looked like. They had something the sages with all their learning would never have—unity and love.

When she first woke up after Morgo found her, her mind was completely blank. She was filled with fear even though she did not know what fear was at the time. She felt completely alone, like the moon might feel without the stars surrounding it and the sun to greet it in the morning and evening. Just a moon in an endless black sky. But Voddie's face came into her view, and she watched as Voddie smiled and mumbled words. She did not understand the words, but she felt the joy in them. Amorfia had clung onto that joy, and little by little, her ears recognized the words Voddie spoke and she began to not feel alone. The stars and sun had finally joined her endless black sky. Voddie had given her something she desperately needed: an identity.

"Morfie," she heard a voice whisper.

Amorfia looked and saw Voddie's little brother, Boru, appearing out from behind a tree. She smiled. "Boru," she exclaimed. She had met Boru when he was building her room. Although he tried to talk with her, they never really conversed long. He was different from Voddie. Voddie would talk and talk and never tire of offering words. He, on the other hand, would ask her how she was doing. When she said she was doing well, there was an awkward silence until he finally got back to working on her room.

He wore a long tunic and pants, but nothing warmer. Amorfia could tell he was cold. His chin-length brown hair was swept back with perspiration like he had been running, but his nose and cheeks were pink from the chill. Somehow, she saw him with different eyes. He had the same sweetness about him like Voddie, but he seemed more shy about showing it.

"My sister wanted me to bring you this," he said, handing her a netted sack with foods from home.

Amorfia took the sack. "Tell her thank you from me. I do miss her cooking."

"Did you know that my brother and I, we are building an inn—just like the one that the old innkeeper runs in South Basin? He let us look at the building to see how it was constructed. We will follow a similar plan but with a few changes to suit us."

"That is wonderful," Amorfia said. "I'm guessing that Voddie has found a use for the coins that the Supreme Sage gave her."

He grinned. "Aye, our family has all decided to invest each of our portions into an inn for East Basin. Looks like I'll have a busy winter building after all."

"I wish I could watch the construction take place. I'm sure it will entertain the fishermen and their families while their work is done for the season."

The pair walked in silence for a while, allowing the sounds of the forest to speak their turn.

Boru finally broke the silence. "Ah—my sister also wanted to see how you were. She—actually, all of us are worried about you. Did you want to come back home? Your room is waiting for you."

Those words sounded like a beautiful song to Amorfia. "I would love to, but the Supreme Sage is not done with me yet. We are trying something in the morning to help me remember. Nothing has worked so far, but I do know much more about the Lake-keepers and their history."

"That's really good, I think. We have a lot of history—some good and some bad. I bet you've learned about all the territory rivalries we have endured? So many that I don't think I even know about them all."

She nodded in agreement. "Lots of those. The chieftains are always fighting. If they could see from my perspective, they wouldn't fight anymore."

Boru crossed his arms and rubbed them to keep them warm. "I agree with that," he said and thought. "I never told anyone this, not Voddie and especially not my older brother, but I came to the Temple of the Sages once when I still had my youth memories. I hammered the disk and everything."

Amorfia's eyes opened with surprise. "You did? How did it go? I had to sing to get them to come out."

Boru smiled. "I heard. Morgo told us all about it. I can't wait to hear you sing one day."

Something about the way he said those words and looked at her made Amorfia's heart speed up and her cheeks feel hot. "I've only sung that one time. I don't know if I could do it again, but I would like to try. It felt comfortable to sing, like I have done it before. Why did you come to the temple?"

"I had a dream that I didn't understand. When I told it to the sages, they didn't understand it either. Nothing in their youth memories could explain it, so they said it was simply my childish imagination. But I know it wasn't. It felt real and I could feel the power of it."

Amorfia stepped closer to Boru. "What was your dream?"

He looked embarrassed. "It might not be anything, but it is locked in my youth memories, so I can feel it just like I had the dream yesterday."

He closed his eyes, and she waited for the image to pull up in his memory.

"I saw a Chieftain. He looked strong and confident—the strongest and most confident man I have ever seen. I knew instantly He was the most powerful Chieftain to ever live and who would ever live. He was riding on a massive red Swarve that was flying over Domus Lake. He had a sword in one hand and a sphere of light, like a sphere, in the other. All the colors of the six moons were around Him, and I bowed to worship Him. Not like I bow to the chieftains when they pass by me. Everything in me needed to bow."

As Amorfia listened, she was drawn to Boru's words. Something deep within her longed to connect with what he was saying, but like the lifeless fur of the Swarves, she couldn't reach it. She didn't know how to bring that dead part of her back to life.

"I didn't mean to make you cry," Boru said. He rubbed his fingers gently across her cheek. "It's probably nothing."

"No, don't say that. I feel what you are saying is truth, but how can we find this Chieftain? Is He real or is He a symbol of something else? Who is He?" she asked, staring into Boru's hazel eyes. She was desperate to find the truth that nagged at her every moment, and he carried a tiny piece of it.

"I don't know," he said, shaking his head. "But I suspect that these sages are as lost as we are."

Chapter 18

THE SEARCH BEGINS

Weston heard the screech over the howl of the wind. The temperatures had dropped, and he had finally harvested every plant that could be ruined by the cold. He only hoped the fruit tree sapling would survive; though, he doubted it. He wrapped it in an old tunic of his. Maybe the fabric would keep the cold out enough to help the young tree survive. Maybe.

He heard the screech again. It was Banthem.
"That is strange," he said to himself. Banthem would
normally stay at F'lorna's Achion cluster for a few
nights to rest. F'lorna had a tendency to feed him well,
and the falcon enjoyed the extra food. He wasn't
expecting him for at least another week. He brought his
hand above his eyes to shade the sun's rays, so he could
get a better look. Sure enough, it was Banthem. There
was a light-colored parchment tucked into the band
around his leg. He didn't look fatter. Instead, he looked
on the scrawny side like he hadn't eaten much during his
travels.

Banthem finally hovered over the low hanging
branch and landed on the limb, wrapping his talons
around the piece of leather Weston left for him. The limb
swayed a bit, and Banthem looked at him attentively.

"Banthem, you looked starved. I have some dried
marsh rabbit. Let me get it for you. I know that the cold
has caused many of the animals to hibernate, but after
this, you are going to have to find your food. I can't feed
you everything I have or else I won't make it through the
winter." Weston walked to the ground storage he had
created for his meat. He bent down and lifted the lid. All
of his stored meats were there. He grabbed a hefty chunk
of the rabbit and secured the lid back on the hole. He
then threw it directly at Banthem's beak and he quickly
caught it and greedily gulped it down. The falcon
continued to stare at Weston for more. "You are hungry.
Okay, I will get you one more piece, but that is all I can
spare for now."

He went back to the ground storage and grabbed
one more slightly smaller piece of meat. "Here," he said

throwing it to Banthem. "Now let me see what F'lorna has to say and why she sent you back so soon."

Weston walked to the tree and reached up. Banthem ignored him as he swallowed his last piece of meat. He clasped the parchment with his thumb and finger and slid it out. He always treated F'lorna's notes like they were more precious than auraium. Once he opened the parchment, he knew right away that F'lorna had not written the symbols. He skimmed to the bottom of the page to see if the symbols made up F'lorna's mother's name. Maybe she had finally decided to write the symbols. However, to his surprise, the symbols made out the name, *Zelara*.

"Zelara?" he said out loud. "Wasn't she the girl who hated F'lorna?" He quickly read the note and felt his hands begin to shake. "No, it can't be!"

"What is it, Brother?" Merriton asked, as he entered Weston's land. "I saw Banthem flying above. Isn't it too early for F'lorna's response?"

"She's fallen," Weston said, rereading the note in disbelief.

"What?" Merriton said, taking the note from his brother. He read it quickly. "Who is this Zelara? How can we trust her?"

"She says that she and F'lorna are friends. Jaquarn and T'maya have gone to South Village with Lemmeck and his brothers, Sage and Le'ana. I think that River-dweller village is the first one we visited after we crossed over the land bridge. She says that F'lorna has fallen off the land bridge. But they believe that there is a chance she still lives." He turned to his brother. "How can that be? How could anyone survive that fall? And even if she did survive, there is nothing down the river except the desert. She would never survive out there alone."

"Jaquarn would not be looking for her if he did not feel there was hope," Merriton said, placing his hand on his brother's shoulder. "There is always hope."

"But what was she doing there anyway? Eline said she would keep her away from the land bridge because of F'lorna's Mountain Terror. How could she have been so careless with her niece?" Weston felt anger fill him. Just when he believed his life was starting to turn around, he lost the one girl he had liked since coming to the marshlands. He balled his fists and began to beat the sides of his legs.

Merriton reread the parchment. "No, it says that F'lorna saw her friend, Raecli. Remember, Sage told us about her. She was F'lorna's best friend who was taken from her over a year ago. Her grandfather is the rich merchant from the coastal cities."

"Merriton, do you know what this means?" Weston said, turning to his brother. "The Sand-shapers! They have come down to the land bridge. They are in our territory. If they venture to the marshlands, they will find our village!"

Merriton froze. "We can't let them find us. We have families depending on us. My wife, my son. They can't go back to the landowners. They would be made an example to the rest of the farmhands. And you and I, we wouldn't survive the steward's beatings for long."

"I must go to the village at the other end of the land bridge. If Jaquarn and Lemmeck are meeting with the leaders there, I must ask for help. They need to unite with us, so we can protect all of our lands. And if F'lorna did survive, I can help to find her. Banthem can fly for days. I will release him into the desert lands. If he can't find her, no one will."

Raecli loved this day, the end-day, when all the servants were free from work. She enjoyed Lainie's company, but it was nice to be away from her for at least one day a week. Today she wanted to be alone with her thoughts. The weather was chilly, and she enjoyed having an excuse to wear a thick wool cape and a scarf around her neck. She could almost disappear from the world around her. She had finally grown accustomed to having no horns. She could see why the Sand-shaper extracted them. She didn't realize their weight until they were gone. But she still felt there was a reason why Ra'ash created them—maybe a reminder of His strength over them. She hadn't given voiceless words to Ra'ash for some time, and after she saw F'lorna fall into the waterfall, she experienced the same emotions of losing her once more. But now there was one who shared her loss, the grey-eyed grandfather. She knew that he had to be T'maya's father. He had the same eyes. He had visited the Northeastern Mountains and met someone. Then the woman he loved had his baby, a daughter. The daughter grew up and left the mountains and met Jaquarn. And they had a daughter, F'lorna. A granddaughter he would never meet. He felt the loss of

F'lorna by never meeting her. Raecli was no longer alone in her grief. Another shared it.

Her mind went to Lord Sabien. They had exchanged a few words, but she could tell that he would never love her—even though she knew he may marry her to appease his parents. It was difficult to look at him. His hair was a shade lighter than hers, but his eyes were the same grey as F'lorna and her mother's eyes. *Cousins,* she thought. *F'lorna and Sabien were cousins.* Raecli looked around at the sprawling estate. So much land to the north, south, west and east. She could probably walk for days and not find the end of it. If T'maya would have grown up on this land, she would have never met Jaquarn at the pillar in the north villages just under the mountains. F'lorna would never have existed, and she would have not known her best birth friend. It was good that the grandfather did not take T'maya back to his home—though, he could have done better at visiting his daughter when he could.

Raecli stopped and listened. She heard raised voices. One was Sabien's, but she didn't recognize the female voice. They were behind the steward's storeroom. She crept slowly to the front wall to listen. She didn't want to eavesdrop, but she was curious who he would be arguing with. He was normally a very quiet person. She peered through one of the glass windows. She could see the two on the other side in a heated conversation. Raecli did recognize the girl. It was the steward's daughter, Kysha. She was tall and thin with chestnut hair, dark eyes and exotic features. She looked nothing like the steward, but Lainie told her that the steward's wife was a beauty who died tragically too young.

"If you marry her, I will not keep seeing you. I will not be a mistress to a married Lord. I would rather stay in my father's home, and you know how much I hate him!" Kysha yelled.

Now everything made sense. Lainie had hinted that Sabien had been in love before, but Raecli never thought he was still in love, and to the steward's daughter.

"We can still stay together. Your father always looks away. This girl means nothing to me. She just has the connections my father wants and the violet eyes my mother wants. That is all. I will never love her," Sabien said.

Raecli had never heard so much passion in his voice. She realized now that his apathy toward her had been a demonstration of his love for Kysha.

"Do you know how twisted my father is? He hurts his people. The farmhands are his people and he treats them worse than the mongrels you keep. The only reason he says nothing about us is because he is keeping the information for bribery later. He will use it against you once you become Lord over this estate."

"That is not going to happen for some time. My grandfather is still alive, and my father is not handing anything over to me until he's dead. We have years to worry about that." Sabien grabbed Kysha. "Look, if you want to leave, let us leave tonight. I will give everything away to have you. The only way we can be together is if we are willing to lose it all."

Kysha said nothing. "Where would we go? To the coastal cities and be workers there? To the mountains? Or maybe we can become River-dwellers and live in trees? What is our life away from the estate?"

He drew the girl close to him. "What is our life without each other?"

She threw her arms around his neck and cried into his shoulder. "Why can't I have violet eyes?"

Suddenly, a loud bark startled Raecli. She looked down. It was one of Sabien's mongrels. "Good boy," she whispered, trying to quiet it.

"Who is there?" Sabien yelled. He ran around the storeroom and caught up to her. "Oh, Raecli. I didn't mean to yell at you."

There was a rustling sound and Raecli looked through the window and saw Kysha running back toward the steward's house.

"I'm sorry. I didn't mean to intrude. I was taking a walk and heard voices. I just wanted to ensure everything was alright." Raecli said, hoping the covering around her face hid her embarrassment.

Sabien looked angry but quickly tried to cover up his feelings. "What did you hear?"

Raecli tried to think of something to say, but she was a horrible liar, and she didn't have persuasive speech Lainie possessed. Deep down she was still a River-dweller, and they were honest people for the most part. She felt the tears begin to flow. "I'm so sorry! I didn't mean to hear so much. I'm so upset for Kysha and you. I wish there was something I could do to help. But I'm trapped too by my grandfather. I know what it feels like to lose everything, so I know why Kysha is struggling."

Sabien stared at Raecli for a moment. Then he sighed and crossed his arms. "Look at us. A Lord and Lady both trapped."

"Honestly, I'm not much of a Lady. All my life I was a River-dweller. Those were the best years of my life—before my mother died," she said. So many emotions were coming at her. She had coped as well as she could, but she couldn't bear another blow. Sabien was in love with someone else, so there was no way they would marry. Her grandfather and Lord Tarmian had already formed a partnership. Lady Rosarian was already having baby clothes made. Her grandfather would be outraged. They all would be. Highborns did not marry servants and stay in the family long.

"I'm sorry I have been ignoring you. I knew that you being here wasn't your choice either. I could see it when you first arrived. You looked sick and close to death. I can't believe your grandfather had your horns pulled out so late. I'm sure the pain was unbearable," he said.

More tears threatened to come. "Not as unbearable as losing my friend. She fell off the land bridge trying to save me."

"I heard mention of that from your grandfather's steward, Moirel. Who was she?" he asked.

"Her name was F'lorna. She is no one you would know. Just a River-dweller with eyes like yours."

"River-dwellers have grey eyes?" he asked, surprised. "I didn't know that."

"No, they don't. They have eyes of gold, blue, green, brown and even emerald. But not grey. She inherited her grey eyes from her mother."

"Who was her mother? She must have been a landowner's daughter who left to love who she wanted."

Raecli shrugged. "We don't know the full story of her mother's family." She didn't want to divulge too much information. If the grandfather had kept the secret all these years, she would too. "All we know is that her mother has grey eyes and no horns—obviously a Sand-shaper. She would braid twigs into her hair to look like us. She would have F'lorna and I recite the *Divine Oracle* to her because she did not have the words in her Eternal Memory. I'm glad for that. It taught me most of the *Divine Oracle* early. I guess Ra'ash knew I would be taken away from my home at a young age."

"What is her name? Your friend's mother?" he asked.

She hesitated to give too many details, but the grandfather did not know her name, so it wouldn't matter if she said it. "Her name is T'maya." Raecli smiled and wiped away the glistening tears that threatened to slip down the creases of her eyes. It felt good to talk about who she use to be. She had tried to hide it for so long. She looked back at Sabien and he was backing away from her with a slight look of panic on his face. "I'm sorry. Did I say too much? Please don't be angry. I was only trying to give you hope. I see how much you love Kysha. My mother was a Sand-shaper and she moved to the villages and found happiness. It can be difficult, but you will be able to join with Kysha."

"How did your friend's parents meet?" he asked.

182

Raecli wondered at his curiosity, but she thought maybe her words were helping him with his decision to leave. "When T'maya's mother died, she traveled south to live with the River-dwellers. That is when she met Jaquarn. He was traveling north learning as a Spiritual Elder. She journeyed with him to Right River Hook and they joined—or married as you say it. The village is the same location as your lands except on the east side of the River."

"T'maya is her name. Who was her father? Did she ever mention that he may be a landowner?"

"T'maya never met him," Raecli said. This was the truth. T'maya had no idea who her father was beyond that he was a Sand-shaper.

"Did she travel from the coastal cities?" Sabien pressed.

"Oh no, that's where my mother was from and the reason why she died. She got Smoke Sickness. T'maya was from the Northeastern Mountains where the rural workers live. She would shape little glass jewels. Why do you look upset? Have I said something to offend you?" Raecli asked.

"Not purposefully," he whispered.

Raecli thought over her words. "What did I say?"

"You said my great-grandmother's name, T'maya. She was my grandfather's mother. And if what you say is true, then your friend may be my grandfather's illegitimate granddaughter, born from the baby he fathered in the mountains. I have lost a cousin I never knew I had."

Chapter 19

MEETING THE AUNT

"Morfie! Morfie!" Range yelled when he saw Amorfia walking up the path to the house. "Range!" Amorfia yelled when she saw him. She set her pack down and knelt to let him collide into her arms. She squeezed his little body and he squeezed her back. The weather was cold and he wore a wooly jacket, but she could tell that he had worked up a sweat from running outside. She finally put him down and stared into his hazel eyes. They looked a lot like Boru's eyes.

"Morfie! You are here!" Voddie came from the house carrying Paxton in her arms. He looked like a stuffed cushion with all of the blankets around him. "I was monitoring Range from the window, and he disappeared. My heart stopped until I heard your voice. Oh, look at you! You look like a sage!" Voddie embraced Amorfia with her free arm.

"Let me hold that baby," Amorfia said. "My arms have been missing his squishy, little body." She took Paxton and brought him into her arms. His face instantly recognized hers and he squealed with delight. She rubbed her nose against his. The heat from all his coverings permeated his face. "Look how much you have grown, Paxie. I missed you!"

"Come into the house, Morfie. It is too cold out here, and I want to hear about everything. You are staying with us from now on, are you? I see you have brought a pack along."

Amorfia walked beside her toward the house. "I can only stay for a few days. The Supreme Sage has run out of things to do with me. She is meeting with the Supreme Sages from both the South Basin and the Highland Cliffs to discuss what to do next. Is Morgo home?"

"No, he left to the innkeeper's home in South Basin. He and my brothers are helping their family brew ale, so they will have enough to last through winter. They are also building a secret passageway behind the counter to hide the extra food and barrels. That way, if that blasted Rathtar and his friends try to steal everything again, they will only get what's out in the open."

Amorfia could tell by Voddie's voice that she was not happy about what the chieftain's son had done to the poor innkeeper. "Let me guess," Amorfia jested. "There is a couple of barrels of ale in return for their hard work?"

"Aye, they are using the ale to bribe the fisherman to help them build the inn while they are bored at home with nothing to do. Boru told you about the inn, didn't he?"

Amorfia nodded. "Yes, and I think it is a brilliant idea."

"We have already purchased all the lumber, building supplies and the land. East Basin does get a lot of visitors from other parts of Domus Lake looking to buy fish and whatnot. An inn here would do well. Morgo is planning on trading his fish for some of the innkeeper's ale. His inn and our inn will not be competitors in the same village, so the trade will benefit all of us."

When Amorfia walked into the small house, memories flooded back. This was the place where her life began—the only life she could remember. It had been several weeks since she left, and now she felt like she had somewhat of a past. She had matured much during her short time at the temple. She felt older— though, she knew she was physically about the same age. As she looked around the only home she could remember, she knew deep down that this was not the home of her childhood. Something beautiful was still

186

missing, but she could do nothing to regain it on her own.

"Here, let me take Paxton. It is the boys' naptime. Take off your cape and set down your pack. Make yourself comfortable. We have your room waiting for you. I want to hear about everything. My itching ears need more information than my little brother can offer me. He's such a quiet fellow—always has been. When he comes back from visiting you at the temple, I ask him a boatload of questions, and he gives me such skimpy answers." She took the baby and held her hand out to Range.

"I don't want to take a nap," he whined.

"Yes, but you have played hard today, and I can see that your eyes are puffy and red. Take a short nap for Mommy, so you will be full of energy when Amorfia eats dinner with us tonight."

Range's eyes lit up. "Okay! And I will show her the new design I created with the sticks and string she made me."

Voddie took the baby and the boy's hand and led them to their room. "Yes, you can show her your design, but only after you sleep."

After the three entered the room, Amorfia took off her cape. Voddie had a large fire going in the fireplace. The house was small and tidy, and Amorfia stared at all the little trinkets, cushions and candle holders that Voddie used to decorate her home. The home was full of peace and love. She felt like she needed to offer thanks to someone, but she didn't know to who. "Thank You," she whispered, hoping that her words reached the ears of the One who deserved to hear them.

187

She finally sat down on Morgo's cushion in front of the fireplace. She had sat there often when Morgo was fishing.

She heard the soft footsteps of Voddie coming into the main room of the house. "They were really tired. Range has been at it all day. It's all I could do to monitor him and feed Paxton." She walked over and sat on her cushion next to Amorfia.

"I'm sorry, I am not here to help you," she said.

"Oh, Morfie! You have been offering me much more than simply help now that you are with the sages. You have turned everything upside down. The sages are in an uproar over you. Suits them right. They always looked down on the rest of us, like we are simpletons. Well, you are showing them. I heard you have memorized the youth memories of dozens and dozens of sages. And can you believe it? When you came to my home, you knew not a single word. But I did not fear. I could see intelligence in your eyes. I always knew there was something about you that was special. So how is it going with Boru? I know he has visited you several times now that things have slowed in the village."

Amorfia blushed. "He talks with me when I have my breaks from training."

"And—" she waited. "You sound just like him but worse. You are giving me no details to work with."

Amorfia tried not to look embarrassed. "I enjoy his company. He is quiet and he doesn't mind if we just walk for a while or pet the Swarves in silence. But when we do talk, we talk about things that you can't see or do. We talk about life and its meaning. Just a bunch of stuff that some might think is boring."

"Aye," Voddie thought. "That's my little brother. He was always thinking, and then when he would ask our dad a question, the question would be something no one could answer—not even the sages."

"I like his questions," Amorfia confessed.

"Morfie, you don't have to tell me that. I can already see it in your face. You like Boru, don't you?"

Amorfia looked at the fire as it consumed the wood that gave it life. "There's something about him that knows me. I can't fully explain it, but he has a piece of what I've been looking for."

Voddie leaned back in her chair. "That's called love, my friend. When the other person draws you to them, and there's just nothing you can do about it."

An abrupt bang on the door startled them. "By the orders of Chieftess Dalia bar Haven, you are commanded to open the door! I need to speak with the sage, Amorfia."

Paxton began to cry and Range started yelling, "Mommy! Mommy!"

Voddie looked at Amorfia. "You get the door, and I'll go to the boys—and, Morfie, when it comes to the chieftains, they have all sovereignty. Dalia is not like her brother, but you would do well not to cross her."

Amorfia nodded. When she saw Voddie close the door of the boys' room behind her, she got up to answer the door. A large swordsman with a scarred face looked down at her. "Are you who the sages call, *Morfie?*" he asked.

"Yes," she nodded.

"Chieftess Dalia would like to see you. She is waiting for you at the Highland Cliffs Fortress."

"Let me get my cape and pack," she said. She quickly looked around the house. She didn't know why, but she felt like it would be her last time there. She wanted to slam the door and run to her room, but she had a sense that she was being beckoned further onto her journey for truth. "Goodbye, Range and Paxton, I love you," she whispered. "And you Voddie and Morgo too. Tell Boru that—that I will miss him." She turned and left, wondering if that was the first time she had whispered those words or had she said them to someone else in a different life.

When she exited the house, the large man was waiting for her. He was wearing thick leather and furs with a sword by his side. He had four other men with him. Why was she being so heavily guarded?

"We came by boat. Follow us," he said, gruffly.

She followed him around the outskirts of the village and down to the shore. Every so often, he would look back at her. Was he making sure she wasn't going to run away? Where would she go? She would not dare go back to Voddie's home and endanger the safety of Paxton and Range. Would she go back to the temple? No, the temple had become a prison for her that held no answers, just more and more information that felt empty and lifeless. She thought of Chieftess Dalia. The Highland Cliff sages had come to the Temple of the Sages in Atlatl Forest. She learned almost everything about the bar Haven family—except for the bar Haven swordcraft. That was knowledge that was only passed down to family members.

"We are here, Morfie of the sages," the swordsman said.

190

Amorfia couldn't help but stare. The wooden boat, although small, was beautifully carved with the flag of the Highland Cliffs flapping on the top of a silver pole at the back of the boat. The seats in the back and the front were cushioned, and the wooden ones in the middle were located by the oars. Now she knew why so many men were needed.

"Sit there," the aged warrior said, pointing to the back of the boat. Amorfia complied. She noted the sun was going down and the air had gotten colder. She knew from the sages that Domus lake had frozen over a few times, but only during very severe winters. She wrapped the cape tightly around her body and got into the boat. She set her pack on the cushion beside her. The swordsman stepped into the front of the boat and sat down, while the other four men piled in the middle. Each man sat down next to an oar. Then they waited for the signal.

"Rowers! Heave!" the warrior yelled.

The four men simultaneously and harmoniously pulled the oars. They pushed the oars inches above the water and pulled in a flat circle-like motion. She wondered if they would get to the fortress before the darkness blanketed the sky. She looked out on the water. She hadn't been there since Morgo found her—but even then, she didn't remember. She preferred staying home with Voddie and the boys. The space there was safe and secure, a perfect place for an injured person to heal.

She looked around her as the last of the sun's rays glistened along the current, making shimmering reflections like Morgo's metal tankard did in the light of the fireplace. By the time they finally got to the shore, the light of the sun had been replaced by the violet light of the moon, but winter clouds had muted the glow. She saw torches in the distance, and they looked like they were attached to a long pier. The swordsman was directing the men alongside it.

"More to the left! Hurry or you'll damage the chieftain's boat!" The boat jerked to the left. "That's too much! I can't reach the ropes." It moved slightly back to the right. "There now, ease up." Finally, the boat slowed enough and the four men grabbed ropes that were tucked under their chairs and jumped out.

Amorfia couldn't see the cliffs, let alone the fortress, because of the darkness that blanketed them. They had been described to her, but without a point of reference, she had no idea what they looked like. She grabbed her pack and put the long strap around her head. She would be needing to use both hands to get out of the boat. She got up and looked to the aged warrior reaching for her.

"Now watch your step. Chieftess Dalia would not be happy if I brought her guest back harmed."

Amorfia noted a slight tenderness in the swordsman's voice. She extended her hand, and he grabbed her with his rough hands and pulled her straight up. Her feet landed softly on the wooden pier.

"Oh, thank you," she said, finding her balance.

"Follow me. On the other side of the tree line are the steps that will take us up the cliffs to the fortress. Once we get there, you will follow my men, and I'll walk behind to ensure you don't fall. The steps were made uneven to cause our enemy to trip, so be careful."

"Yes, I will be careful," she said. She followed him down the pier and into the dark abyss beyond the torchlight of the piers. She could hear the sound of the waves from the shore becoming more distant. The men in front of her carried small torches, but the light they gave could do little to illuminate the night. She barely saw a faint outline of the trees as they walked by the forest rim. When they finally made it around the tree line, everything looked black.

"Here is the first step. Follow my men's feet, not their torchlight. It will cause you to stumble to look beyond the first step. I will be right behind you."

She nodded. Once the four men went in front of her, she focused on the noise that leather-clad boots in front of her made at each step. When the boots stepped, she stepped. When the boots slowed, she slowed. Up. Down. Pause. Step. They seemed to be stepping for a long time before the men's steps flattened on a level surface. They must have arrived at the fortress. She looked up and her throat instantly tightened. The clouds had dissipated, and she gaped at the mighty stone building cut out of the cliffs. The fortress caused her head to become dizzy and the cliffs mocked her. It felt like the structure was bearing down on her, pushing her into the ground with its intimidating, harsh size.

"No!" she screamed.

"What is it?" the warrior asked.

"They scare me! The cliffs! They are hurt!" she yelled just as her body collapsed. The old swordsman caught her before she fell down the hundreds of stone-cut steps they scaled.

Chapter 20

THE FOREST ROOM

Amorfia did not want to wake up. The stuffed
mattress engulfed her and the blankets around her
willed her to stay asleep. She heard a crackling
fire only a few steps away from her. Where was she? She
was having trouble recalling the day before. The days
had been a blur of study with the sages and the Supreme

Sage becoming so frustrated with her that she sent her
away. She was allowed to go visit Voddie and the boys
for a few days. Yes, that was it. She was in her room in
Voddie's home. But why did the bed feel so soft, and
why did the fireplace sound so close to her? Finally, the
memories of yesterday's events came back. She had
gone to that terrible fortress in the cliffs. Just thinking of
it made her shudder. The last thing she remembered was
walking up those dreaded steps and beholding the cliffs.
Did she cry out?

"Are you thinking about waking up, Morfie? Or
shall I wait some more?" she heard a woman's voice ask.

Her eyes fluttered open, and she looked around.
Small trees in large wooden pots were all around her,
and the floor of the room resembled the ground of Atlatl
Forest. The walls were covered in ornate wood slats,
much like the ones she saw on the chieftain's boat. A
large, overstuffed cushion rested near a low wooden
table, and behind that was a wooden armoire that
reached from floor to ceiling. An aged woman dressed in
a thick, green gown with bell sleeves stared down at her.
She had a horn cuff on her left horn with the same image
of the cliffs that was sewn into the boat's flag. Her eyes
were a deep blue and her silver hair draped over a fur
pelt she wore across her shoulders. Golden bracelets
clanked upon her wrist and an opulent necklace dangled
from her neck.

"Where am I?" Amorfia asked.

"You, my dear, are in the Forest Room. It was
made for Chieftess Tarsha, my sister-in-law. Her
husband and my brother, Chieftain Vandar, made it for

her when she moved here from South Basin. You have her same condition—the Fear of Cliffs."

"I do?" Amorfia asked. She had learned about that fear from the Highland Cliff sages that recited to her their stored memories. It was a rare sickness that only formed in those who had never seen the cliffs before their youth memories finished.

Amorfia shook her head. "But that doesn't make sense. My youth memories are available. Why would I fear the cliffs if I can still accept them?"

"Precisely," the woman said. "You are an enigma. You are too old to have youth memories available, yet I have been told that you have the deepest set of memories any sage has ever seen. Yet you still have this fear—though, according to your youth memories, you should not."

Amorfia looked at the woman and thought. "You are Chieftess Dalia, the aunt of Chieftain Lothar bar Haven of the Highland Cliffs. Your sages have told me about you and much of your family legacy."

The old woman suppressed a frown. "The Supreme Sage from Atlatl Forest sent for our cliff sages. We were quite angry at first until the forest sages told us about your unique abilities. Very impressive. You have soaked up much information about our history, and I know all about that poor fisherman finding you on our shores."

"Morgo is not poor. He is very rich with a wealth unknown to the sages," Amorfia said, defensively.

"And now I see that you are loyal and wise," the woman said. "I sent for a Swarve hatchling for you. Not a brown or bronze one, but one of beautiful gold—the color of the auraium that hides in the cliffs," she said, wiggling her wrist and allowing the stacked bracelets to clank together.

Amorfia blinked. "A Swarve? Like Chieftess Tarsha?"

"Ah yes, like my fragile sister-in-law whose beauty was renown, who wound up not being so fragile after all for she ran away into the caverns with her Swarve." Dalia sat on the corner of the mattress where Amorfia lay and stared at her. "Your beauty will be just as renown. You favor her a bit. But how spectacular are your eyes? I've heard the sages speak of them, and they are exactly right. They have no color whatsoever. Who would have thought such a girl existed? You have assuredly been marked by the Befores."

Amorfia felt uncomfortable under Chieftess Dalia's gaze.

"The sages think the Befores brought you. What do you think?" the old Chieftess queried.

"I don't think the Befores have as much control as the sages give them credit for," Amorfia said.

Chieftess Dalia smiled. "I seem to agree with you," she said, reaching into a fold of her dress. She brought out a clear, circular canister. Do you know what this is?" She handed it to Amorfia.

When Amorfia took the canister, she was amazed at how smooth it was, like a stone washed up from the lake but even glossier. It was translucent like water when you cupped it into your hands. "It seems different but familiar."

"Many of those have washed into our lake from the river. We are the first to find them, and we have been gathering them ever since. We don't want to cause commotion with the people. There is already too much unrest as it is. As of now, only my nephew and I and a few trusted servants know that these exist."

"Where do they come from?" Amorfia asked.

"It seems that the speculations about a foreign land and distant people are actually true. We are thinking, my dear, they come from the same place you come from—beyond the desert in a land we thought was lost during the Shaking. I was hoping the translucent canister would help you remember, but maybe this will offer you a better perspective." She brought her other hand out and opened it. Inside was a rolled, thin fabric sheet that looked firm. She handed it to Amorfia. "Unroll it and see what's inside."

Amorfia sat up and unrolled the sheet, gasping. "There are markings."

"Yes, we have looked at many of these sheets and found that there are forty-four different markings to be exact. However, we have no reference point to decipher them. We think they are a written form of language—a way to document stories and procedures without having to remember them or rely on the sages. This is why we have kept it a secret up to now. If the sages were to find out, they would surely try to halt our research."

"Why would they stop it?" Amorfia asked.

"Because we wouldn't need them anymore if we could document information without them. Wouldn't that be something? Instead of the bar Haven family having to call on the sages, we could gather our translucent canisters with their rolled sheets and symbols. We would never forget our family lineage, and we could easily document more. If the bar Haven had the key to unlocking these symbols, we would be the strongest family of all the Lake-keepers, not just in force but in intelligence."

"Why are you telling me all this?" Amorfia asked. What she had learned about the chieftains was that they were a highly private people, keeping secrets that were only for their immediate family members. The sages kept their well-known history, but other things, like the bar Haven swordcraft, were kept hidden.

"Morfie of the Shores, your naivety surprises me. You are a girl who has lost her people, and we happen to be a people who need to find a girl. We will make the arrangements official with the sages once we receive your Swarve and you have prepared, but you will be Amorfia bar Haven before too long." She looked at Amorfia's horns. "And I think your horns are just long enough to bear our crest with your very own horn cuff. We have much work to do before we can present you to my nephew, but I have a feeling he will agree with my choice."

Amorfia paced the Forest Room. She tired of being trapped inside. She missed the crisp air and taking long walks—but, truth be told, she did not miss the sages. She never wanted to return to the temple in Atlatl Forest and the control of the Supreme Sage. She continued pacing the floor. She couldn't leave until she receive her

Swarve, but it had not hatched yet and the process must not be rushed.

She looked at the rolled sheets on the low desk. She had analyzed the symbols for hours just as Chieftess Dalia instructed her, but she couldn't translate them. She was missing a key element, but it was nowhere in her memory. They had brought her a flat box filled to the rim with sand, and she traced the symbols over and over again until each shape was in her youth memories. However, nothing came to her. As of now, they were useless designs much like the ones Range made with his sticks and string.

She looked at the tall armoire that now held several dresses and her warfighting leathers—all specifically designed for her. In the last few months, she went from wearing the humble dress that Voddie gave her to donning the simple tunic of the sages. Now she wore a layered gown of the Highland Cliffs Chieftess. She thought of what Dalia had told her. She may have come from the land where the translucent canisters flowed in from. Although she never beheld the river that fed into Dumas Lake, she heard its rumble from a distance. There must be people living beyond the desert, but she wondered why they were just now finding proof. Did something happen over there? Unless she remembered, though, she would never find the people she had lost—or had they lost her?

She heard a knock on her door. "Amorfia, are you dressed? We have your Swarve, and he is in much distress."

Amorfia quickly opened the door. The old warrior who had saved her from falling off the cliffs held a long, two-pronged stick and was pushing the Swarve in front of him. Even though the Swarve had just been hatched, he was already almost too big to enter through the doors that led to the Forest Room. He had golden fur, and the individual strands were searching. He grunted and whined and sniffed with his wide, black nose.

"Push him in, Garth," Dalia said to the old swordsmen.

Garth placed the two-prongs around his neck and pushed him into the Forest Room. Dalia whipped the door shut. Then she spoke from the other side of the door. "Now, be calm. Just pet him like you pet the Swarves at the Temple of the Sages. He will calm once he senses you."

Amorfia's heart raced a bit. She had to remind herself that he was more scared then she was. She talked to the Swarves at the temple, and this was no different. She slowly made her way to her mattress and sat down. The Swarve swayed from side to side grunting, and the fur on his body continued to move.

"Come here," she whispered. "I won't hurt you." She needed to name him. She thought through the history of the Lake-keepers and found a name for what was believed to be the first Swarve ridden by a Chieftain. "Croga," she said, reaching out her hand. "Come here. My name is Amorfia, but friends call me Morfie."

The golden Swarve whined and began to amble toward her. His strands of fur were all facing her now, longing to find someone to connect with. She reached out her hand, and he nuzzled it with his moist nose. Then he drew beside her arm and his fur began to tickle her skin. Then they each wrapped around her arm in a warm embrace. Suddenly, she was filled with feelings of well-being and safety. All her fears vanished, and she felt courage and a sense of adventure rise up within her. Croga's whines stopped and were replaced with the peaceful grunting sound that she had grown accustomed to hearing. The rest of his fur gently rested while the ones around her arm continued to hold on.

"Morfie, has he connected? Is his fur still now?"

"Yes, Chieftess Dalia. He is resting." Morfie stroked his back, and his large body leaned against her leg and shoved her back into the mattress. "He's is very large for being just a hatchling."

Dalia walked in holding a potted plant. "Oh good. I'm so glad the connection went well. Do you feel better now?"

Amorfia nodded. "Yes, I have no fear at all. The Fear of the Cliffs is completely gone."

Dalia set the plant on the ground. "Yes, it should last two or three days. You will need to visit your Swarve anytime time you begin to feel even the slightest bit weary. We have made its stable ready. He will have the finest grasses and the best care. Though, it is best that no one else but you touch him for at least a few weeks just to make sure he doesn't connect with two people. It's been known to happen before. I'll show you to the stables when we leave." She looked at the rolled sheets on the low table. "So how did the deciphering go?"

"There is still something missing. There must be some ancient history on the markings, but I haven't found any information from the sages you have sent me."

"The only sages you haven't consulted with now are the ones from the Lowland Cliffs, and we are not on friendly terms with them. Their sages have some of the oldest history of all the Lake-keepers. They hide it greedily. However, I do know of a sage who might be able to help us. I have worked with him before when I sought help for my brother," Dalia said. "I shall meet with him, and see if he can find a sage with the information you need." She walked over to the armoire and opened it. "Good, I see that your clothing has been delivered. When you meet Lothar, I want you to look like a chieftess. If he accepts you, we shall perform your rights of adoption."

Amorfia looked back down at Croga who seemed to be sleeping on her arm and against her legs. He was very warm and she couldn't help smiling as his wispy golden fur rose and fell along with his low snores. Finally, she looked back up at the chieftess. "But I have a people across the desert."

"Yes and you can't remember anything about them, and even if you did, it would be impossible to travel the river upstream unless you have a multitude of rowers," Dalia said.

Amorfia could tell that Dalia was prepared for this argument.

"Besides, once you are a Highland Cliffs Chieftess, and my nephew and I are traveling with the Befores, you can do what you want. You can amass an entire army and build the biggest ship to take you up the river and beyond the desert. That would bode well with us—our family line being the first to discover new lands and conquer new people. But you could never do that as a fisherman's daughter or even a sage. I am offering you power and resources that can eventually help you find your way home. It is the only way."

Amorfia thought over Dalia's words. They made sense now that she comprehended the full scope of her situation. If she were to stay with Voddie, she would never return to her people. She would probably stay, marry Boru and become a wife and mother, like Voddie. But would she be content with that now that she knew that one day she could find her true home? Would she be satisfied staring at Domus Lake knowing that her real-life was awaiting her beyond the desert? "I think you are right, Chieftess Dalia. I will do as you say."

Dalia clapped her hands. "Good, now you can call me Grand Dalia for you are to become my grandniece. It will be nice to have a young woman to spend time with. Your uncle is not the type who enjoys keeping company. And I must begin your training of the bar Haven swordcraft. We wouldn't want your youth memories shutting on us too soon, now would we? I may be old, but I can still wield a sword. And before we go to the stables, let me show you the special plant I brought."

Dalia walked over to the small potted plant she first brought in and picked it up. "This is a plant only found in the caverns that run along the river. No one but I and my trusted servant, Garth, know about it, so please keep it secret." Dalia plucked one of the green leaves growing from it and handed it to her. "Here. What do you think?"

Amorfia brought the leaf close to her and examined it. "I've never seen it, yet it seems familiar."

"They never grow very big, and they only last a year or so, but if you feed your Swarve a few leaves a week, he will have a longer life."

"Is that why Chieftess Tarsha's Swarve lived so long? They think he was around fifteen years old before she escaped to the caverns."

"As a girl, I would wander through the caverns after my studies with the sages and my swordcraft training were over. I stumbled on one of these trees. They are very small and only grow deep within the caverns. I brought it home and fed it to my favorite Swarve in the stables. He loved the leaves and sucked down every one I brought him. As I got older, I noticed he kept living longer than the other Swarves. He continued living until I was an adult. When we discovered that Tarsha had the fear, I made sure to feed her Swarve the same leaves."

"Why did she run away to the caverns?" Amorfia found herself asking. "What would make her run away from being a Highland Cliffs Chieftess?"

Amalia frowned. "That is a conversation for another time. Let's just say for now that she made the wrong choice and the Befores judged her for it. Now we must wake up this sleeping Swarve and get it to the stable. We have training to do."

Chapter 21

THE DECOY HEIR

"So my mother had not gone mad after all," Chieftain Lothar said, holding a large translucent canister in his hands. He sat in the treasury deep under his fortress. All of the canisters with their written symbols had been brought down there for protection and secrecy. "There are people on the other end of the river

206

who have their very own written language. I need to
learn everything I can about them. Has the girl made any
progress in translating their language?"

Dalia sighed. She looked at the piles of treasure
surrounding them hidden deep within the rock, but all
they cared about were the canisters with the sheets of
clues to where Chieftess Tarsha had fled. "No, but I'm
seeking information from my source in the Temple of
the Lowland Cliffs. There must be information about the
lands before the Shaking. There were several people
groups then. We Lake-keepers were not the only ones on
Rodesh. We simply need to find the people group who
made these symbols and get Amorfia to remember,"
Dalia finished and thought. "She believes we are going
to adopt her."

"We will go along with the proper ritual of
adoption once I meet her. I need to put on a show of
accepting her, so she believes she holds value. But make
sure every sage present does not have any youth
memories available. Their memories must all be
finished, so her false adoption is not written down in our
history."

Dalia set down the canister she had been holding.
"Do you really think we can find your mother? What if
there's nothing out there but sand?"

Lothar pointed to a bunch of branches in the
corner. "That tree floated down the river into our lake. It
doesn't come from here, so we know that, at the very
least, the lands have trees. And if they have trees, I am
certain they have other plants and animals and people."

"Then what if the lands are so vast that it's
impossible to find her?"

"My aunt, you forget that people like to tell stories. And a woman with child coming out from the caverns in the desert is something people will talk about. There will be stories and there will be speculations. And eventually, those speculations will lead to my mother, my sibling and possibly a nephew or a niece, the rightful heir to the Highland Cliffs. She also took our family heirloom with her. The dagger that has been passed down to each chieftess that stood near the throne. When we find the dagger, we will find her."

"What if we do find them, but they don't want to return with us?" she asked.

"Why would they not want to be the most powerful chieftain family of all the Lake-keepers? Besides, I am not leaving without absorbing the new land into my territory. I plan on taking over every land my army's feet tread upon. The Lake-keepers have always been warriors. My sibling and nieces or nephews will have no choice but to join us. All I need now is to have the markings on the sheets in the translucent canisters translated, so I can see what I'm up against. Do they have metal swords like we do or are they still using bow and spear-like the people of Lake Basin? Are they peaceful people or people of war? This is why we need that girl to remember. Once we decipher the symbols, we can learn everything we need to know about them from the canisters we have."

"Garth, is patrolling for more in the boat. He should be back soon." She looked around the treasury. "We have collected hundreds. Once we have learned how these symbols work, we can write down our own history and save them in stronger metal canisters. We won't need the sages anymore."

"Everything depends on that girl," Lothar said. "Do what you need to do to make her feel like she is one of us now."

"I've started training her in the bar Haven swordcraft. Chieftain Darmin and his son expect it, and they will be arriving to meet and approve of her all too quickly. When they do come, we can expect they'll want a wedding right away," Dalia said. "Amorfia is quite pretty, and her youth memories are filled with stories and information of our people. I think they'll ignore the fact that she was found by a fisherman."

"The wedding can't take place until she figures out the symbols. You must delay it if necessary."

"I know Rathtar is desperate to be married. No matter. I will simply tell them that she hasn't learned all of our swordcraft—though, I doubt it will take her much longer. Morfie is actually quite good with the sword. She is tall, agile and getting stronger every day. If I did have to choose from the Lake-keepers an heir, I would have chosen her. She's smarter than all the sages combined, and she is naïve enough to not be suspicious. We could use her as a backup heir if we do not find your mother. She was found on our shores, so she is technically from the Highland Cliffs."

"We will find my mother if she is alive. If not, we will find my sibling. I will have no need for the girl. She is merely my decoy. She can marry that insufferable boy, Rathtar. And when I return with the true heir, he will probably kill her himself along with any children she has given him. So go ahead and teach her the bar

Haven swordcraft. It will perish when she does. The bar
Holthens will never gain our family secrets, let alone our
skill of the sword."

Dalia frowned. "But why keep up the charade?
Why not change your mind? The bar Holthens are half
expecting it anyway," Dalia said. She began liking the
girl and wanted to avoid unnecessary harm.

"Because I will be away from my lands for some
time searching for my mother. I will need the bar
Holthen family on my side protecting my lands from
Chieftain Rugar and the Lowland Cliffs. You will rule
the throne in my stead, and keep the girl in your
confidences after she marries Rathtar and goes back to
the East Basin Fortress where she belongs. I will tell
them that I'm on an expedition of discovery—an heirless
old chieftain's last dying need for adventure."

"I'm sure they'll believe it too," Dalia said and
sighed. "They are an ignorant people blinded by their
desire to have more power. When you meet Amorfia, I
will have her perform a sword routine for you. Then you
will see why I am impressed with her. I can't help but
think the Befores have sent her to us. She has to be more
useful than simply to be a fake heir. She has the Fear of
Cliffs that your mother had. Do you not think that it is a
sign?"

"All it means is that she was not exposed to the
cliffs as a child and nothing more," he answered, gruffly.
"We have no idea where this girl comes from, but she
must not have been highly esteemed if she so easily
washed up on our shores," he thought. "Does she really
have colorless eyes like they say?"

"Yes, they look like the lake on a cloudy calm day. I wonder if Chieftain Darmin and his son will approve of them. I fear their preference could go either way. I dare say you will like her eyes. I find myself staring at them often."

"I seriously doubt they will mesmerize me," he said. "All I want before my eyes is the real heir to the bar Haven family. Have you told her she is to be married?"

"Not yet," she hesitated. "I have discovered from personal conversations with her that she may not want to marry Chieftain Rathtar."

"Why not? The girls from the entire Lake Basin admire his good looks," he said.

"Yes, but she is not one to swoon over handsome features. He has done something to an innkeeper at South Basin that angers her, and it has affected the fisherman and his family that took her in. She loves that family, which makes Chieftain Rathtar's case worse."

"I heard about the incident. He left the comforts of his East Basin Fortress to venture off for some fun in a South Basin village. Seems that Darmin bar Holthen is unable to pay his son's debts. I know exactly how to use this information to benefit my position with the bar Holthens and to show the girl that I can be trusted," he said with a smirk.

Dalia looked back at the glass cylinders, a wealth of information stored up with symbols. She wondered what kind of people these symbol makers were and how they would respond to a confrontation from the Lake-keepers. Then she thought of Amorfia. It was impossible to spend so much time with her and not begin to like her. She had an aged maturity mixed with a young innocence.

If her nephew didn't want her, maybe she could eventually adopt her. As of now, she could do nothing outside of Lothar's control.

Amorfia walked the shores near the fortress just where the tree line bustled up against the cliffs. The sand of the shores crunched under her leather boots. The breeze was wet and cold, and she appreciated the thick gown and long fur cape she wore with a hood that wrapped around her horns. They were almost full-grown now, and she would get her horn cuff signifying that she was a part of the bar Haven family. Once she had resources and information at her disposal, she would try to discover who she was and where her family was located. Everything seemed to be too easy, though. She was nervous about meeting Chieftain Lothar that evening. She may be on trial in his eyes, but she too wanted to see what his true intentions were.

She had just finished petting Croga, and he extended his feelings of well-being and peace to her. She visited him almost every day. The bar Haven swordcraft was a brutal and tiresome skill to learn. Although Dalia was old, she was still strong and had quick reflexes. She easily made her mark on Amorfia's warfighting leathers. Every muscle in Amorfia's body ached for days, but she quickly grew accustomed to the rigorous movements. Dalia had been obviously impressed by Amorfia's dexterity. She was limber and could move with ease once she learned the routine. It was almost like her body flowed to an unheard rhythm.

She looked across the lake. There were no fishing boats this close to the Highland Cliffs. Garth had prevented the boats to pass through because they were still gathering the translucent canisters. She felt Dalia's pressure to decipher them, but nothing came. She hoped the sage that Dalia was working with from the Lowland Cliffs would find some new information. Until then, she would learn the swordcraft and enjoy Croga's company. She wondered if Boru would visit her. He had found a way to spend time with her at the Temple of the Sages, and she believed he would find a way to visit her at the fortress.

She heard voices and looked up to see Garth coming in around the cliffs to the chiseled stone steps that met up with the tree line and notched their way to the fortress. The very same place he had saved her life the night she came to the fortress. There were several men following him with barrels. She knew the barrels did not hold fish. They held the translucent canisters with sheets of symbols on them. He noticed her and held up his hand for her to wait. He gave out several orders to the men before he turned to face her. His face softened when he saw her.

"I see you no longer have the Fear of the Cliffs. The Swarve is doing the trick, now is he?"

She liked how his leathery face transformed from being fierce to showing kindness. She had heard stories about him from the sages—namely, that he is the one who helped bring down the Goliathans that Chieftain Lothar had on his throne wall. Of course, he wasn't given public credit, but the sages kept the truth hidden in their stories.

She nodded. "I named him Croga."

"Do you need any more of them leaves? I can go fetch you a few more saplings?"

"Yes, I would like more. I'm only supposed to feed him a few leaves a week, but Croga loves them. He always whines for more, like he would eat the entire tree for one meal if I would let him."

"Yes, they do like them. I remember Chieftess Tarsha always sending me to the caverns to get more leaves for her Swarve. He was already so old. When she found out she was pregnant again, I think she feared losing him even more," Garth said.

Amorfia could tell that he had been fond of the chieftess who ran away. "Why did she run away to the caverns?"

The old warrior came out of his reverie. "I can't much talk about it. Though, I'm sure a few sages have some stories about what happened in their youth memories."

She shook her head. "No, it's like much of her history has not been stored up by the sages or they are not sharing it, which would be unusual since they relish sharing their memories. The years leading up to her second pregnancy and her running away into the caverns are blank. I've asked Grand Dalia, but she won't share the information with me."

Garth fidgeted with the clasps on his warfighting leathers. She could tell he was uneasy with the conversation, but she needed to know why Chieftess Tarsha would leave. Not only leave but go into the heart of her biggest fear—the caverns were just like cliffs but underground. She continued. "I've been able to only come up with two conclusions."

He looked at her. "What are your conclusions?"

"Either she somehow knew before everyone else that there were lands on the other side of the river with people who would take her in…or," she hesitated.

"Or what?" he asked.

"Or life for her in the fortress was so bad that she would rather risk the life of her and her baby than stay a moment longer."

"Maybe it was both," he said, eyeing her.

"I think you are right," she said, thinking about Voddie's baby boy, Paxton. Voddie would never do anything to risk his life unless she had no other choice. "So then my next question is what was happening in the fortress to cause her to take that risk?"

"What do you think was happening?" Garth asked.

She noticed that although he wasn't confirming her conclusions, he wasn't countering them either. "My only assumption is that her husband, Chieftain Vandar, was cruel to her—so cruel that she feared for her life and the life of her unborn child. I know you know what happened, Garth. You've been with the family since before Lothar became the chieftain."

Garth immediately replaced his tense expression with an easy-going smile. "There's no need to be thinking about all this. What's done is done. You best be thinking about your future as the Chieftess of the Highland Cliffs and not worry about the past. No use fretting over a history that can't be undone."

"I know that's easy to say, Garth. But what I've learned from all the sages is that the past repeats itself if we do nothing to stop it," she finished. She could see that the conversation was over. He was not a sage. She couldn't expect him to tell her family secrets, especially the ones that have somehow been made void to the sages.

"We best get in. If Chieftess Dalia sees me keeping you out in the cold, she'll have me mounted on the throne wall. I hear you will be performing for Chieftain Lothar and the sages this evening, so you better be ready."

"I'm sorry if I've made you uncomfortable, Garth," she whispered. "I'm just trying to figure everything out. So much is missing, and I think If I can understand, at least, what's in front of me now, then maybe my own history will come back to me."

"I know," he said. "But some things will never be understood no matter how hard you try. Do you want me to walk you up to the fortress?"

"No, but thank you. I know you have a lot to do. I'll come in shortly. Dalia wants to meet with me to go over my routine with the musicians, so I want to look at the lake one more time. It's so flat and peaceful that I feel that I could walk on it all the way to where I came from."

"Okay," he said. "I will see you in the throne chamber. I'll fetch those saplings for you in the morning."

"Thank you," she said, bowing slightly.

He smiled and turned to walk back up the sand toward the stairs. She watched his large footprints mark a path up the shore and to the first step. Then she stared at his footprint closest to her and wondered how many times his feet had made the same trek. How many times would hers? Suddenly, she noticed something glimmering on the edge of his footprint halfway buried. She reached down and picked it up. It looked like one of the translucent canisters, but this one was smaller and misshapen. It didn't have the rolled sheet inside. Instead, it contained shimmering silver strands that shined different colors in the light. It looked like some kind of hair, but not hair from a person—at least, not a person she'd ever seen.

She looked toward the end of the water where the river met Domus Lake and began to snake its way through the desert. She knew the canister had come from there, but she didn't know why the hair within seemed so familiar to her, giving her almost the same feelings that her Swarve offered. She looked back toward the tiny canister and gently shook the hair within. The hair didn't belong there, yet there it stayed—trapped. She couldn't help feeling the same way. Trapped in a false existence, like her eyes were open but she continued to sleep.

Chapter 22

SWORD CRAFT

A morfia walked into the throne chamber. The smells of the dinner cooking wafted into the great hall. She felt hunger pains hit her, and she wished the kitchen wasn't so close to the throne chamber. She should have eaten earlier, but she had been too nervous. The sky holes in the ceiling allowed the rays of the moon to stream in. The violet rays of the moon mixed with the yellow of the torchlights that were anchored on all four walls of the hall. Sages lined the right side of the stonewall. Most of them wore the more elaborate patterns of the older sages. She noted that the Supreme Sage from Atlatl Forest was present. She wondered why none of the younger sages had come with her.

On the left wall were the trumpet blowers and drummers, the instruments of the Highland Cliffs. The Lowland Cliffs shared the same instruments, but the Lake Basin people had to use wooden pipes since the metal of the cliffs was too difficult for them to get. She preferred the sweet sound of the pipes versus the sharp sound of the trumpets. The musicians were dressed in traditional dark green uniforms. They held their instruments poised waiting for her first move and their cue to begin. Amorfia had only practiced with them once, but Dalia said that would be enough. But she had memorized their music, allowing the melody to repeat in her mind as she practiced her routine until she believed she had it perfect.

Other than the sages, the musicians and a few swordsmen, the throne chamber was relatively empty. Chieftain Lothar's stone throne stood at the front of the great hall. She noticed the large Goliathan heads mounted above the throne. With their sharp hides and monstrous features, she could see why it would take at least two men to bring one down. She wondered if they were the reason Garth's face held many scars. Dalia stood to the right of the throne and Garth to the left. On the throne sat Chieftain Lothar. She had not met him yet—only seeing him from a distance—and he was much fiercer looking than Garth. She searched the Chieftain's face to see if the same tenderness she had found in Garth was also in him, but either the atmosphere was too dim for her to see or he was nothing like Garth. He sat silently on his throne staring at her.

She walked to the center of the room as Dalia had instructed her to do earlier that day. She wore the warfighting leathers and she had a sword sheathed by her side. The sword was nothing special—just one of the spare youth swords found in the armory. But she had practiced with it and found it acceptable. Once she was adopted, she would be gifted a Chieftess Dagger— though, not the one that was lost with Chieftess Tarsha.

Once she made her way to the middle of the hall, she slid her right foot behind her and gave the traditional low bow. She stood back up and waited for Chieftain Lothar to raise his right hand for her to begin. She slowed her breathing and allowed the draft from the winter breeze slipping in through the cracks of the fortress to cool her body. Dalia had told her that she would do well, but Amorfia wanted to do better than well. She did not have a family and she did not remember who she was nor where she came from, but she felt a deep sense of value like she had a purpose. Even if Chieftain Lothar rejected her and she went back home to Voddie and Morgo, she wanted them all to know that she carried worth within her with or without their approval.

Chieftain Lothar finally gave the signal, and she instantly unsheathed her sword and swept into the first stance. The music came in right as she landed her thrust. Then she took her time with her second move as the drummers maintained the beat. She jumped onto one foot and jabbed the opposite leg out with a sideswipe of her sword. She continued each step without rushing but using power in the moments of attack. She felt the sweat dripping down her back and chest, but she kept her breath steady and her expression emotionless as the warrior. Her routine brought her closer to the throne, and she could see she had captivated Chieftain Lothar's attention. Dalia stood without showing emotion, but she too did not look away. Garth, on the other hand, allowed his mouth to gape. She guessed he was impressed.

Amorfia allowed the attention to give her the courage to make her moves more expansive yet concise. Finally, she entered her last move. The drums pounded their beat and the trumpet exploded their wail. She slid her body upon the smooth stone ground sweeping her sword in a complete low circle. Then she ended with a low bow before standing and sheathing her sword in a single move.

The music instantly halted and all was quiet. She did not look away from the throne and waited patiently as Garth, Dalia and the Chieftain stared at her. She would not allow herself to feel intimidated. Finally, Chieftain Lothar rose and began to applaud, and she gave another bow.

"My aunt, you were correct to assume that I would be impressed with Amorfia. I have never seen the bar Haven swordcraft look so fluid, almost like she was dancing."

As he continued clapping, he walked toward her. He wore his warfighting leathers and a black pelt around his shoulders. He had a sword with red stones adorning the hilt sheathed by his side. His face was aged, but he looked several years younger than his aunt. As he drew closer, Amorfia could see his indifference was now usurped with curiosity, but he still lacked the tenderness that she has seen in Garth. Suddenly, she recognized his cobalt blue eyes, but when she searched her memory, she couldn't understand why. Nothing she had learned so far suggested why his eyes looked familiar.

He stood before her. Although she was tall, he was about two hand-widths taller than she. She could tell he was analyzing her colorless eyes. She had grown accustomed to the stares—even the sages seemed startled by their lack of color. She stared back, so she could seek to find the answer to why his face looked so familiar to her, like something she once cared about. She couldn't help it. She reached her hand up and touched the side of his face, hoping to reignite some hidden memory. But she felt nothing. Then the feeling vanished like steam from a boiling pot of water.

Her touched startled him. He stepped back several paces. "Why did you touch me?" he demanded.

She blinked. "I-I don't know. You seemed familiar to me. I apologize. I did not mean to offend you." Amorfia could see more fear in his eyes than anger.

"You are to adopt her after all. She must accept us as we must accept her," Dalia said. She walked up next to the Chieftain holding a horn cuff in her hand and a white robe draped over her arm. "So what do you say, my nephew. I can tell you truthfully there is not a girl of all the Lake-keepers who could compare to her beauty, her knowledge and her artistry. The sages are here ready to fulfill the requirements of adoption. Does Amorfia meet your demands as a daughter? Do you believe she is worthy to represent the bar Haven family lineage? You have already seen how well she performs our swordcraft, and she has not yet finished her studies. She has more to learn, but already she is exceeding my expectations."

The Chieftain regained his composure and walked back up to her. His fear now replaced with resolve. "Amorfia, if you are to become my daughter and be woven into the fabric of the bar Haven family, you will have to commit to all the demands of the Highland Cliffs Chieftain family line. As my daughter, I am your voice of authority, protection and influence. You can no longer simply look out for your own interests but the interests of our bar Haven legacy. Do you understand the profound duty you have to uphold all the days of your life as a chieftess?"

Amorfia nodded, though she felt unsure. Dalia had never spoken of the enormous responsibility she would have as Highland Cliffs Chieftess. She now felt the weight of adoption and wondered if she would not be better off with Voddie in the small village. However, if she did not take this step, she would seal her fate of never discovering her past.

"I now recognize you as my daughter," he said. Then he reach his hand to Dalia and she placed the golden horn cuff in his hand. The horn cuff resembled Dalia's with the imprint of the cliffs upon its metal. It had a clasp on one end and tiny needle-like protrusion along the inside. He took the cuff and wrapped it around her left horn and squeeze the needles into the bone. Dalia reached over and secured the clasps. Then she swept the white robe over Amorfia's shoulders.

"You are now Amorfia bar Haven, daughter of Chieftain Lothar. Niece of Chieftess Dalia. You will continue the bar Haven legacy," Dalia said.

Amorfia bowed. "I will fulfill my calling."

"Good. You will start by marrying Rathtar bar Holthen and uniting our two territories," Chieftain declared for all to hear. "You will meet them on the end-day of this week." With those words, he turned and walked passed the sages and out of the throne chamber.

Amorfia stared at Dalia. "You never said anything about marriage."

"You have heard our history from the sages. How could you not possibly think marriage wasn't part of your destiny here?" Dalia said, sounding surprised.

"But I've told you what the chieftain's son did to the innkeeper," Amorfia whispered. She felt stunned, like the sun's rays had suddenly pierced through the clouds and into her eyes.

"Your father knows about what Rathtar has done, and he has a plan to vindicate the innkeeper and the family that found you. Now, follow me. It is time to dine as a family."

Amorfia followed behind her grand aunt. She spied the Supreme Sage staring at her, but she did not look back. She was no longer a sage and didn't have to answer to the powers of the temple. She was officially a Highland Cliffs Chieftess and now had other concerns to worry about.

Snow started falling before the sun rose that morning, but by late morning, the sun's rays had already melted the white dusting away. The arduous work of building the inn was easier when the coolness kept the heat at bay, and Boru was thankful for the mixture of a sunny day and a chilly wind. He and his brother had already laid the gravel bed and driven in the foundation stakes. Now they had to put in the foundation walls before they laid the floors.

They hired out fishermen to help with the building—paying them with free ale and promises of free rooms when the in-laws visited. The men had nothing better to do now since the fishing was done, and they wanted to get out of the house from the wives and kids for a while. None of them stayed all day. Some would come in before lunch, and others would arrive just after. Some helped with the vigorous work of cutting the slats of wood with double-handed saws. While others preferred the easier work of sanding down the wood planks. Either way, the men enjoyed their hearty work in the cold with their ale and friends.

Boru looked at his brother-in-law, Morgo. He especially liked the work of building. He didn't have any of the skills in his youth memories, but once he was shown what to do, he worked with eagerness. Morgo also liked the fact that he didn't have to be the boss for the project. During fishing season, everyone came to him for answers and direction, but now he could relax, work and stay busy. Boru also knew another reason why

Morgo wanted to get out of the house for a bit every day. His wife enjoyed talking. Boru had been raised all his childhood with his sister's constant gab. She could talk for hours without running out of things to discuss. Morgo was more like him—quiet and reserved—which is probably why he fell in love with Voddie in the first place. Well, her beauty first and then her talent for gab. She quickly put shy people at ease because they knew that they didn't have to add to the conversation if they didn't want to. A simple nod and smile and "Oh, is that so?" would suffice.

"Men! Builders and fishermen alike!" Jayston, his older brother, shouted while holding a large wooden tankard of ale. He enjoyed talking just as much as Voddie, and he loved being the center of attention. Voddie's son, Range, was at his side. Range would benefit from having two skillsets in his youth memories—fishing and building. Jayston waited for everyone's attention and then continued. "What you are about to see is the foundation come into completion! You have worked hard, but the fun is just beginning!"

Cheers were heard all around him. He noticed some bystanders coming to watch the speech. The inn was located near enough to the lake and only a short distance's walk from the village market, a perfect location for people traveling through East Basin. The family had been given coins from the sages in Atlatl Forest. The cost of the land had absorbed almost all of it, but the prime location would eventually bring more coins to the family. "My brother, Boru, and I have not discussed this, but I'm suddenly hit with inspiration!"

Now Jayston had his full attention. He hoped what his brother said next would not jeopardize their innkeeping business before it had even begun. He could be too generous at times, which would cause them to barely break even on projects. This didn't cause too much strife between them because neither of them was married, but when they had wives and families to support, they needed to be more business savvy.

Jayston looked at him and smiled. "Brother, we have not discussed the name of our inn yet, but I think with all the help we are getting from these fine fishermen, we should offer a name in their honor: The Fishermen's Inn!"

Again cheers erupted. Boru smiled too. He rather liked the name. East Basin was mostly full of fishermen, so the name did fit well. His brother held up his tankard and waited for his approval. When Boru nodded his consent, applause reigned once more. He watched his little nephew, Range, hoot and holler next to Jayston. He could see the merge of tradesmen in the young man's mind. It was a perfect way to lead the next generation of East Basin—one of unification and mutual respect.

He soon realized no more work would get done for the rest of the day when the wood pipes came out. There would be music and dancing. The wives and children would be called out from their homes to join the celebration. The Fishermen's Inn would hold its first gathering with no floors, no walls and no roof; but with a crowd of merry friends.

Boru decided that he would go fetch himself an ale and sit back and watch the fun. Then he could think on Amorfia and her eyes that looked like the large stones he had seen at the bottom of the lake on a clear day. She had been taken by the barren Chieftain of the Highland Cliffs. Would Lothar bar Haven really adopt a girl with no family and with no knowledge of who she is? He took his mug and walked to the nearest tree to think. No one would notice him there. He leaned up against the bark and allowed his mind to envision Amorfia. He had gotten to know her when she was at the Temple of the Sages. He only wished he had visited her more while she was living with Voddie. Sometimes he hated his shyness. Instead of talking to her while he and his brother built her room, he let his sister chatter on about the village happenings.

He wanted to visit her at the Highland Cliffs Fortress, but he also didn't want to be ran through by a sword. No man visited a chieftess—or even a chieftess to be—without an invitation and lived to tell about it. How could one girl go from a fisherman's home, to a sage temple and to a chieftain fortress so quickly? Nothing about her made sense, but he loved being with her. She didn't talk so much and enjoyed the quiet with him. She also had an inner sense of worth that was based on nothing more than that she existed—not on what she could do or offer. She had something special deep within her that he couldn't explain but he wanted. When he talked with her as they walked through Atlatl Forest, he kept expecting it to suddenly burst out of her. But her memory had been blocked by something—maybe tragedy, maybe injury, maybe both.

"Are you Boru the builder?" he heard a voice say above him.

He looked up. It was a young sage dressed in a plain tunic and pants. "Who wants to know?"

"The Supreme Sage of the Temple of Sages in Atlatl Forest would like to speak with you. The matter is urgent. She has requested that I bring you to the temple immediately."

Boru looked at his brother and brother-in-law. They were enjoying the music and dancing. Voddie had just arrived with her baby bundled in her arms. They probably wouldn't notice his absence for the rest of the day. "I will join you," he said. He got up and followed the sage. He knew there was only one reason the Supreme Sage would contact him. Something must be terribly wrong with Morfie.

Chapter 23

HOPE IS BORN

Jaquarn held his mother's dagger in his hand. The blade itself was composed of a material he had never seen before. The hilt of the dagger had red stones embedded in ivory. Eline used the blade to cut his mother's womb and pull him out of her dying body. Everything made sense now. His parents' old age. Their inability to play with him while he was a youngling.

He'd always toddle to the other villagers' Achion clusters to play with any mother or father or friend willing to give him attention. Was that why he had such a desperate need to please the villagers? His adopted parents did love and care for him, but they never looked at him like the other parents looked at their younglings. He always thought it was their age, but now he knew the truth. He was not really their son. Eline had always doted on him, but she traveled much. She would have stayed in the village and raised him as her own if she had been joined.

"What are you thinking about, my husband?" T'maya asked. "Are you worried we won't find the cavern where your mother came through? The ground shudders have changed the landscape so much, I fear we will never find a way through."

He sighed and placed the dagger back on the notched shelf above him. They slept in a wide Achion tree that was meant for visitors to South Village. The Violet Moon streamed in through the hole. The air was cold, and T'maya curled up next to him. They had two fiber coverings—one atop of the other—to keep them both warm. They had searched for too many rises hoping to find the cavern where the Spiritual Elder of South Village, Limmian, found the dagger, but as of yet, they had not discovered it. They needed to act quickly because the Sand-shapers would be back. The South Village hunters chased them away for attacking one of their Novice Elders and stealing their food. But the peace they enjoyed for the moment would soon be replaced with a fight.

"I'm worried about a lot of things, and I'm struggling with my words to Ra'ash. I fear for South Village. In fact, I fear for all the River-dwellers. When the Sand-shapers come back, they will increase in number and carry those obsidian blades. That golden stone they crave is all over the face of the cliff. They will not stop coming south until they have harvested all of it."

He looked at his wife to see if his words caused her discomfort. She stared quietly at him. "Continue. I want to hear your thoughts," she whispered.

"Then I'm curious about where I came from. I am not a River-dweller by birth. I come from the other side of the Desert Plains from the Lake-keepers. If they are indeed the Lake-keepers we thought we lost in the *Great Engulfing*, I want to find them. I want to experience how they live and get to know their customs. I feel this yearning to meet them now. Do they have all the *Divine Oracle* or portions of it or none of it? And I feel so silly. All this time I've been worried about making peace with Elder Trenton and the villagers of Right River Hook when there is an entire population that may need me." He paused. "And—" he broke into tears.

T'maya got onto her elbow and grabbed his face gently between her two palms. "Do not mourn for our daughter yet. Eline believed F'lorna is still alive. We must have faith in what she said."

"It's so hard to believe when I look at the land bridge and peer down the vast waterfall. The force of the water causes the ground to shake and produce a mist in the air. How could she survive unless Ra'ash Himself caught her fall and carried her down the River?" He

232

hated his words, but the image of F'lorna falling contradicted the hope wanting to awake inside of him. Could he look beyond the reality of the situation and believe despite what his eyes and mind told him?

"I may not have the *Chants of Jeyshen* memorized, but the themes have embedded themselves into my spirit. And one of those themes is faith. Do we believe Ra'ash has more power than our circumstance? What is stronger? The things we see with our mind or the things we see with our heart? I feel the Indwelling within me, and it is saying that F'lorna is alive. I don't know why Ra'ash sent her to the Lake-keepers, but I know that He has a purpose for her there. I give voiceless words constantly that she is protected and safe, but even so, I want her back. We will find her."

Jaquarn took his wife's hand and kissed it. "I will have faith in your faith." He then took her back into his arms. He would choose to believe until he had proof otherwise. As his eyes began to droop close, he heard a loud screech overhead. He instantly opened his eyes and listened for the sound again.

"Is that Weston's falcon?" his wife asked.

"I believe it is. Come! Let's go to the Village Achion cluster," he reached up and retrieved the dagger. He wouldn't want anyone taking his one connection to his people and to his daughter.

Jaquarn helped his wife out of the tree and they both walked to the bridge that would lead them into the heart of South Village. The cloudless night allowed for the Violet Moon to shine down on their steps. Lemmeck and the twins came up beside them.

"We heard Banthem," Dashion said. He and Rashion had their bows out. Lemmeck carried a sphere gifted him from the villagers of South Village.

"Why are your weapons out if it is only Weston?" he asked.

"In case he was followed," Lemmeck answered. "The villagers here know Merriton and Weston because they came to this village when they traveled up the River, but others may not know them and have followed to see where he goes."

Jaquarn was not accustomed to so much precaution being used with weapons, but he knew that he needed to get used to it. He looked at the dagger in his hand. It wasn't simply a clue to discovering his past; it was a weapon to protect his future.

Before they got to the bridge, Le'ana and Sage caught up with them.

"We heard Weston's falcon," Sage said.

"He must have gotten the Sand-shaper symbols we sent him," Le'ana added.

"How could you possibly write him the symbols, Le'ana? You do not know them. Nor do you, Sage!" T'maya said and stopped walking. She crossed her arms. "Girls, what are you not telling us?"

Jaquarn looked at each young face. They each looked like they were hiding something. "The only ones I know that can write the Sand-shaper symbols are my wife and my daughter, so how did you all write to Weston?"

"Someone else knows the symbols," Le'ana said, hurriedly. "But we have been sworn to secrecy. Not to worry. She is on our side."

"There are more villagers on our side than you realize, and we will need everyone's help to find F'lorna and get her home," Sage added.

Jaquarn looked at his wife. "Looks like our village is filled with secrets," he said. Then he turned back to the others. "I will trust you on this one, but no more secrets after this."

"Yes, Spiritual Elder," Sage and Le'ana said simultaneously.

"Now, let's go find Weston and see what he has to say," Jaquarn said, leading the way over the bridge.

When they got to the village center, Limmian was already speaking to Weston. There were several hunters with spears ready. Banthem was resting on a branch that Weston had covered with a worn piece of leather.

"Where is Merriton?" Jaquarn asked when he reached Weston.

"He had to stay back in the marshlands. We fear that the Sand-shapers will discover our village soon. There is talk of more coming downriver, and Limmian has verified it."

Limmian stepped in. "I will leave you all for now. The hunters will be surveying the area to make sure the village is safe. I must go to each Achion cluster to speak with every family in our village. Weston and his falcon made them uncomfortable the first time they arrived in South Village. I should reassure them once more."

"Yes, we understand," Jaquarn said and watched the band of hunters disperse. He knew the duties of a Spiritual Elder too well. The burden had only been

235

recently lifted from him, but even now he felt a freedom he hadn't had for some time.

When Limmian left, Jaquarn reached his hand out and squeezed Weston's shoulder. "I offer you my apology of healing. I will give voiceless words for your village's protection, but I fear that none of us is safe now that the Sand-shapers have found the auraium in the cliffs of the waterfall."

"I received a note from someone who claims to be F'lorna's friend. I didn't know anyone else knew the symbols," Weston said, looking at Sage and Le'ana.

"She accidentally learned them when she was a girl. A friend taught them to her without realizing what she was doing," Sage said. "She has kept it a secret until F'lorna discovered that she knew them."

T'maya shook her head with disbelief. "I know now who you speak of—though, I struggle to see how she kept knowing the symbols a secret this long."

Jaquarn looked at his wife. "Who could it be? We live so far away from anyone who could write them." Suddenly, an image of Elder Trenton moving to Right River Hook came into his mind. They once lived in a north village just under the Northeaster Mountains. "Ah, now I see who it is. Does her father know?" He looked from Sage to Le'ana.

They shook their heads. "No," Le'ana said. "And she fears what would happen if he did find out, which is why her writing Sand-shaper symbols shows just how much she cares for F'lorna."

"It helps knowing that we have a way to communicate with Right River Hook if anything were to happen. We can warn them," Jaquarn said. He began to realize just how valuable written language could be. "Maybe Ra'ash has allowed the Sand-shaper symbols to come to the River-dwellers for this time."

"I have written F'lorna another note. I want to send Banthem out in the morning. He can fly long distances. If she is beyond the desert lands, he will find her."

"Yes, that is a good idea! If she can write back, she may be able to tell us how to find her," Jaquarn said. "We must get to her before the Sand-shapers come back to the land bridge."

"I saw what they did when I crossed over the bridge this evening. They have mined out much of the auraium on the cliffs that edge the waterfall. When I was a child, a man from the mountains described to me what the mines of the Northeastern Mountains look like. They plan to rip apart these cliffs for auraium just like they ripped apart the mountains for smoke stone. What is the name of the Sand-shaper that comes to harvest it? All the note told me was that he is Raecli's grandfather."

T'maya spoke up. "His name is Lord Rencon."

Weston nodded. "Yes, I know of him. He is a powerful merchant. He has lost much in the ground shudders. I have retrieved several of his cylinders—some of them family heirlooms. That must be the reason why he came all the way south to see the auraium for himself. If he has gone back to the coastal cities to get reinforcements, it will take him some time to make his way back downriver. I think we will have the time we need to find F'lorna. Raecli is his granddaughter with the violet eyes? The one who was taken from Right River Hook?"

"Yes, Eline was able to get word to us before she died that Lord Rencon was extracting Raecli's horns. F'lorna heard her scream out, so she tried to save her."

"Spiritual Elder Limmian told me about your loss. I am sorry about Eline," Weston said.

"Thank you," Jaquarn said and hesitated. "She was a wonderful sister."

Weston nodded with agreement. Then he thought for a moment. "And you are sure Eline said they were extracting Raecli's horns?"

"Yes, they pulled one out, which is why F'lorna heard her scream," T'maya said. "Then they pulled out the other. They asked Eline to give her some herbs for the pain. Why?"

"There would be no reason for him to extract her horns without proper precautions unless it was an emergency. Why would the merchant make such a hasty decision when he was just about to return home to the coastal cities? They normally would never allow a River-dweller healer to attend to their needs unless they had no other choice."

Jaquarn hadn't thought of that. "Was he simply being cruel?"

T'maya shook her head. "No, she is his only heir. He would not compromise her health unless he needed her horns out for some reason right away. The only thing I can think of was that her horns were sick, but that is very rare in a girl her age, especially a highborn one who is being carried in a traveling case."

Weston abruptly slapped his thigh. "I know what is going on!"

"What?" Jaquarn asked. He was completely lost when it came to Sand-shapers' ways.

"What would a wealthy, powerful merchant do with piles of auraium and an heiress? He will need more help to mine the rest, and he will want to find a family to merge with."

Weston looked at the blank stares around him. "He extracted Raecli's horns because—"

"He wants her to join!" T'maya exclaimed. "But why would he extract them now? He could have still waited to return to the Northwestern Coast."

Weston frowned. "Unless he wasn't taking her home. Now that he's rich with auraium, he could unite his family with a wealthy landowner." He stopped. "Oh no! It can't be!"

"What?" Jaquarn asked, barely able to keep up.

"I know of one wealthy landowner who owns much of the land above the marshlands, and he has a son who is of the age to marry. And this landowner is looking to make an alliance with a powerful merchant."

"Why is that troubling to you?" T'maya asked. "Don't merchant and landowner families merge often?"

He rubbed the back of his neck with worry. "Yes, but if the landowner is who I think he is, his presence down here will not be good. Lord Tarmian is our old master from before we escaped and claimed the marshlands as our new home. His steward is the one who gave my brother his scar. If he discovers us, we will no longer be Marsh-landers. We will be enslaved as farmhands again—or worse, we will be killed to be made an example of."

"Oh no!" T'maya exclaimed.

"And if Raecli's grandfather is getting help from Lord Tarmian, they could be back down at the land bridge much sooner than we thought."

"We will have to warn Elder Limmian and the South Village," Lemmeck said, holding up his spear.

"No," Weston said so softly that Jaquarn had trouble hearing him. "If those two families unite, we will have to warn all the villages."

As the atmosphere grew quiet, Jaquarn felt an urgency to make a decision.

"Lemmeck," he said with finality. "You will stay here with your brothers and travel to all the villages you can. You must warn them and prepare them."

Lemmeck hesitated.

"I know you want to help find F'lorna, but trust me when I say this: no one wants to find her more than I do. I will get my daughter back."

Lemmeck nodded his head. "I will send up many voiceless words for your journey."

"T'maya, you will stay here with Le'ana and Sage. Elder Limmian will protect you all. Keep looking for that cavern."

"Where are you going?" T'maya asked.

Jaquarn felt hope birth inside of him. "I believe my daughter is out there. I will cross the Desert Plains to find her." He looked at Weston. "I know your people may be in grave danger, but do you think your falcon can locate her?"

"He usually looks for the swatch of leather to land on, but if I send him across the desert, he may be able to pinpoint her. It's not like there is anything else out there."

Jaquarn reached out and squeezed Weston shoulder once more. "There is much more for me to tell you about what's on the other side of the Desert Plains"

"You can tell me in the morning when we begin our journey," Weston said and smiled. "Because both Banthem I will be joining you."

Chapter 24

THE CAPTURE

"So you really think the Laker-keepers are over there?" Weston shouted above the noise of the waterfall. He handed the dagger back to Jaquarn and then adjusted Banthem whose talons were squeezing his leather-clad left arm. "I've never seen any material like that. If the Sand-shapers find out about it, they will want to discover where it came from. They are always looking for a stronger material than the fortified obsidian they use. That tool could chip away rock without breaking."

"That is why we must never let them find out about it," Jaquarn shouted back over the ruckus of the water. He wrapped the dagger with a leather strip and placed it back into his pack.

Weston looked at the main river winding up the desert lands. The morning was cold and his breath could be seen when he spoke. Limmian was able to obtain a heavier jacket for him. He had been in such a rush to get to South Village that he didn't think of the weather turning colder. He liked the cold when he was working the fields of the farms, but now he wished for warmer weather while they traveled. They would be forced to create a hearth fire every night, which would keep away critters but draw the attention of other Rodeshians.

"Here you go," Le'ana shouted. She stood holding a long rope. "We tied the ropes securely together. I'm glad the Sand-shapers left these here. There is more than enough slack to get you to the bottom." She peered over the edge. "It is good that you are going down now. If it gets any colder, some of the water on the rocks may freeze and become too slippery to climb down."

"Thank you," Jaquarn said loudly, taking the rope. He looked to his wife. "Keep looking for the cavern. And remember if you find it, just mark it. Don't try to go through the caverns alone. It is too dangerous. If the Desert Plains end up being a dead-end, I'll come back. And we can take the caverns together."

T'maya said nothing but fell into Jaquarn's arms. When she started to cry, Weston took it as his cue to give them some room. He motioned to Sage and Le'ana to follow him away from the cliff where it was quieter.

When they got several paces away from the roar, he asked, "Has Lemmeck already begun his journey?" His respect for Lemmeck had increased yet again. He knew that Lemmeck wanted to look for F'lorna, but he stayed willingly because he was needed to warn the villagers that the Sand-shapers would be coming back sooner and with more force than they had anticipated.

"He is staying until the Heat Source rises in the morning," Sage said. "He is teaching the South Village hunters how to make bows and arrows. Then he will show them how to shoot an arrow properly. He has several younglings in his group of students. That way the village will have both the skill of the spear and the bow."

"Yes, they must know both if they are able to fight back those who would assume to take their lands," Weston said. He thought of his brother and the other Marsh-landers. None of them had any hunting skills. Only farming. They knew how to set traps to catch their meat and furs, but that would not help them fight an enemy trying to take their lands. The best they could do for now was to stay hidden.

"Are you worried about Marshland Village?" Le'ana asked. "Sage and I may be able to travel to find it if you draw us one of your images like you did the land bridge. We can warn them."

"Thank you, Le'ana, but I would not want to jeopardize your and Sage's safety. Besides, we don't want visitors coming into our lands yet because our village could be exposed. My brother knows I'm looking for F'lorna, so he won't be expecting me anytime soon. Our village is safe as long as it stays hidden. The Sand-shapers think our marsh has no value. It's the auraium they want. And that is here." The weight of the falcon on his left arm began to get heavy. "I should release Banthem now."

Weston checked the note that Banthem wore in the band around his leg. "Everything looks good. Let's see if he is willing to fly through the desert lands. "Banthem, go to F'lorna," he shouted as he pushed his arm into the air. Banthem flew up and soared over the waterfall. Then he made a wide circle before landing on a thick branch on the opposite side of the River.

"Banthem!" Weston shouted while pointing to the desert. "Over there!"

"Maybe once he sees you and Jaquarn start your journey, he'll be more comfortable flying that way," Sage suggested.

Weston stared at his falcon. He seemed agitated. He began to flap his wings and screech. "Something is wrong. Banthem sees someone."

Weston scanned the other side of the River where the rocky land met up with the forest rim. He saw movement. "Sand-shapers," he said. "Several of them, and they are coming this way."

Jaquarn must have seen them too because he ran toward them. "Sage! Le'ana! Go with T'maya. She is going back to the village!"

T'maya was running toward the forest, and she kept looking back and waving to the girls to catch up. It didn't take long for Sage and Le'ana to reach her side, and then all three disappeared behind the veil of the woods.

"Let me do the talking," Jaquarn said. "Do you recognize them? Would any of them recognize you?"

Weston looked again. The Sand-shapers were making their way to the land bridge "I don't think so. Their clothing looks to be from the coastal cities. That big man. He looks like a steward of some sort. He is very well dressed for a servant. I don't think any of them come from the farmlands. Wait," he said, squinting his eyes. "There is someone else coming out of the trees."

"Who is it?" Jaquarn asked.

Weston stared until he recognized him. "He comes from the farmlands. He is the snitch. If they reach me, they will take me back to the Lord Tarmian, and they will torture me for information on where the rest of our people are."

"You must run then!" Jaquarn said. "Quick before they come!"

"They will also come after you for helping me. Hurry! Give me your rope. I will hold it and help you down the cliff. Then I will run to safety."

"No! There isn't enough time!"

Weston grabbed the rope. "If you don't make it down, F'lorna will not be found." He tied the rope around his waist and sat down on the hard ground in front of a large boulder. He pressed his feet against the rocky surface and looked back at Jaquarn.

Jaquarn hesitated until he heard the Sand-shapers shouting. He looked to the land bridge. "They are crossing!" He strapped his pack around his neck.

"Now go! I will feed you rope until you get to the bottom."

Jaquarn grabbed the end of the rope. Then he walked to the ledge and laid down flat on his stomach. He scooted himself over the edge while holding the rope tightly in both hands. Jaquarn's tall, strong body was heavy, but Weston knew he had the strength to hold him. He began to steadily feed him the rope with long sweeps of his arms. His hands were burning, but he wouldn't allow the pain to make him stop. He quickly eyed the big man coming over the land bridge. He made it to the other side and started to run toward him. "Just a little further," he whispered to himself.

Weston fed the rope faster. The man was almost to him. Finally, he knew he needed to let go. He hoped Jaquarn was close enough to the bottom that the fall wouldn't hurt him. The man grabbed his arm just as he loosened his grip. The rope spun out a few feet then stopped. Weston and the man stared. Finally, the rope was yanked over the ledge. Weston smiled. "Looks like he made it."

The man growled, clenched his fist and punched Weston in the face. Everything went black.

Lemmeck ate his late lunch quietly. His brothers had taken the hunters on their first bow hunt. Dashion and Rashion were patient teachers. He smiled. Probably from having to deal with their younger brother who always wanted to tag along. They made bows and arrows early that morning. Then they practiced shooting those arrows into large fabric pouches filled with grasses that they mounted on trees. The younglings caught on faster than the seasoned hunters. Skills are always easier to learn with those who had their Eternal Memory opened. He thought of Limmian's granddaughter, Dezzy. She had dark skin like her grandmother, but her hair was a deep burgundy color. It reminded him of Sage's hair color but a little darker. She was just a few turns younger than he and eager to learn the skill of the bow while her Eternal Memory allowed it.

"May I join you?"

He looked up and saw Elder Limmian looking down at him.

"Yes," he said. "Thank you for my lunch. I didn't have time to eat it earlier."

She carefully sat down an arm's width away from him. "My age is catching up with me. The ground is much softer in the spring and summer. So how did my granddaughter do?"

"Very well," he answered truthfully. "She is a natural hunter. I was surprised to learn that there are no hunters in your family."

Limmian sighed. "We were all surprised when she chose hunting as her Adoration. We knew she loved to explore, and our Dezzy has always loved animals. She'd bring injured animals home and nurse them to health again. Then she'd release them back into the forest. I believe her love of animals grew into deep respect for how they nourish our village. When she speared her first tree squirrel, she gave voiceless words over it. Of course, she is taught the words to say from the

Hunting Elders, but she would create her words according to how she felt at the moment."

"That sounds familiar," Lemmeck said. "It is good for the hunters to have a deep respect for what they take from Rodesh."

Limmian looked away. Lemmeck could sense that she carried a deep heaviness. "What is it that concerns you?"

"I don't want to add to your burden since you have only started your first turn as a Novice Elder, but I must have the opinion of someone younger and who still has color in his hair," she laughed, pointing to her grey bun. "It is your generation who will be leading our villages after the leaders now have all gone to their Eternal Dwelling. You will be forced to deal with the decision that we make today. My spirit is deeply troubled, and my granddaughter has made my decisions that much more difficult."

Lemmeck stared at his food. He had lost his appetite. "I know what concerns you."

Limmian nodded. "I thought you would."

"It is the same struggle we face as hunters and even farmers. How can you love something yet hurt it out of necessity? I have hunted many animals for food, and their meat feeds and sustains my village. Their skins and furs clothe us and keep us warm. I don't harvest them with anger or malice in my spirit. I do it out of my great love for my family and friends and an awareness of the provision of Ra'ash. That is why I give voiceless words over every animal I hunt and kill. I want Ra'ash to know my intentions are good, and I'm thankful for His provision."

Limmian stretched out her legs and leaned back on her palms. A few silver strands of her hair had pulled out from the knot she wore at the back. "And now I have an enemy at the foot of my village. I don't know much about Sand-shapers, but the *Divine Oracle* is in my Eternal Memory. I can see what happens when those full of greed and selfishness are let loose in Rodesh. They devour and dominate and destroy. They will try to take our lands. They will try to enslave my village to harvest their yellow stones. And if what Jaquarn has told us is true, the Sand-shapers are uniting together—the ones from the coastal cities and the ones from the farmlands. Soon they will be so powerful that we won't be able to stop them. The only reason we have lived in peace so long is that they have been too busy enslaving each other. But now they have their gaze fixed on us peaceful River-dwellers."

"And do the peaceful River-dwellers allow themselves and their villages to become enslaved or do they fight back?" Lemmeck asked. Then he thought about Dezzy. "And you fear not only the choices you must make, but the choices your granddaughter must make as a hunter."

"Yes," Limmian admitted. "My decisions would be so much easier if I didn't have to worry about someone I love fighting to keep our village protected and our villagers free to live as Ra'ash wills them. Dezzy has a tender heart, and she cares very deeply. But could she harm another to defend what she loves? Or would she hesitate and become captured or harmed herself?"

Lemmeck considered his words carefully. He knew they carried weight in the Spiritual Elder's ears. "I

250

don't think any of us will know the answer to that question until the moment of decision has arrived. But I can tell you with all sincerity that my generation would tell you that we need to fight. I would rather go to my Eternal Dwelling fighting to protect our way of life than live all my years enslaved to another."

"I knew that would be your answer, but I needed to be sure. Thank you, Lemmeck. The decisions I have to make aren't easy, but at least I know they are right."

A sharp whistle pierced through the village.

"What is that?" Limmian asked, looking around.

"That is one of my brothers. Something has happened. We must find them." Lemmeck quickly got up and extended his hand to help Elder Limmian. "He came from the south."

Lemmeck began running toward the land bridge. He kept a steady pace for the Spiritual Elder to keep up.

"Just go ahead of me, Lemmeck. I will catch up," she said between breaths.

He darted forward with all his speed. He knew his brothers would not use the whistle unless something very wrong had happened. He thought of his friends, Sage and Le'ana, and gave voiceless words for their safety. He got to the bridge that led over the circled tributary and saw Dashion and Rashion coming his way on the other side of the water. They had T'maya, Sage and Le'ana with them. He sighed in relief. Something must have happened to Jaquarn and Weston as they scaled down the cliff face of the waterfall. He rushed over the bridge and stopped in front of his brothers. "What has happened to Jaquarn and Weston?"

Rashion spoke first. "Sand-shapers came from the other side of the waterfall. They must have known who Weston was because they practically ran across the land bridge to get to him."

"Where is Jaquarn?"

"Weston helped him get down the waterfall just before they got to him," T'maya said. "My husband is alone and Weston has been captured!"

"The big Sand-shaper didn't ask him any questions. He just threw his fist into Weston's face, and he fell over," Sage said, crying.

"Then the other Sand-shapers picked him up and carried him back over the land bridge," Le'ana added with tears streaming down her flushed face.

"Do you think they've already started taking villagers?" Dashion asked. "Have they begun to take us for their workforce?"

Lemmeck thought for a moment. "No, this was a direct attack. If they had started taking villagers, they would gather us in groups, not individually. This was a purposeful attack just to get Weston. I think his old master has finally found him."

"What are we going to do?" Sage asked. "We can't let them take him. They will use him to find the rest of the Marsh-landers!"

Elder Limmian finally caught up with the group. "What has happened?" she asked breathlessly.

"Weston has been captured by his old master," Lemmeck said. "And I must leave now to get him back while the trail is fresh." He looked to his brothers. "Keep warning and preparing the villages. I will not return without our friend."

Chapter 25

THE SONG OF FEAR

Amorfia allowed Dalia to adjust the golden headpiece around her forehead. "Must I wear so much jewelry Grand Aunt? The metal on my sword should be enough and the golden cuff on my horn?"

"Amorfia, you always intrigue me. Are you not happy with your gifts from your father? He had the headpiece and bracelets made especially for you."

"Why would he not give me something from the family's treasury as customary? It is not usual for him to create new pieces for children." Amorfia heard many stories from the sages, and she knew the history of the bar Haven family. They passed down their jewelry—only making new items for those who married into the family.

"I forget that you know more of our history than both my nephew and I combined. Don't fret over it. I'm sure Lothar has something picked out for you, but the new gifts are fitting, are they not? Since you are a special gift to us from the Befores."

Amorfia smiled. "Yes, Grand Aunt. You are probably right. My gown is very beautiful. It is the color of the stones in Father's sword," she said. She hoped her Grand Aunt wouldn't be hesitant about sharing more information.

"Yes, the ruby stones are only found in the Highland Cliffs. We have the same golden stones and silver metals that the Lowland Cliffs have in their lands, but they have not found red stones like ours yet. It is very sacred to our family, and the bar Hathway family of the Lowland Cliffs envy us for it. Their leader, Chieftain Rugar bar Hathway, covets our lands."

"Is that why I must marry Rathtar bar Holthen of East Basin? Does Father want to unite our lands as a defense against our enemies in the Lowland Cliffs?"

"Yes, Grand Niece, that is exactly why." Dalia finished adjusting the head peace. "You look stunning. I dare say that Rathtar will be enamored by your beauty."

"I dislike what I know about him so far. He sounds like a spoiled young chieftain who gets away with too much. I still don't fully see why I must marry him. It is not a Lake-keeper custom to unite lands. We would rather die fighting for what is ours."

Dalia hesitated. "Sometimes change is good, Amorfia. Your father senses that a union would benefit both territories. Once you are married, your father will have his quest to see what is on the other side of the sands. I will hold the throne until he comes back, and then you and Rathtar can rule the united territory once your father joins the Befores."

"I would very much like to go with him. What if it helps me to remember who I am? Then I can decipher the forty-four symbols for father." Amorfia wanted to find her way back to where she had come from—somewhere on the other end of the river. But Dalia told her she would have to wait until her father walked with the Befores. She worried that she would be too old to be recognized by the time she traveled there.

"You are needed here to protect his lands in his absence, Amorfia. You know this too well. You must quit asking to join him on his quest or you will irritate him."

Amorfia looked down. She felt trapped again like the silver hair in the translucent canister she carried in the folds of her gown.

"Amorfia, you look distressed." Dalia placed her hands along Amorfia's arms. "Have you gone to your

Swarve today? You need to be rested and of good spirits tonight. You meet your future husband and father-in-law."

"Yes," she nodded. "I went to see Croga this morning. Garth brought me more of the saplings he loves, so I fed him a few leaves."

"Be sparing with those leaves. There are not many of the saplings left. Garth must go deeper and deeper into the caverns to find them."

"Yes, Grand Aunt."

"Oh, I do have news that may cheer you up!"

"Have you heard from Voddie?"

Dalia frowned. "No, they are not to summon you. I have heard from the sage from the Lowland Cliffs. He has found an old sage who may have a bit of history about the people who make those markings. He has sent word that he will be arriving in few days. You may decipher those symbols very soon. Your father needs to know what information is hidden in those canisters."

"It may even help me remember who I am and where I come from," Amorfia said, excitedly.

"There now. You are all cheered up and looking beautiful. I think it is time to venture to the dining hall to meet your future husband. Bring your sword along. They may ask for a demonstration of the bar Haven swordcraft after we dine. Just perform the routine that you did for your father. It will quite impress them."

Amorfia bowed. "Yes, Grand Aunt." She walked slowly from the Forest Room down the cool, stone passages of the fortress. The rays from the moon poured in through the sky holes, and the torches lining the walls were lit. She hadn't realized how many servants tended the fortress until she walked the halls one day. Most of the people who lived in the barren lands behind the Highland Cliffs served the chieftain. Many of the men served as swordsmen and the women served within the fortress walls. There were a few farmers who struggled to grow vegetables on large plots of gravelly soil. All their produce came to the fortress.

"We are almost here, Amorfia. Pick up your chin and walk in like you are the chieftain's daughter."

"But I am the chieftain's daughter," Amorfia said.

"Exactly, so act like it."

As they entered the dining hall, she could hear her father laughing. He was drinking ale and in a jovial mood. The room was filled with servants to illustrate the wealth and power of the Highland Cliffs. The musicians were on the far wall, but very few sages lingered next to them. The Supreme Sage was not present. Her father sat at one end of the table with Garth and a few other swordsmen standing guard behind him. Chieftain Darmin bar Holthen was sitting on the other end of the table with his son next to him. The East Basin bowmen were standing behind them both.

Lothar stood up. "Ah, I would like to introduce you to my gift from the Befores. They placed her on my shores just in the nick of time. She is tall and beautiful like our Highland Cliffs people, and she has youth memories to beat all of the Supreme Sages combined. Let me introduce you to Amorfia bar Haven, my daughter."

Amorfia walked to her father and then turned to face her future husband and father-in-law and bowed.

She stood and waited for the reaction of the East Basin Chieftain. After several seconds, he began to clap.

"Rathtar, you have outdone yourself. She is a worthy beauty." Chieftain Darmin got out of his seat. "I need to see if what they whisper about her is true." He walked up to her and stared unabashedly into her eyes. "By the Befores, her eyes have absolutely no color. They are grey like the hairs on your head, Rathtar. To have grandsons and granddaughters with such eyes would truly be a gift. And I expect many of those, my future daughter-in-law," he said, winking at her. "This calls for a feast! Lothar, do feed us. We are famished!" he shouted, as he walked back to his chair.

Her father raised his hand, and the servants began setting down large trays of meats and cooked vegetables.

"My aunt and daughter, please sit at the table and join me. We celebrate," he said, lifting up his golden tankard.

Amorfia sat down at the table next to her father on the opposite side of her grand aunt. She looked at Rathtar. He did not look amused by his father's words. She allowed the servants to portion out her food. She pinched a green vegetable and placed it in her mouth.

The atmosphere was busy with the clanking of the dishes. When the movement subsided, Lothar broke the silence. "Darmin," Lothar began. "I have heard some distressing news about your finances."

Darmin instantly stopped chewing his food. "There is absolutely nothing wrong with our treasury, Lothar bar Haven. You assume too much."

Lothar shook his head. "I know what I have heard to be true. I sent out my best scouts to investigate.

Now that you will be marrying my daughter and we will be uniting our two territories, I worry that your financial problems have become mine."

Darmin slammed the table. "Your accusations are unfounded!"

Lothar continued to slowly chew his food. Then he took a long drink of his ale. "I am speaking of a certain innkeeper from a South Basin village that your son left destitute for the winter. He and his friends drank all this man's ale and ate all his food, promising repayment. But when the morning came, no coins were left."

Darmin turned to look at his son. His cheeks were red with furry. "I told you to pay the innkeeper and to never do that again!"

Rathtar looked down at his food. "I am sorry, Father. I didn't think the innkeeper deserved our coins. The food and ale he served were not worthy of my consumption."

"Yet, you consumed all of it! You embarrass our family when you do not pay your debts—frivolous as they were. Now the youth memories of all the children of East and South Basin will have the story of the drunkard chieftain's son who cannot pay his debts!"

"Don't be angry with your son," Lothar said, eyeing the young man. "I see now that he was merely having fun with his friends. We are only young once, are we not? And I'm sure he was busy preparing to meet his future wife and forgot about sending the payment. Were you not, Rathtar?"

Rathtar vigorously nodded his head. "Yes, there was much to do."

"You see," Lothar said with a smile. "That is exactly what my servant, Garth, told the innkeeper when he paid the debt for you on my behalf. I believed it was an innocent oversight—easy to do with the insignificant village folk. And I did not want my daughter to come into a marriage that may be cursed by the Befores. Now the children with youth memories will talk about the innocent oversight of Rathtar and the generosity of Chieftain Lothar bar Haven of the Highland Cliffs."

"Thank you, Chieftain Lothar. It will not happen again," Rathtar asserted.

Amorfia watched the hue of Darmin bar Holthen's cheeks turn back to their normal pale color. Her father had paid the debt to the innkeeper. Maybe he did care about her after all. She had told her grand aunt about what happened to the innkeeper and how Voddie and Morgo helped him. Dalia told her not to worry about it. Lothar would take care of it, and now he has done just that. Maybe there was nothing for her on the other end of the river. At least, here she was wanted and cared for.

Amorfia tasted a honeyed nut, and its sweetness alluded her. When she smelled them roasting at the village market in East Basin all those months ago, she couldn't wait to have one. Their aroma seemed like delight flavoring the wind. Now a platter filled with honeyed nuts lay before her, and their scent no longer pleased her senses. She wondered if she was back with Voddie in her small home eating the honeyed nuts would they taste sweet as she had imagined.

"Lothar, you have done a good deed for us. We are truly family now," Darmin said, grabbing a large bone with meat and taking a greedy bite.

"Yes, we are," Lothar agreed.

"Speaking of children talking. I heard a story about young Amorfia here. When she went to the Temple of the Sages in Atlatl Forest, she hammered the golden disk, but none of the sages opened the great double door."

"Is that so," Lothar said. "I have not heard this story yet."

"Good, I will tell it! So the story goes that she waited and waited but no one walked down the steps. So to entice them to come out, she sang a song about a local village builder. And guess who opened the door?"

"Who?"

"The Supreme Sage herself. Not only that! She gave a bag of coins to the young man Amorfia was with!"

"Who was this man?" he demanded, turning to her.

"It was only Morgo, the fisherman who found me. He was bringing me to the temple to seek knowledge," she said. She noticed that his face went from tense to relaxed quickly. She wondered if his moods always changed so drastically.

"Why did she give away a bag of coins? Supreme Sages are quite tight-fisted with their money."

"I sang a song that Voddie taught me about her Great Uncle Shardon. He designed the temple but never received full payment. The Supreme Sage was paying the debt."

Lothar pounded the table and laughed. "Is that so! Seems like all debts have been paid!"

"We would very much like to hear her sing. If she could bring out the Supreme Sage, she must have an amazing voice. I remember hearing your mother sing when I dined with your parents. Her voice echoed the voices of the Befores!"

The room became quiet. "I did not know that you dined with my parents," Lothar said.

"I was very young. My head barely reached the top of this table, but your mother's voice is seared into my memory. How beautifully she sang. I would have wept if my father was not watching me," he said. "Amorfia, my future daughter-in-law, I demand you stand and sing for us. But not a song about the village people. Sing me a royal song—one of the Highland Cliffs Chieftains!"

She looked to her father for what he would say.

"Go, ahead and sing a song, but make sure to make it sad, so we can see Chieftain Darmin weep," he said and lifted his tankard toward opposite side of the table. "My daughter will sing in your honor!"

Amorfia took a sip of water and stood. She looked at Rathtar. His expression was indifferent. She thought over the songs she had learned. The saddest one to her was "The Song of Fear," composed by Chieftess Tarsha when she discovered she had the Fear of the Cliffs. She sang it before a young sage who was now aged and living in the Highland Cliffs Temple. The old sage repeated to Amorfia once she discovered she too had the same fear. The sage couldn't repeat the high notes of the melody, but she explained the pitch of each note. Amorfia believed she could sing it almost as it was originally sung.

She cleared her throat and remembered to act like a chieftess like her grand aunt had reminded her. They needed to see her confidence in her position, not simply in who she was as Amorfia. She began with the first quivering words. They were full of timidity and fear of the cliffs, but as the song continued, the words grew in the strength of the Swarves. Feelings of fearlessness flowed from her mouth, like a bird of prey taking flight in the moonlight. She hit the high notes with so much power that her voice ricocheted off the platters on the table in front of her. She closed her eyes and the final words poured from an abundance of force deep within her that she feared she would hurt the ears of her listeners—but that was how Chieftess Tarsha sang the song. When she finished, she felt tears wetting her cheeks. She opened her eyes and saw fear on Chieftain Darmin's face.

He stood up so quickly that he knocked over his chair. "What kind of game is this, Lothar!" he demanded. "Why does she sound exactly like your mother, Chieftess Tarsha? Her voice is locked within my youth memories, and that girl has it!"

"I didn't mean to offend you. I only tried to pick the saddest song I knew. Since I too have the Fear of the Cliffs, that song fills me with sadness, but in the end, it reassures me."

Darmin said nothing and gaped at her. She looked at Dalia. "Grand Aunt, what is going on?"

"I don't know, Amorfia. But when you sang, you became like my sister-in-law. I didn't see it before because of your grey eyes, but you look so much like Tarsha," she said in awe.

"You told me to act like a chieftess," Amorfia whispered.

"Yes, but this is different. You became one."

Amorfia looked toward Lothar. "Father? Am I in trouble?" He stared in a way she had never seen before like he recognized her.

"The day you touched my face," he said. "Why did you do it?"

Amorfia remembered the first time she saw Lothar. She sensed that she knew him. There was something about his eyes that were familiar to her. "It felt like I knew you," she said, quietly.

Lothar stood up slowly, keeping his eyes on her. "You really are a gift from the Befores. They brought you straight to my shores, but I did not have time to find you before that fisherman stole you away from me! The Befores are finally paying me back for all that they have taken from me! All debts are being paid!" He turned to look at Chieftain Darmin and his son. "You will leave my fortress this very moment! My daughter will never marry an East Basin Chieftain. The marriage between Amorfia bar Haven and Rathtar is hereby annulled. Consider the debt I paid to the innkeeper my payment of regret!"

Amorfia allowed Croga's fur to embrace her arm as she fed him another one of his favorite leaves. The other Swarves were sleeping in their stables, but Croga hadn't minded when she snuck in his stall to pet him. That evening she watched as Darmin and his son stomped out of the fortress. There were demands of retribution and declarations of war, but Lothar scoffed at them all. In fact, he seemed to revel in Darmin's threats.

She thought of Lothar, and the way he looked at her after she sung his mother's son. There was recognition in his eyes, and something more—affection. She had desired for him to look at her like that as a father would his daughter. But something was off, like the time she touched his face. He did not completely fit the expectation she had buried deep in her heart and hidden away from her memory.

"You've eaten almost all of your leaves," she whispered to Croga. "Now I will have to send Garth to find me some more saplings."

Croga sensed something first. He looked toward the door of his stable.

"What is it, Croga?"

She heard movement of the dried grasses. She thought it may be a Swarve having a nighttime snack, but the soft sweeping noise was coming from outside.

"Morfie, it's Boru," a low voice said.

"Boru?" She waited for Croga to relax the fur wrapped around her arm. Then she got up to open the wooden stable door. "What are you doing here? If you get caught, they could have you thrown in the fortress prison underground."

"I had to come warn you," he whispered. He entered the stable and walked right up to her. She was surprised when he took her into his arms. He had never shown such physical affection before, but his embrace felt warm and genuine.

She let him hold her for several moments, but she knew that they didn't have much time. The stable servants would be arriving soon. "Has something happened to Voddie or one of her boys?"

"No," he said. "He clasped her shoulders and stared into her eyes. "The Supreme Sage contacted me. It's about your adoption. There were no young sages present, so your adoption is not recorded in the bar Haven history."

"What does that mean?" Amorfia asked.

"It means that it was a fake adoption," he said. "Chieftain Lothar is using you for some reason. If he hasn't really adopted you, he will get rid of you sooner or later."

Amorfia looked down. "I knew something did not feel right, so I am not truly his adopted daughter."

"All he wants to do is marry you off to Chieftain Rathtar for personal gain. You can't marry him."

She looked back at Boru. She could barely see his hazel eyes in the light of the moon coming in from the windows. "I won't be marrying into the bar Holthen family."

"Did the bar Holthen family call off the wedding?"

"No, my father has," she answered simply.

"Why do you call him your father?" Boru asked, obviously irritated. "He is nothing to you. He doesn't even want to adopt you."

"I know," she said. "But he may be my only key to discovering who I truly am."

Chapter 26

SECRET DISCOVERED

"Girls, you better come outside to the front of the house. I'm sure Lord Tarmian will want everyone to see," Marva said, poking her head into Raecli's room. "Lainie, get Lady Raecli bundled up. The snow is still falling and there is a mighty chill in the wind."

"Yes, Miss Marva," Lainie said with a curtsey. Once Marva left, Lainie ran to the window and peered out.

"What is going on?" Raecli asked. She had been dreading the day since Lady Rosarian wanted to go over fabrics for children's clothes. Raecli couldn't use the excuse to take her daily walk because the snow began to fall. She would be forced to keep company with Lady Rosarian all day with no reprieve, but maybe this interruption would halt her plans.

"Oh my goodness, several workers have been rounded up. It looks like the heads of each working family are there. They are all standing in a half-circle in front of the porch waiting. Your grandfather is there on the porch with Lord Tarmian and Lord Sabien—even the steward is there, Mr. Barton, and his daughter Kysha! Now Lady Rosarian is coming out. She looks to be almost swooning. I wonder what's going on?"

"Is Sabien's grandfather out there?" Raecli asked. The family almost never insisted that the old grandfather attend family events or dinners. It suited them fine to let him stay in his room or ramble around the courtyard grounds.

Lainie leaned closer to the glass pane of the window. "No, I don't see Lord Dexarian. And I don't see your grandfather's steward either. What's his name?"

"Moirel," Raecli said. "He's been away for many days. I think my grandfather sent him to the land bridge to inspect what was going on there. I heard that the River-dwellers chased away the remaining Sand-shapers." Raecli was surprised that the River-dwellers fought back, but she knew it would only cause her grandfather to fight harder. He always got what he wanted.

"We better get you down there. I can see Lady Rosarian looking for you. Let me grab the wool cape she had made for you. I hope it isn't too long as the other dresses. I don't want it dragging in the snow and picking up moisture." Lainie got up and walked to the armoire. She gently pulled down the thick wool cape and brought it to Raecli. "I hope you are feeling strong today because this cape is very heavy."

Raecli allowed Lainie to wrap the cape around her. It was interesting how easy it became to let Lainie do the menial tasks for her. Not even in her coastal home with her grandfather's servants did one of them dress her and keep her company all day. But Raecli had to admit she enjoyed the attention. It felt good for someone to dote over her and be concerned for her. She also liked the attention Lady Rosarian gave her—though, not when it came to having babies. At least, she fretted over Raecli and sent her gifts of clothing. She slightly regretted that Lord Sabien was in love with someone else. She didn't love him either, but life here was better than her life with her grandfather.

"Come on, Lady Raecli, or we'll miss what's happening down there, and Lady Rosarian will send me to the farmhouses. I forgot one more thing!" She ran to the top drawer of the dresser and opened it. She pulled out two fur-rimmed wool gloves and handed them to Raecli. "Put them on as we walk," Lainie said, and she took Raecli's elbow. She led her out of the room and down the hallway. "Mind each step. I don't know if I could catch you with you wearing that heavy cape."

They reached the bottom of the steps facing the kitchen. "Let's take you through the house to the front. I want that cape to have as little contact with the ground as possible." They made their way through the drawing room, the parlor and into the front lobby.

"There you are, Raecli! I've been looking for you," Lady Rosarian said, opening the front door. "Lainie, why have you detained her?"

Lainie gave a curtsey. "My apologies, Lady Rosarian, but I wanted to make sure she was good and warm. Miss Marva warned us that it was quite chilly outside."

Lady Rosarian grabbed Raecli's gloved hand and brought her through the door onto the porch. "I see," she smiled too broadly. "Now you can go prepare us some hot tea and a few snacks. Be waiting with them in the drawing room. We will be famished once this is over."

Lainie pressed her lips together trying to avoid frowning. She bowed slightly. "Yes, Lady Rosarian."

Raecli watched her go. She knew that Lady Rosarian was punishing her by not letting her see what was happening in the front yard. She would have to describe the event in full detail this evening when Lainie helped her ready for bed.

"Lord Rencon, not to worry! I have your granddaughter here with me. I would not want her to miss this gift that you have given our family," Lady Rosarian said. "It must be nice to have a steward who comes through with what he promises."

Raecli felt uncomfortable. She knew Lady Rosarian was slighting Lord Tarmian's steward, Mr. Barton. She looked toward Sabien. He tried to appear indifferent, but she could see that he was holding back an array of emotions. Kysha stood on the step to his left, and Raecli stood on the porch to his right. He was stuck in the middle between the one he wanted to love and the one he needed to marry. She didn't envy his choice. She was almost grateful that she hadn't fallen in love with anyone. She noticed that Kysha did not have a cape or robe over her dress. She looked cold, but she stood resolutely next to her father.

"Just wait until you see what Mr. Moirel has brought us and so quickly too," Lady Rosarian began.

"Quiet, Rosi," Lord Tarmian said in a harsh voice. "Everyone can hear you. Just wait until Moirel arrives."

Lady Rosarian was about to say something but changed her mind. Instead, she huffed and forcefully put her hands into the pockets of her robe. Raecli looked around one more time for Lord Dexarian. She couldn't find him, so the old man was probably in his room. His room faced the front and not the courtyards in the back, so maybe he was looking from his window. She looked back through the glass of the front door and smiled. Lainie was hiding behind the parlor wall, gazing at the front yard. She might not miss the event after all.

"Here he comes!" Lady Rosarian whispered, excitedly in her ear. "And look who he brings."

"Who is he?" Raecli asked. The two men were still in the distance walking away from one of the storerooms.

"He is one of the leaders who led a revolt against our family. He and his brother left with several of our hardest working servants. I believe he is the younger one, Weston. Lady Rosarian nodded. "Yes, it is him. Merriton has a scar on his face from Mr. Barton."

"Why did Mr. Barton cut his face?" Raecli asked.

"Because he was demanding more liberties for the workers. They are all getting lazy, the lot of them. They are their own people. They only work for us. If they get sick, they need to manage it. If their women have babies, they need to figure out how to care for them and keep working. If their clothes get worn, they need to sew them. We already shelter and feed them. What more can they expect from us?"

Raecli thought of the wealthy merchants in the coastal city. The servants who worked for them got paid in credits which were written down on ledgers. If the servants needed food or clothing, they would use their credits. The only problem with the system was that the highborns controlled it. And they could plus and minus credits whenever they wanted.

"Can they not use their credits to pay for healers if they are sick or to purchase new clothes?"

Lady Rosarian laughed. "We stopped keeping ledgers years ago."

"Why?" Raecli asked, confused. "The coastal cities still use them."

"Because the workers actually began to owe us more on the ledger than we owed them. So my husband graciously said he would get rid of the ledger. He ensures that the workers have enough to eat and place to live, and they work for us. What more do they need?"

"Yes, but how would they purchase more clothing or what if they want to buy a gift for their children?"

"We give them fabric if the need arises, and they are a creative people. They make presents for their children from the land, which we own by the way. So there is generosity right there. Plus," Lady Rosarian said, becoming agitated. "Each family has a small plot of land that they can farm after their work for us is done. We have been very good to our workers—almost too good, I believe."

Raecli nodded. "I see." She said nothing more. She could see Lady Rosarian did not like the conversation. She thought of her room, which was filled with trinkets and clothes. She thought of the table she dined at every evening—always brimming with all kinds of foods, even cake with thinly sliced auraium. Then she looked at the workers surrounding her. Their clothes were threadbare, and they looked half-starved. Raecli wouldn't say it out loud, but the workers seemed more like slaves than servants.

Moirel made a show of walking in front of the circle of workers and walking to the front of the porch. He pushed the young man onto the first step. "I have found one of the brothers you have been looking for. He was at the land bridge cooperating with those River-dwellers from the village that chased our men away from our position at the bridge. One of the women with him was clearly a Sand-shaper. I didn't get a good look at her because the three women ran away when they saw us coming, but she did not have horns."

"Thank you, Moirel. You have done well finding this criminal," Lord Rencon said loudly. He turned to Lord Tarmian. "It pleases me to offer you this traitor as a sign of goodwill from us. I am determined to look out for your interests, as I know you will look out for mine. They say he is the younger brother, Weston."

Lord Tarmian walked down the steps to the young man. "You have put my steward to shame," he said, looking at Mr. Barton. "He has been looking for those traitors for over a year now. At last, one stands before me. Where are your brother and the rest of my people?"

Weston looked up. His right eye was almost closed shut with bruising and swelling, and his hands were bound behind his back. "They do not belong to you! We are a free people!"

As Raecli watched the scene, she realized that the mother and son she had seen near the rim of the marshlands by the land bridge were part of this group of dissenters. They were the farmhand families that ran away from the estate to claim freedom and to live like River-dwellers. She feared now that they caught one of them, Lord Tarmian and her grandfather would find them all and force them to leave their new lands and return to their forced work on the estate.

"Mr. Barton, please remind Weston who he is," Lord Tarmian said.

Mr. Barton walked down the steps to Weston and kicked him in the stomach. Weston buckled over wheezing and coughing.

"Father, no!" Kysha cried.

"Go back to the house if you can't stomach the discipline that must be given to a traitor."

"You are the traitor!" she yelled and ran down the steps toward the steward's home.

Moirel handed Lord Tarmian a leather pack. "We found this on him. You will see something interesting inside."

Lord Tarmian grabbed the pack and started searching inside. He brought out several parchments. "You have been drawing again. You know it is forbidden." He held up one of the parchments. "Is this the land bridge?"

Weston looked up. "Yes."

Raecli knew his words to be true. That was the place her grandfather had extracted her horns, and F'lorna had tried to rescue her. And it was the last time she would see her birth friend again.

"Lord Rencon, come look at this," he said, handing the drawing of the land bridge to him. "We can use this for our future work on the bridge."

Lord Rencon took the drawing and stared at it. "Yes, this could be quite useful."

Lord Tarmian continued to look through the parchments and stopped. "Who is this beautiful River-dweller?" he asked, holding the parchment in front of Weston.

Raecli couldn't see the drawing because her grandfather had blocked her view.

"That is no one," Weston said.

"It can't be no one if you took this much time to detail her face."

"Let me see that," Lord Recon said, taking the parchment. Then he looked at her. "Raecli come here."

She walked down the steps. "Yes, Grandfather?"

He showed her the drawing. "Is this not the girl who tried to take you at the land bridge. The one who fell into the waterfall?"

Raecli took the parchment. "It's F'lorna," she whispered." She couldn't hold back the tears. "She died trying to save me."

Lord Sabien jumped from the porch to the ground. "Let me see," he said, grabbing the parchment from her. "Is this the River-dweller with grey eyes?"

Raecli nodded. "Yes."

"Lord Rencon, did you not see that this girl had grey eyes?"

"Yes, I knew they were grey when I fetched my granddaughter from that dreaded village over a year ago. I thought it was a waste then, and it's still a waste now. Highborns living as River-dwellers. It's preposterous! And to think my daughter would choose to live in a tree over the homes I provided her. Well, it won't be so with my granddaughter."

Lord Sabien looked back to Moirel. You said there was a Sand-shaper with him. A woman?"

Moirel nodded his head. "I did not get a good look at her face, but she maybe was in her late thirties. She had two young horned girls with her. They were running to the forest on the other side of the land bridge. And there was another man with him. Weston helped him escape. They used our rope, and Weston held onto it while the man scaled down the cliff. He ran off into the desert lands, but I don't know why. There is nothing out there."

Lord Sabien kneeled down next to Weston. "Why did you help that man down the cliffs?"

Weston said nothing and looked away.

"Is he the father of the girl who fell? This girl that you drew on this parchment. Her name was

F'lorna," he said and held up the parchment. "Why would you risk going to the land bridge during the day when you knew you could be exposed?"

Weston stared back at Lord Sabien. "Why don't you tell me, my childhood friend?"

"How dare you call him that!" Lady Rosarian yelled.

"Mother! Quiet!" Lord Sabien shouted to his mother. "He has a right to call me his friend because we were friends for almost fourteen years before you forced him and his mother to leave our home."

"And you see why? Look how attached you've become to a servant!"

Lord Sabien glared at his mother. She closed her mouth and crossed her arms.

He looked back to Weston. "And this Sand-shaper woman? That was her mother, wasn't she? Did she have grey eyes too?"

"My son, what are you speaking of? How do you know this girl?" Lord Tarmian said, interrupting. "Why are you asking these foolish questions?"

Lord Sabien looked at his father. "I ask because of a story my grandfather told me when I was young when he believed me to be asleep."

Lord Tarmian stared at his son and took the drawing of the young girl from his hands. "Mr. Barton, send the workers back to the storehouses. Have them finish canning the goods," he said, looking down at the parchment.

"You heard him!" Mr. Barton yelled. "Get back to work!"

"You too, Mr. Barton. Go check on your distressed daughter. I fear you do leave her alone far too often."

Mr. Barton stood stunned. "Yes, Lord Tarmian. Right away."

Raecli watched as the workers and Mr. Barton left. The tension on the porch mounted quickly. Everyone left stood in silence waiting to see what would be said next.

"Marva, go retrieve my father would you?" Lord Tarmian said, coolly.

"Yes, Lord Tarmian." She curtseyed and quickly went into the house.

Lord Tarmian stood for several moments in thought. "So," he began. "We have a young girl who fell off the cliffs and into the water. We have a father scaling the cliffs to find her. We have a traitor willing to risk being seen to help this father. We have a Sand-shaper woman running back into the forest with young River-dwellers. Did we discover her eye color yet?" He looked back at Weston. "Tell me the color of her eyes."

Weston looked away.

"No matter. I'm sure Raecli knows this information since the young girl was her friend," he said, turning to face her.

"We are back," Marva said from the door.

"Ah, Father. I'm glad you have joined us. We have found out a bit of interesting information."

"What is it? Why have you woken me?"

"Here, Father, look at this drawing," he said, handing Lord Dexarian the parchment.

"You have missed much, but let me recap quickly. The girl you are looking at has grey eyes. She is Raecli's friend from one of the villages. Her mother is a Sand-shaper and her father is a River-dweller. She fell over the waterfall and her father is going after her. My son is asking questions like he knows something that I do not. He says you told him a story when he was a child and you thought him asleep. There. Now I think you are all caught up."

He looked at Raecli. "What color are her mother's eyes?"

Raecli looked at the grandfather. "They are grey."

"Where is her mother from?"

"The Northeastern Mountains."

Lord Tarmian looked at his father. "You visited the mountains quite often. In fact, I do believe you spent almost a year there, did you not? About forty years ago when I was yet a young boy."

The old man nodded but continued to stare at the parchment.

"What is her mother's name?" Lord Tarmian asked.

Raecli looked at Sabien, but she couldn't decipher what he was thinking.

"Her mother's name is T'maya," she answered.

"What did you say?" the grandfather asked.

"My friend's mother," Raecli repeated. "Her name is T'maya."

"Isn't that interesting, Father?" Lord Tarmian said with anger twisting his expression. "Why would this

Sand-shaper from the mountains who has grey eyes have the same name as your mother?"

"I must have told her," the grandfather said.

"Told who?"

"My sweet love from the mountains. I must have told her about my mother. And she remembered. When I left her, she must have named our daughter after her."

Lord Tarmian looked at his son. "Is this the story your grandfather told you when you were young?"

Lord Sabien nodded. "Yes, Father."

Raecli could see the heat on Lord Tarmian's face simmering. For the first time she had known him, he looked confused and hurt. He glared at his father once more before walking back into the house and slamming the doors. His mood contradicted her own. She had just found out her best birth friend may still be alive. If her father was looking for her, there must be a chance she survived the fall. She had hope inside of her that she had never experienced before. Maybe Ra'ash was with her after all.

Chapter 27

THE ESCAPE

R aecli tiptoed down each step quietly. She wore a long cape over her elegant nightgown. She knew the cook's room was adjoined to the other side of the kitchen. Thankfully, the old woman snored so loudly that Raecli could tell when she was asleep. She was glad the snow continued to fall. It would cover up her footsteps to the holding cell where Weston was locked up. She crept to the table where the cook showcased her baked goods. She grabbed several rolls and tarts and slipped them into the pockets of her robe. Then she walked to the door and opened it quietly, slipping out onto the back porch without a noise. She pushed the door closed and it shut with a low click.

She walked through the snow and felt the crunch of the cold crystals under her leather moccasins. She saw two guards sitting next to the holding cell with a large basin between them and a small fire in front of him. They looked half asleep. When she reached the first guard, she nudged him softly. "I want to speak to the prisoner for a moment."

The young man darted up in his seat. "No one is allowed in or out," he said a little too loudly.

The second guard woke up. "What are you doing here, Lady Raecli? You want to get us in trouble?"

"I only want to speak to the prisoner for a moment. I'm sure you both heard what happened by now. This man knew my best birth friend. I just want to ask him a few questions," she said, trying to look very innocent. "Also, I brought you both something to eat from the kitchen. I'm sure you are hungry." She reached into her pocket and pulled out two tarts and handed one to each man.

They both looked around and then took the tarts. "Okay, Lady Raecli," the second guard said. "But just for a bit. We don't want to get into no trouble. Lord Tarmian is not in a good mood. We wouldn't want to get on his bad side."

"I promise, it will be just a moment," she said, smiling. "And here," she reached into her pocket. "I was going to eat these later, but why don't you two have them. Make sure to eat them both slowly, so you can savor every bite."

The guards took the additional rolls she handed them and nodded hungrily.

She opened the door to the holding cell and walked in. She saw a big pile of old vegetable bags filled with dried grass. "Weston, are you under there?" The bags moved until one rolled over.

"Yes, I'm trying to keep warm," he said, sitting up. "What are you doing here?"

"I brought you a roll and a tart," she said, bringing them out of her pocket. "I only have a moment with you, but I wanted to ask you about F'lorna. How do you know her?"

He grabbed the roll and tart and set them on his lap. He took a big bite from a roll before talking. "She was traveling to the river with Lemmeck and his brothers and Sage, Le'ana and Ralona. They were harvesting sinews of the animals that died during the earthquakes, so we helped them."

"What did they need them for?"

"They were building some kind of bridge for their village," he said. "That's when we found out that F'lorna had Mountain Terror."

She nodded. "Yes, that is why she fell down the waterfall. Her father thinks she is alive?"

Weston hesitated. "Look, I don't know how much I can trust you. You are one of them."

"I am here because I was forced to leave my village after my mother died. F'lorna was all I had, and my grandfather took me away from her. Besides, I know where your people are hiding. I saw a mother and a son near the marshlands, and I didn't say anything then, and I won't say anything now."

Her confession seemed to convince him. "I apologize for being cautious. I now see that you are a friend. F'lorna did talk about you. She missed you very much."

"But how could she be alive? Even if she survived the fall, there is nothing on the other end of the River."

He continued eating. "We have reason to believe that there are people on the other side of the desert lands."

"What? That's impossible. Who would be there?" she stopped. She thought of some of the *Songs of the Prophets*. "Unless the Lake-keepers survived the Great Engulfing."

"That's them. I couldn't remember their names, but they found evidence that there are people over there."

"What kind of evidence?" she asked still skeptical.

"A dagger with a shining blade made of a material we've never seen before. And—" he began. "It's a long story, but just know that one of them came to our lands through the caverns that run alongside the river."

"Do you think her father will find her?"

"I don't know," he said, finishing his last bite. "But everyone seems to think so. They have this hope that doesn't make sense, but they have me believing it too."

"It is Ra'ash," she whispered.

"Yes, that's His name. And something about His dwelling."

"It's called the Indwelling. When you told us today that Jaquarn was looking for F'lorna, I felt hope come to life inside of me. It must have been that—the Indwelling."

Weston dusted the crumbs from his lap. "Raecli, you better go now. If they find you here with me, we will both get into trouble."

"They are going to torture you tomorrow," she whispered. "Mr. Barton will not stop hurting you until you tell him where the others have gone. My servant girl told me before bed. You have to leave."

"The guards have a large drum basin between them. They will pound it if I try to sneak out. Then I will have thirty men after me and no way of escaping. And look what they took from me," he said, pulling up his bare feet. "They have my boots and my jacket. I would freeze before morning. I will never tell them where my people are, so they will just have to kill me."

"There must be something we can do," she said.

"What was that?" he asked, getting up.

Raecli listened. Suddenly, she heard a strangled voice, like someone was choking.

"There it is again!" he said.

They both stared at the door as it creaked open. Raecli was about to run, but she saw a hand she recognized. Then a face. "Lemmeck? Is that you?"

"How did you get past the guards?" Weston asked.

"Both guards were asleep," he answered. "So I made sure they would stay asleep for a while longer with a large stone I picked up. Don't worry. They should wake up soon with just a little bruising and a headache."

"I should have known. You defeated the River Monster, so two guards are no problem for you."

"Here," Lemmeck said, dropping boots and a jacket on the ground. "I got these for you." He turned his attention to Raecli. He placed his hand on her shoulder. "It is so nice to see you, old friend. You have been greatly missed."

Raecli hugged him. "I have missed you and all of my friends," she whispered.

Weston sat on the ground and started putting on his boots. "You must have been watching us for a while if you learned where they hid my boots and jacket."

"I arrived when you two did just as the Violet Moon awoke, but I've been waiting for a good chance to get you out. I've overheard enough information to fill two Eternal Memories. Good thing mine is shut."

"Did you hear about T'maya?" Raecli asked.

Lemmeck nodded. "Yes, we have discovered who her father is."

"That would be strange if I married Lord Sabien. He's related to F'lorna. If they are cousins, F'lorna would become my family through marriage."

Weston got up and slipped on his jacket. "So you have been arranged to marry Lord Sabien. I thought that might be the reason your grandfather pulled out your horns at the land bridge."

"Yes, but it might not happen. He is in love with another."

"Kysha. I know. He's loved her ever since we were boys. But that marriage is not allowed."

"He may run away with her to the mountains or the villages," she said.

"Raecli, why don't you come with us? I will take you back to South Village. You will be safe there," Lemmeck said.

"I would love to go with you. I want so badly to see F'lorna again. But if I went back, we wouldn't be safe for long. My grandfather will find me, and he will fight anyone who intends to hide me."

Weston looked out the window. "The sun will rise soon. We must go. Did you happen to get my pack?"

Lemmeck shook his head. "No, Lord Recon has it in the house."

Weston thought. "They are going to use my drawings to help mine more auraium from the land bridge." He looked back at Raecli. "Maybe you can help us."

"How? I feel so useless."

"Do you know how to write the Sand-shaper symbols?"

Raecli nodded still trying to fight the shame of knowing them.

"F'lorna knows them too," Weston said.

"That is not possible."

"Yet another thing that is not possible, but is. F'lorna and I communicate with the symbols. We send parchments to each other through my Saber Falcon, Banthem. He carries them on a band attached to his foot." He looked at Raecli's confused expression. "Do you understand me?"

"No, not really, but I'm listening."

"I can send him to you. He knows this place. Just keep a large swatch of leather material tied around the branch of the tree that is close to your window. You are in the guest room facing the courtyard, right?"

She nodded.

"Tie it there, but be careful."

"Does the falcon bite?" she asked.

"No, Banthem is gentle. Be careful that you are not seen and you don't fall out the window."

"Oh, yes. I will be careful."

"I'll let you know when we find F'lorna, and you can keep me updated on what's going on here."

"I can do that. My housemaid, Lainie, keeps me well-informed," she said.

"Lainie is your maid?" he asked.

"Yes, is that good?"

"She can be trusted as long as it doesn't compromise her position. Just be careful what you share with her, and don't let her know about the falcon. Don't let anyone know."

"Okay," she nodded.

"Now go back to your room before everyone wakes up."

"Thank you," she said, giving Weston a hug. "You have given me reason to hope."

Weston bowed slightly. "I am honored."

Then she walked back to Lemmeck and gave him another hug. "It was good to see you. Tell F'lorna and the others that I miss them, and that I hope to see everyone soon. I believe Ra'ash is finding a way. We need only to work together."

"I will tell them, and I will offer voiceless words to Ra'ash for you," he said.

Raecli smiled. Then she picked up her robe and slipped outside. She didn't look at the guards asleep on their chairs. The snow came down harder. It would be difficult for anyone to track Lemmeck and Weston as they escaped. She thought of everything they had told her about F'lorna knowing the symbols and a falcon who carried parchments of communications. It all sounded so far-fetched, but here she was on the estate of her best birth friend's grandfather. She hadn't felt this alive since she was taken from Right River Hook. She finally had something to live for.

Jaquarn pulled the hood over his head tighter and lifted the scarf around his mouth. Even still the wind was fierce and blew sand and snow across his cheeks. This was his third rise to wake up in this foreign, desolate land. Barely anything grew here. Even the Achion saplings he'd seen sprouting from the cracks of rocks would never become the majestic trees they were meant to be. He had already eaten half the food his wife packed him. He would need the rest to return home. If he didn't find the Lake-keepers today, he would have to turn back around.

Thankfully, water was plentiful. The water tasted sweeter and looked clearer along the Desert Plains like the sand had filtered out the dirt. He had seen several fish, but there was no use catching them. Weston had packed the fire stones in his pack, and he never made it down the cliff. Jaquarn hoped that he made it back to the forest before the Sand-shapers captured him.

The ravine that cut through the Desert Plains where the River flowed had many niches and caves for him to sleep in. They kept the wind away, and he stayed fairly warm through the night. He dreaded to leave the protection of the ravine, but he needed to get to higher ground, so he could look ahead. He walked quite a distance when the Heat Source went down the evening before. He kept going until his knees began to give out. He thought of his daughter, and his wife's look if he did not return with her.

"Maybe, I'll see a village now instead of white sands covered in snow," he said to himself. He began to make his way up the ravine to a large boulder that seemed like a perfect look-out spot. The incline became so steep that he had to crawl on his hands and feet. The wind blew harder and he almost lost his footing. When he finally made it to the boulder, he pulled himself up. He stood slowly making sure the boulder was secure. He pushed his hood back, so he could get a good view. He had to shield the bright rays of the Heat Source while trying to keep the sand out of his eyes. When his eyes were able to take in the view around him, his mouth gaped. The River split into three directions. One stayed going south while the other two went east and west.

"Oh no," he whispered. "I don't know which direction my daughter has gone." Jaquarn knew that even if the Lake-keepers were just over the horizon, he had two in three chances to pick the wrong branch of the River that fed into their lake. He didn't have enough food to make that mistake. He had to return back to the land bridge and hope that T'maya discovered the cavern. He felt the hope inside of him waver. "Ra'ash, help me."

Chapter 28

SAGE OF THE ORACLE

"My daughter, how do you feel this morning? Rested I hope. My aunt has not been working you too hard with the bar Haven swordcraft? Although I must confess, the crisp wind on your cheeks gives you a youthful glow and make your colorless eyes bright." Lothar stood from his seat at the front of a long stone table. The servants behind him held platters of food. He woke up that morning and thanked the Befores for the gift that they had given him, a daughter. And not just any daughter—one that was supernaturally marked by the Befores. They drained her eyes of color to show everyone who looked at her that she was extraordinary. Then they gave her youth memories that could swallow up all of the sages' stories combined.

Amorfia smiled. She wore her warfighting leathers and kept her sword sheathed by her side. "I am sorry we are late, Father. We lost track of time. Before we knew it, the sun was already coming over the treetops. I hope you did not delay breakfast on our account." She walked to the seat to the left of Lothar and sat down.

"And it is exactly the opposite of what you say, my nephew. She has been working me too hard. I must confess, she now knows everything I know about the bar Haven swordcraft. There is nothing more I can teach her, so I will have her practice with the trainers. Other than a spectator, my work is done." Dalia set her sword on the table and sat down opposite Amorfia. She too wore her warfighting leathers. "I am famished. Please tell me that one of our servants trapped a land animal. I tire of fish."

The platters were placed down. "Oh good. They have procured us some pheasant. That is exactly what I was hoping for. Lothar, however did you know?" Dalia pinched off a piece of meat and sucked it between her teeth. "Delicious."

"I am glad you are pleased, Aunt," Lothar said. He tried to eat his food, but he couldn't wait any longer. "I have a gift for you, my daughter." He signaled a servant who held something long and wrapped in a large white cloth. Lothar stood and unfolded the cloth. Underneath lay his sword with the ruby stones on the hilt. Its blade was sheathed in a black leather scabbard. "This sword was my father's. He was a powerful chieftain who expanded our territory and subdued our enemies. He used this sword to mortally wound Verdan bar Hathway, the Chieftain of the Lowland Cliffs. He was succeeded by his son, Rugar bar Hathway, and one day I hope you will overthrow him." He picked up the sword with both hands and pulled the blade from the scabbard in one swift move. The metal of the sword hummed as it released from its sheath.

"Lothar, that is your sword! It's meant for a Chieftain, not a Chieftess. She is your daughter, not your son," Dalia said. "Amorfia needs a dagger."

"She is a gift from the Befores to me! She supersedes our traditions, and I will not degrade her with a lowly dagger, like my mother! You said yourself, she has learned the bar Haven swordcraft well, is that right?"

Dalia hesitated. "Yes, she has. Better than anyone I have ever seen. Maybe even better than you."

He turned to Amorfia. "That is why I have chosen to give you my sword. My daughter will not be seen fighting with a youth sword. You must have a mighty weapon to lead the Highland Cliffs. Take that one off."

"Yes, Father," she said. She unclasped her sword from her belt and laid it on the table.

Lothar slid the Chieftain's sword back into its scabbard and handed it to her. "See if it fits."

She took it and tried to buckle it in her belt. "It is too big for my belt."

"Dalia, have another sword belt made for Amorfia immediately."

Dalia nodded.

Amorfia placed the sword back onto the cloth. "Thank you, Father. I will use it well."

"I know you will." Lothar sat back down and continued to eat.

"I have very good news," Dalia said. "The old sage from the Lowland Cliffs arrived late last night. He is the one who may have information about canisters we have found. I've asked him to speak with Amorfia after breakfast today. I think what is stored up in his youth memories may finally help her to remember and decipher the symbols for us."

"Send him away, Dalia. He is not needed anymore," Lothar said and continued to eat his food. He tired of sages filling the mind of his daughter. She needed to focus on learning the practicalities of leading a people as Chieftain.

"Are you sure, Lothar? If we can decipher the symbols, we will have a better idea of who is on the other end of the river in case they arrive at the foot of our cliffs ready for battle. And we may be able to finally save our family history with symbols. We won't need to rely so heavily on the sages."

Lothar threw down the bone he had been chewing. "I will not repeat myself, Dalia. Do as I say! I don't want any more sages filling her head with nonsense, especially ones from the Lowland Cliffs!"

Dalia folded her hands. "I will do as you say. After he has rested, I will send him away."

"And fetch several sages from our temple. I want to hold another adoption ceremony this evening. And this time Amorfia will use my father's sword when she performs her routine from the bar Haven swordcraft. And make sure all the sages are young. I have no use for the older ones," he said. Then he looked at Amorfia. "Tonight, we will show everyone that you are Amorfia bar Haven, the daughter of Lothar bar Haven, the gift from the Befores."

"Yes, Father," she said. "May I be excused? I must check on my Swarve."

"That is a good idea. Get your strength up, my daughter," he said. "But be ready to meet me in the throne chamber this evening. I will have your sword waiting for you."

Amorfia nodded and got up from her seat. She took the youth sword and clasped it back into her belt. Then she turned and exited the dining hall.

As Lothar watched her walk away, he was reminded of his mother. She would often excuse herself from the table to see her Swarve. She'd come back looking calm and refreshed. Amorfia was very much like her. Lothar felt a tightening in his chest. The only difference was that he would make sure that unlike his mother, Amorfia would never run away.

Dalia leaned in and whispered. "I am confused, Lothar. Why have you suddenly changed your mind about deciphering the symbols?"

"I haven't," he said, taking another bite. "In fact, I am more determined now than ever to take the new lands before Chieftain Rugar discovers them first. I don't doubt that he has found some of those canisters floating along his shores, and I will not let the Lowland Cliffs have more land or power than me."

"But why do you want me to send away the sage?" she asked, looking baffled. "You will need to know their written language to overcome them."

"Amorfia needn't bother herself with the symbols. She needs to concentrate on ruling Highland Cliffs in my stead. I will get what I need to interpret them."

"How? There is not one single Lake-keeper who can decipher them."

He looked at Dalia and smirked. "Then I will go to the new lands and take an interpreter."

Amorfia wanted to run to the stables. Every time she passed a servant, she would slow her step, but when she turned a corner, she sprinted down the passageway. Something felt so wrong. She now had the love of a father, but it was not the one her heart was searching for. Even worse, he saw her as more than just a daughter. He saw her as a gift from the Befores. How could she be a gift from those who walked before? Were they so powerful that they could create life, yet not so powerful to save themselves from death? None of Lothar's words made sense to her, and the more she called him, Father, the more she hated herself for saying it. That word didn't belong to him, but she didn't know who else to give it to.

When she finally made it outside behind the fortress, she darted to Croga's stall. He would help her think clearly. He would make her feel better. When she arrived at the stables, she pushed the door open. She saw his golden face and black, wide nose. He was happy to see her and his fur stood up on end. "Croga! You've missed me!" she exclaimed, walking up to him. She normally laid up against him, but this time she decided to climb onto his back. She had only ridden him a few times because she wasn't allowed to leave for long, but he had very much enjoyed their walks.

"Do you mind holding me for a while, Croga?" She laid completely on his back letting his fur wrap around her. She still wore her warfighting leathers, but she could feel his fur wrap around her lower arms and neck. Even though a sense of well-being washed over her, she still had the nagging sensation that she was missing something.

"I don't mean to interrupt you, Morfie. Are you taking a nap now on your Swarve?" Garth asked with a chuckle. "I heard you talking to Croga, so I wanted to check on you and make sure you were okay."

She turned her face toward Garth, pressing her check onto the Swarve's fur. "I'm fine. I'm just relaxing."

"We won't be long. I'm preparing the old sage to head back to the Lowland Cliffs. I feel sorry for him. He came all this way just to turn right around. He's using the Swarve in the stall next to Croga's. I'm taking him down to the dock. He'll take the boat back across Domus Lake. It's a lot faster than traveling all the way around by foot."

Amorfia sat up. "Where is he?"

"He's sitting on a bench right out there," he said, pointing through the door. "You can't miss him. He has the facial tattoo and feathers of the Supreme Sages from the Lowland Cliffs. If you want to keep him company while I get his Swarve ready, I think he would appreciate it. You know how sages are. They love to tell their stories."

"Yes, I think I would like that," Amorfia said, swinging her legs over Croga and landing softly on the floor. "But first let me feed Croga some of his favorite leaves."

"Ah, you may not want to feed him anymore for a while," Garth said. "I know he loves them, but I think they are doing something strange to him."

"What do you mean?" Amorfia asked. She inspected. "I see nothing wrong—though I know he is big for his age."

"Lift up his wings," Garth said.

She bent over to his right wing and spread it open. Long, golden feathers unfurled from it. "Garth, what are those?"

"They look to be feathers like the ones the cliff eagles have," Garth said. "And they don't come out either. I tried. They are longer than my forearm and anchored deep into his wing."

"What are they there for?" she asked, still in awe.

"For flying, of course," she heard an aged voice say.

She looked up, and a dark skin older man with a cane ambled up to her. She looked into his eyes. They were a beautiful emerald color. "I recognize your eyes, yet I have never seen that color before."

"Almost all the Lowland Cliffs people have my color eyes, and my color skin for that matter," he said, giving a toothless grin. "It's nothing special unless you've never seen one of us before."

"But I have, I think. I don't remember," she said, feeling confused.

"Are you the girl with endless youth memories?" he asked.

"Yes," she nodded. "You are the sage Dalia brought me."

"Chieftess Dalia thought what I have stored in my youth memories would be of some help to you. Something about the symbols that you have found. Forty-four of them to be precise."

"She wanted me to decipher them, but I don't know how. I can't remember anything beyond waking up in the fisherman's home."

"That is a tragic thing not to remember who you are," the old sage said, sucking his gums. "You see those feathers?" he asked, pointing with his cane.

"Yes," she said.

"I have stories in my youth memories about Swarves flying. Not only that. I have memories from before the Shaking when others walked among us."

"You mean the Befores?"

The old sage laughed. "The Befores are merely a counterfeit for what was lost—our way of trying to create answers for the questions that we have forgotten to ask."

"What questions?"

"Why are we here? Where do we come from? Who created us? How does it feel not knowing who you are and where you come?" he asked.

"I feel lost," she whispered.

"Exactly!" he said. "We are all lost if we cannot answer those basic questions. But I have the answer. And it is the true answer, which is why the sages shut me out. They feared I would tell people the truth, and they would lose their power."

"What is this truth you speak of?"

"It is the truth about Ra'ash," he said with excitement.

"You mean Rash and Vorn. The fisherman told me about them," she said, feeling her hope slip away.

The old sage shook his head. "No, those stories are merely supplemental. I speak of the heart of Ra'ash. I don't know about the forty-four symbols you speak of, but I do know the forty-four *Chants of Jeyshen*. Jeyshen was a gift from Ra'ash to us, so we could love the One who is love.

"A gift," she repeated. She thought of Lothar. He kept calling her a *gift*, but she knew she couldn't live up to that call. "What are the *Chants of Jeyshen*?"

"They tell of a Creator who had so much love that He created Rodesh and filled it with plants, animals and fish. Then He created two masterpieces in His image, and He put His spirit within him and her. And He so loved them, but He would not force their love back."

"What happened to the masterpieces?"

"They disobeyed and brought shame onto Rodesh. But even in their shame, Ra'ash longed to be

301

with them, which is why He sent Jeyshen as His gift to all of Rodesh."

Suddenly, an image of Boru's dream flashed through her mind. A Chieftain flying on a red Swarve over Domus Lake. "Jeyshen," she whispered.

"Would you like me to tell you the chants?" the old sage asked.

"We don't have time," Garth said, looking out the door. "I don't know if I was allowed to even let you speak to Amorfia since they were sending you home."

"Please, at least let him tell me one chant," Amorfia pleaded.

"Okay, just one, but make it short."

The sage closed his eyes. "I will recite to you *Jeyshen's Chant of Acceptance*. It is the shortest of all the chants but just as powerful."

Amorfia watched as the old sage recited the chant. She didn't listen to each word. Instead, she let the melody of the chant fill her mind. She could feel a memory pressing against her, imploring her to let it out. Several feelings came to her. Feelings of peace and anguish, and love and loss. Images began to blur like fading moonlight in her mind. She saw fragments of people—smiles, smells, embraces—all swirling in a current of emotion that she couldn't seem to grasp. Finally, the chant was over and the old sage opened his eyes.

"So be it," she whispered.

"Exactly right," he said. "So be it. How did you know?"

Suddenly, a searing pain sliced through her mind down into the core of her body, and she fell to her knees. "Mother! Father!" she yelled. Her mind overflowed with memories and her heart swam in a sea of emotion. "Why, Ra'ash? How could You let this happen?" She cried for each loss she received as she began to remember. Croga came and laid by her side, embracing her in his peaceful presence. But nothing could take the heartache away of the life she had forgotten and the burden of the two memories she now carried.

F'lorna finally woke up.

Chapter 29

THE TRUE HEIR

F'lorna made long strides next to her Swarve as they followed Garth. Her amber hair swished behind her from the wind and her fast pace. Before she left, she snuck back into the Forest Room to retrieve her pendant from Lemmeck and her two horn bulbs from Voddie. Those would be the only things she brought with her beside food and her sword. She decided to keep her warfighting leathers on because they were warm, and Garth gave her his large fur pelt that he normally wore over his shoulders. He told her she could use it as a coat and a blanket to keep warm.

She felt her left horn. She had grown accustomed to having two horns and watching them grow. But now that her memory was back, she had flashes of fear that one was missing. She tried to take the horn cuff off of her left horn, but Lothar had squeezed the sharp prongs into the bone and clamped it shut. She was able, however, to take off her horn brace. Her horns were almost fully grown. So much growth in such a short amount of time—much like the growth of her mind and heart while with the Lake-keepers. She eyed the large, golden Swarve next to her. He seemed happy to get out of his stable and away from the limiting grounds of the fortress.

They hiked a secret path that Garth had discovered, which cut through the cliffs away from the fortress. It led to where the River fed into Dumas Lake from the Desert Plains. F'lorna worried that Croga wouldn't fit through some of the narrow trails, but much of his bulk was due to his lightweight wispy fur. She looked at his wings. The large golden feathers that protruded out were definitely not wispy. She would feed him more of the sapling leaves as she found them in the cavern. Maybe he would grow more feathers on his wings.

The old warrior looked back to her. "What did you whisper to the old sage before he left?"

She smiled. "I sent him to my friends, the fisherman and his wife. I told him to request the room they built for me. I know Voddie won't mind. She loves the company. I want the old sage to share the chants with their sons, so they can have at least a piece of the *Divine Oracle.*"

"They are important to you, these chants?"

"Yes," she nodded and thought. "Why are you helping me?" she asked. "If Lothar finds out, he will kill you."

Garth slowed his pace to come alongside of her. "I know that he will never let you return home, and now that you have your memory, he will use you to decipher what those symbols say."

"But he told Dalia this morning that he didn't care about the symbols anymore," F'lorna said. "That's why he sent the old sage away."

The old warrior looked at F'lorna. "Chieftain Lothar did not want you to remember because he had decided to keep you. But that wasn't going to stop him from interpreting the symbols. He was sending me and a few of my men up the river on boats to discover your lands. I was to find some of your people and take them back with us."

"He can't just steal River-dwellers!"

"He can and he will," Garth said, flatly

"Will you do as he commands?" F'lorna asked.

Garth said nothing for several steps. "I will go, but the boats will never make it. There are two rivers to the west of us that intersect with ours. Once they unite, they disappear under the sands."

"I am not sure if that is still true," she said.

306

He turned to her. "Why?"

"The River no longer goes underground on our side. We had great ground shudders that exposed its path through the sands. That is how I fell. Where the River disappeared underground is now a large land bridge, and you can see the River wind its way up to the horizon."

"If that is true, your people are very much in danger," Garth said. "I know them to be simple and peaceful. They live in trees and use the bow or spear to hunt. They are no match for our people and our metals when it comes to war."

F'lorna stopped walking. "Garth, how do you know so much about the River-dwellers? You have been to our lands, haven't you?"

"Yes," he admitted.

"You are the one who helped Chieftess Tarsha escape to the caverns."

Garth exhaled deeply and wrung the back of his neck with his hand. "I told her she should wait until the baby was born, then she could leave to the new lands that I found. There were forests in the new lands and people who lived in trees and never spoke of war."

"Why did she want to leave?" F'lorna asked. "I tried to discuss the matter with Dalia, but she always avoids answering my questions."

"Her husband, Chieftain Vandar, had gone completely mad. He began hitting her and locking her up. She feared he would kill her and the baby before it was born. She wanted to take Lothar. He was a young man at the time, but she knew he wouldn't go with her. She made me promise to stay and watch over him. Several days after she left, I searched the caverns to make sure she made it across. I found her Swarve dead, but she wasn't there. I believed she had made it until I discovered her body in the Domus Lake. When I pulled her out, I saw that her womb had been cut open and her baby taken. I buried her body in Atlatl Forest."

"I'm sorry. It sounds like you cared for her."

"You asked me why I'm helping you. That is the reason. I see Lothar following the same patterns of his father. It is only a matter of time before he begins to go mad like him. When I first met you at the fisherman's house and learned you were to be our chieftess, I promised myself I would not let myself care about you like I cared for Tarsha. But then you suffered the Fear of the Cliffs like her, and I had to save you too from falling. Now I do care, and I don't want you to suffer her same fate. Amorfia—I'm sorry. I mean, F'lorna, you are strong and smart. You will make it through the caverns. And you will find your people, the River-dwellers. And warn them that Chieftain Lothar is coming to their lands."

"I will make it. I promise," she said, taking his hand.

He smiled. "And if you ever hear of stories of a baby found in the caverns around forty-two years ago, tell him that his mother died to protect him."

F'lorna laughed. "That's the age of my father."

Garth's smile faded. "Do you know your grandparents?"

"No, they were very old when they had him, so they died before I was born. But my aunt still lives— though she is double the age of my father. He is what we call Onefold because he's seen all seven years of each of the six-colored moons once. She is Twofold, which is eighty-four of your years. That means she's seen the six-colored moons twice."

"Is it normal for your people to have babies at such an age? Your grandparents had to be at almost sixty or older when they had your father."

"No, it is not," she said, hesitantly. "When I first met Lothar, I touched his face because it seemed familiar to me. Now I know why. He has the cobalt blue eyes like my father."

"It can't be possible," Garth said and began pacing the ground. "What does your aunt do? Where does she live? Does she have kids?"

"She's a Healing Elder, and she travels the River teaching other healers. She never joined, so she could never have babies."

Garth stopped. "F'lorna, I don't want to speculate, but the way you sing like her and you have the Fear of Cliffs like her. You even look like Tarsha except for your colorless eyes."

"My eyes are grey," she whispered. "I get them from my mother. Everything else about me looks like my father."

"What is his name?" he asked.

"Jaquarn. He is the Spiritual Elder of my village."

Garth looked at the sky. "The sun is starting to descend. We must run. If you are who I think you are, Chieftain Lothar will stop at nothing to get you back, for you truly are the heir to his throne."

Lothar sat on his throne holding his ruby studded sword. It was fitted in its scabbard and clasped to the new sword belt he had made for Amorfia, an adoption gift for his daughter. A real gift for a real adoption. The throne halls were empty except for his aunt, Garth and three of his swordsmen. He threw everyone else out—the sages, the musicians and the servants. There would be no celebration tonight.

"Where do you think she would have gone? To the Fisherman's house?" Dalia asked.

"I sent some of my men to check, but I doubt she would go there. She wouldn't jeopardize that family. She cares about them too much."

"Maybe she left on a boat," Garth suggested.

"Her Swarve is gone too. She wouldn't be able to fit him on any of our boats," Dalia said.

"When was the last time you saw her?" Lothar asked, turning to Garth.

"I was sending the sage home, and she was resting next to her Swarve. That was the last time I saw her."

"I checked her room, and I didn't see anything missing, but she did leave her horn brace. Maybe she left to Atlatl Forest. Those woodsmen might take her in," Dalia said.

Lothar got up from his chair. "If one of those appalling woodsmen so much as touches her, I will burn down their entire forest!"

"Would you like me to search for her there?" Garth asked.

"No, I've already sent every one of my swordsmen to find her. I will need you here if they come back empty-handed. You will have to search the caverns."

"Why would she go to the caverns? She doesn't remember who she is or where she came from. Even if she made it to the other side, she is in a worse position than she is here. She has given me no indication that her memory has been restored," Dalia said.

"She has no other memory!" Lothar lashed out. "She is a gift to me from the Befores. Must I repeat myself? They have given me a daughter to replace all they have taken. This will be the story of my legacy. This will be how the sages remember me!"

"I'm sorry, Lothar. I didn't mean to offend you. I know how you feel. I just want to make sure we consider all the options."

The door to the hall opened, and several swordsmen came in dragging an old sage. They dropped him on the ground in front of Lothar.

"He was on his way to an East Basin fishing village. He won't tell us more than that," one of the guards said.

Lothar tucked the sword and belt he carried under his arm. "So this is the old sage. Let me see your eyes."

The old sage looked up.

"Dark skin, emerald eyes and an archaic facial tattoo—you must be a sage from the Lowland Cliffs. What are you hiding?"

"I am hiding nothing," the old sage said and looked back at the ground.

"Why were you going to East Basin?"

The sage said nothing and continued to stare. Lothar swung his leg and kicked his side, causing him to roll onto his back and yell in pain.

"I asked you a simple question. Where were you going? You were supposed to get into a boat and float back to that groveling territory of Rugar bar Hathway. But it appears that your traveling plans have changed."

The old sage looked at Garth.

"Stop looking at my swordsman and answer me! Before I kick you again!"

"She sent me," the old sage said. "That is all. She wanted me to tell them my stories."

Lothar crossed his arms. "What stories?"

"The forty-four *Chants of Jeyshen*."

"Forty-four of them," he looked to Dalia. "It seems you were right, my aunt. This sage did have the missing clue. Forty-four symbols and forty-four chants."

"Did you say your chants to my daughter?"

The sage looked at Garth again.

"Stop looking at him!"

He nodded.

"And did anything change in her?"

"She remembered who she is."

"And who is she?"

"Her name is F'lorna."

Lothar unsheathed his sword and dropped the new sword belt on the ground. He kicked it away and knelt next to the sage. "So you took my Amorfia away from me."

312

"Stop!" Garth yelled. "Don't hurt him. It is my fault. I didn't think she would regain her memory."

Lothar stood and walked to Garth, keeping his sword unsheathed. "I never intended on killing the old sage. I don't blame him for stealing my daughter. I blame you. I just needed to see if my suspicions were true. You led my mother to the caverns, didn't you?"

"Your father was going to kill her and her baby!"

Lothar looked to his three swordsmen and gave the signal. Before Garth could take out his sword, they seized him and bound his hands.

Lothar took the hilt of the sword and thrust it into Garth's stomach. "How dare you say that about my father. He loved my mother."

Garth tried to bend over, but the men pulled him back. "Is that why he beat her?"

Lothar thrust the hilt into his stomach again. "You speak lies! You wanted my mother for yourself, so you stole her from me. And now you have stolen my daughter!"

Lothar moved the blade of the sword under Garth's chin.

"Stop it, Lothar!" Dalia yelled. "There is some truth in what he says."

"Get my aunt out of here before she angers me!" he yelled to the swordsmen who had brought in the old sage.

He looked back down at Garth. "You are going to show me where those caverns are, and I will get that wretched girl back."

"Why do you still need her now that you know she isn't a gift from the Befores? Just let her go back home."

"Because if she remembers, she can now decipher the forty-four symbols. I will use her to interpret them, and then I will kill her for tricking me into caring for her."

"F'lorna didn't trick you. You tricked yourself!" Garth said.

Lothar took his sword and sliced it across Garth's face. "I won't need you. My aunt knows the caverns. She will show me." He drew the sword back to plunge the blade into Garth's stomach.

"Wait! There's something you should know about F'lorna."

Lothar halted his thrust. "Why would I care?"

"I believe you were right."

"Right about what?"

"She is a gift from the Befores, but not like you thought."

"Do not anger me!"

"No, please! I only tell you for her sake, not mine. I would rather die before you knew, but I have no other choice since you mean to kill her."

"I'm listening," Lothar said, mockingly. "I do enjoy a good story."

"F'lorna sings like your mother. She has the Fear of Cliffs like your mother. She even looks like your mother except for her eyes."

"I know this! That is why I thought she was a gift from the Befores!"

"Let me tell you the rest. She recognized you that day when she touched your face. It's because you have the same color eyes as her father."

"Many people have my color," he spat.

"Yes, but her father is forty-two years old. And his parents were almost sixty when he was a baby. His aunt is a healer who traveled the river. She is twice his age and never married."

"What are you trying to say? That this F'lorna is my niece? How dare you lie to me!" Lothar took his sword and plunged it into Garth's body.

Garth instantly spat up blood, but he kept moving his lips. "I found her body," he whispered hoarsely.

Lothar leaned in towards Garth's face. "What did you say?"

"I found your mother's body in the lake, and I buried it."

"So you see, she and the baby never made it to the other side. Now I know you are lying."

Garth shook his head and coughed up more blood. "Her womb had been cut open. The baby was gone. The healer. She must have taken your brother, Jaquarn." Garth's eyes roll and he slumped over.

Lothar stared at him for several moments. "Take him away," he told the swordsmen. He walked back to his throne and sat down. He stared at the old sage who was still on the floor guarded by a single swordsman.

"So what do you think old sage? Tell me honestly, and I'll let you go to the fisherman's house and offer your chants. Do you think this F'lorna is my niece?"

315

The old sage got up and dusted off his robe. "From the first moment I saw the young lady, I knew she was a Highland Cliffs Chieftess."

"How can you be so sure?" Lothar asked.

"The same way you knew I was a Lowland Cliffs Sage. She looks like one," the old sage said simply.

Chapter 30

DIGGING CAVERNS

T'maya held the torch out in front of her and edged around the large rock blocking her way. She could see that the ground shudders had shifted the cavern, causing rocks to fall from the ceiling of the cave. Everything was dark and they could hear the rush of the River all around them. The roaring current sounded so close that if she chipped at the rocky wall for just a moment, the water would come gushing in.

"Elder T'maya," Sage whispered. She walked behind T'maya with her torch and Le'ana followed behind her.

"Yes, Sage," T'maya whispered back as if the sound of her voice would cause the entire cave to collapse.

"We didn't bring any food or supplies. We've been walking this cave all morning and maybe even afternoon. Are you intending on us walking all the way to the Lake-keepers?"

"I brought some food," Le'ana whispered.

"I know. You always have food," Sage said, looking back at her friend with an irritated look. "But whatever you packed is not enough for all of us for an entire journey! Plus, though I can hear the water, we cannot reach it. We will die of thirst before hunger!"

"Don't worry, Sage. I'm not planning on taking us very far."

"Then where are you taking us?" Sage asked.

T'maya stopped and turned. "I'm looking for bones."

"Bones!" the girls said simultaneously.

"Yes, an animal died in here with Jaquarn's mother. If we can find the bones, then I will know that this is the right cavern for when Jaquarn returns."

"Why didn't you tell us?" Sage asked.

T'maya exhaled. "I taught both of you the Cooking Adoration for a time. Don't you remember? Sage the singer and Le'ana the planter. Neither of you enjoyed working with meat. I didn't want to worry you, but now that you know, look around for bones sticking out from under rocks or the ground."

"Aren't the bones old?" Le'ana asked. "Will they still be here?"

T'maya tried not to be exasperated with the young girls. At almost fifteen turns of the moon, they thought anything over thirty was ancient. "Jaquarn's bones are still intact, so I am fairly certain these bones will be too. Though, there won't be any skin or flesh on them."

"You were right. I wish I didn't know what we were looking for," Sage said.

T'maya continued looking. She knew it was getting late. If she hadn't brought Sage and Le'ana, she could continue her search longer. But she also knew that Jaquarn would not be pleased if she walked the cavern alone. What if something happened? What if she got stuck? It was safer to not go alone, and it kept her mother's heart from risking too much to find her daughter. She thought of Jaquarn and gave voiceless words that he had either found her or he was returning home. If she could just ensure this was the cavern, the hope she carried would stay alive.

"What is that?" Sage asked, pointing with her torch.

T'maya followed the light of Sage's torch. Something greyish white protruded from the ground to the left. "It looks like a large bone!" she whispered, excitedly. She crawled to the bone and inspected it. "Yes! It is!" She grabbed the bone and pulled as hard as she could. "It's stuck."

"I brought a small planting shovel," Le'ana said, reaching into her tunic belt.

"Food. Shovels. What else did you bring?" Sage asked.

"I am a Planting Novice Elder, Sage. We always come prepared. Here, take my forked digger and help me dig," Le'ana said and handed Sage the tool.

The three of them stuck their torches into crevices of the cavern near the bone's location. Then they crawled to where the bone stuck out of the ground. Le'ana and Sage dug around the bone while T'maya held it ready to pull.

"It's a really long bone. You see those notches? It looks like a spine—a very big spine," T'maya said. "You'll have to dig further down."

Sage and Le'ana continued to dig a deep circle around the spine. Soon they had to lean the upper half of their bodies into the hole just to keep digging.

Sage stopped and wiped the sweat from her forehead with the back of her arm. "Can we just break it in half and take what we can?"

"We'll need the entire thing, so I can compare it to other animals. Right now, I am fairly certain I've never seen an animal this big besides the River Monster." T'maya looked at the girls. "Come here and grab the spine and help me pull it up."

"I really don't want to touch it," Sage said, backing up.

"It's either we keep digging or we pull," Le'ana said. She took Sage's tool and placed it next to hers on the ground.

"Okay, I'll just close my eyes," Sage said.

The three of them grabbed the spine and stood up.

"Okay, lean into it, girls. And pull!" T'maya said.

The three pulled with all of their might until they all fell back and tumbled on top of each other with the spine in their hands.

"Get it off of me!" Sage cried. She crawled out from under the spine and wiped her face. "There's dirt in my mouth."

Le'ana crawled up and stared at the spine. "Elder T'maya, that spine is longer than you are!"

T'maya stood up and held the spine above her head. She finally had it. Proof that she had discovered the right cavern. When her husband returned, they could travel the cavern together and find F'lorna. She placed the spine over her shoulder. "Okay, now we can return."

"Wait," Sage said, listening. "I hear something. It sounds like wind."

"It's just the River next to us," Le'ana said.

"No," Sage said, shaking her head. "I may not be prepared with planting tools like you, but I am a Singing Novice Elder, and I can point out tones that most people would miss. I hear wind."

T'maya grabbed her torch and walked back to the hole the girls had dug. She got on her knees and peered down. "It's coming from down here." She took the torch and positioned it down the hole. "It's not stopping."

"What's not?" Le'ana asked.

"The torch. It keeps going! We don't need this one," she whispered and dropped the torch.

As the three peered down the hole, they watched the light falling—getting dimmer and dimmer until it splashed into a watery abyss below.

T'maya gasped. "We need to get out of here now!"

F'lorna walked through the cavern with her Swarve behind her. They were on their third rise of the moon, and she had grown weary of walking in the dark. She had always liked the feeling of being enclosed, like when she slept in her Achion tree, but after being in the cavern for so long, she began to feel tension rise up—tension that even Croga couldn't help with.

"I think you hate it in here more than I do," she said, looking back at him. He made his soft grunting noise and nuzzled her hand with his nose. She allowed him to wrap around her fingers with his wispy fur. Her other hand moved along the cavern wall feeling for saplings for Croga to eat. Finally, her fingertips felt a tender branch, and she pulled the small tree from the cave wall. "Here, I found you some more leaves to eat. I believe you are eating better than I am," she said.

He unwound his fur from her hand, and she plucked all the leaves off of the thin branches. She then held all the leaves in her cupped hands and brought it to his nose where she could hear his soft breathing. "Smell. It's your favorite."

Croga gave a couple of sniffs and them moved his flat face up, so he could let out his wide sticky tongue. She tipped her hands forward and allowed all of the leaves to go into his mouth. He munched the small serving quickly and sniffed for more.

"That's all I have, but I'll keep looking."

She continued her walk until she ran into a hard barrier. "Ouch!" she said. She felt along the rock, and it completely blocked their path. She reached high in the corners and found a small opening. "I can fit through, but you can't, Croga."

As she stood in the darkness, she felt her body begin to tense. She thought of Chieftess Tarsha. If she couldn't make it, how could she? Her breathing became labored, and she placed her hands on her knees and leaned forward. "Calm down, F'lorna. Ra'ash wouldn't bring you all the way here to stop you now. Think. There has to be a direction change. There is something I need to see." She began looking around the cavern, but everything was dark.

"Dig," she heard.

"What?" she asked, looking around.

"Dig," she heard again.

"Dig down?"

"No, dig out."

F'lorna grabbed the hilt of her sword and pulled out the blade. Then she stuck it into the high right corner of the cavern away from the sound of the River. She pulled it out and continued to pierce the side of the cave. "This is not working," she said, frustrated. "It's impossible for me to dig up. I have no leverage."

Croga who had been pacing and grunting came up to her. He reach his front paws at the point she was piercing and began plowing with his front paws so fast that dirt was flying all around her. Finally, light penetrated the darkness, so bright that she had to instantly close her eyes. But Croga kept tunneling until the light engulfed them. He stopped digging and his back legs leaped up and out of the cavern. When she finally climbed her way out, Croga was sprinting a wide circle through the snow-dusted sand. His black tongue flapped to the side, and F'lorna laughed at the sight.

"Croga, come let me get on your back. We've only traveled through forest and rock. I've never seen you run so fast."

Croga slowed and came to her side. She crawled onto his back and his wispy fur engulfed her. She didn't realize how tired she had been. She wrapped her arms as far as she could around him and placed her cheek on the back of his soft neck. "Let's go!" she yelled. He sprang forward with so much force that she screamed with excitement. Free! She was finally free to run and be who she had been created to be. Not a fisherman's wife. Not a sage. Not a Chieftain's daughter. She was F'lorna of Rodesh bearer of the *Divine Oracle* and friend to Swarves. "Go, Croga! Get us home!"

She must have fallen asleep because she woke up to Croga lapping up water from a little stream that veered away from the River. The Heat Source was a finger's width above the horizon and the Violet Moon was just waking up. She sat up and looked around. All she saw was sand, but the River did look more narrow than it had when they dug their way out of the caverns. "How far did you take us?" she asked. Croga continued to lap the water. She shifted her weight and the wispy fur holding her loosened. "I'm thirsty too," she said.

She jumped off Croga's back and walked to the stream. Large stones and boulders lined the water bed, and she leaned on a rock to dip her hands in the cold water. After she rinsed her hands, she cupped the clear liquid and quickly brought it to her mouth. "Oh, the water is so good here." She took several more drinks until the ground shook.

"What was that?" she asked, looking at Croga who began to pace.

The ground shook again. "It's ground shudders!"

The ground shook again so hard that the large boulder rolled over onto her foot. "Ouch! It hurts! It hurts!"

She tried to pull her foot out from under the boulder but whenever she moved, it crushed her foot more. "Croga, push it! Push it!"

Croga continued to pace and whine. The ground shook again and a large cracking noise sounded near the River. F'lorna felt fear rise in her. Then the ground shook again and her foot went deeper under the rock, as the water lapped up to her knees. The cracking noise came closer. She reached her hands to Croga and grabbed onto his thick fur. "Pull!"

He pulled back, but his fur ripped out into her hands. "Oh no!" she yelled.

She pulled out her sword and tried to push the boulder with it, but her strength had run out. She looked around desperately, but there was nothing she could do to save herself. Suddenly, a large bird swooped down and landed on the warfighting leather pants that she wore. It wrapped its talons around her thigh. "Banthem!" she yelled. She heard another crack and the ground shook. When it did, she yanked her foot and it moved back a bit before being caught under the weight of the boulder again. "It hurts!" She yelled looking away. She looked back at Banthem and he stared at her. Then he looked north.

She followed his gaze, and she could see a figure running to her. The ground shook again and she screamed out in pain. The loud cracking sound was coming closer. She looked back at the figure. The man was running to her, getting closer. She reached out her arms. She knew who he was. "Father! Father!" she screamed.

He splashed through the water, squatted next to the boulder and lifted the large rock as he straightened his legs. Banthem flew off.

"Ahhhhhh!" he yelled as the boulder came up.

Croga came to her again and she grabbed two handfuls of his fur. This time when he pulled, her body came out of the water.

Jaquarn dropped the boulder and ran to his daughter. "The land is cracking!" he shouted. "Let me carry you!"

"No! she said. "Get me on Croga! He will carry me and run faster than you can."

Jaquarn looked at the beast concerned, but he listened to his daughter. He laid her on the animals back and its fur engulfed her legs as she sat upright. She felt his fur around her broken foot squeeze the injury. It hurt a bit, but she knew from her aunt that the pressure was good.

"The land bridge is just ahead, but everything is falling! I was about to climb up until I saw Banthem in the distance. He was circling and then he landed. I knew he had found you!"

Another crack sounded and the ground shook causing Jaquarn to stumble. "Go! I'll meet you there!"

F'lorna scooted up on Croga. "Get behind me, Father! Croga is strong and fast. He will hold onto you!"

Jaquarn hesitated but again did as his daughter said. When Jaquarn's bottom half was covered with Croga's wispy fur, the Swarve lurched forward, and he sprinted down the sand.

Jaquarn yelled out in astonishment.

"Hold on, Father!" she shouted.

The ground began to shake continuously and loud cracking noises surrounded them. F'lorna looked to her left and the water from the River was rushing toward them. "Croga! Faster!" she yelled.

Croga opened his wings and spread them to full length. F'lorna was amazed at how long they were and how many large feathers had grown in. The wings began to flap with wide thrusts. F'lorna scooted up to give them more room. "Father, move back a little! Don't block his wings!"

Jaquarn moved back allowing the wings space to move. Croga flapped his wings again, and F'lorna felt a powerful breeze blow across her body. He began to flap them repeatedly, beating them against the wind, faster and faster.

"The land bridge! It's up ahead!" Jaquarn yelled.

She looked up at the bridge that no longer caused her to fear. The waterfall was spilling over the sides of the rockface where the Sand-shapers had mined out the auraium.

"The River is overflowing the Desert Plains," her father yelled.

Croga continued to flap his wings and F'lorna felt his body hover slightly with every bound. The combination of his flapping and sprinting caused them to go faster than she ever imagined like they were about to fly.

"He needs to stop!" Jaquarn yelled. "The others are waiting for us at the top with ropes!"

The water was under them now, and Croga was not stopping. F'lorna saw the land bridge coming, but she trusted that Croga wouldn't do anything to harm them. He continued to flap his wings, as he bounded up the side of the rockface. He jumped from one large protrusion of the cliff to the next while flapping. F'lorna's head yanked back and she closed her eyes. Finally, after several large leaps and flaps, her head fell forward and Croga stopped moving. He tucked his wings back to his side. The ground shudders ceased. F'lorna opened her eyes to a stunned group of her family and friends.

She felt her father's arms embrace her, and her mother came up to her and leaned into her and Croga with tears streaming down her face. Sage and Le'ana gaped. Weston smiled broadly. Lemmeck walked to the edge of the land bridge and looked across the horizon.

"The Desert Plains are gone," he said in awe. "It looks like we found the other end to the Great Expanse."

F'lorna looked back. The River had overflowed the entire landscape. All that was out there was water.

"And it looks like we found a Swarve," Sage said in awe, as she stared at Croga. "One that's alive."

"Just like my dream," Le'ana added.

The old sage sat and held Range on his lap. He enjoyed the peaceful fisherman's house, and the room the young girl gave him. "Do you want to hear another of Jeyshen's Chants?" he asked.

"No," the boy said. "I already know them all. I want to go out and play now."

"Okay," the old sage smiled. "I'll let you down." He placed the young boy on the ground, and he ran off through the door.

"Stay where I can see you, Range!" Voddie yelled. She grabbed two plates with rolls and meat and sat down next to the sage.

"Boru left this morning," she said. "I knew he would, but I held onto a small piece of hope that he would change his mind."

"The boy has to go where he's called," the old sage said.

"He made sure to finish helping with the Fisherman's Inn first. Just like my little brother. He finishes what he starts, which worries me on this journey he has chosen."

"Building boats is a worthy journey," the old sage said.

"Yes, fishing boats. But he's building boats for Chieftain Lothar. Huge boats to sail across the waters that now cover the sands. You know he's only doing it to find her."

The old sage nodded. "I know. They both are."

"Yes, that's what worries me. I don't know who will find her first—Boru or Chieftain Lothar."

The old sage grinned. "Maybe she'll find them first."

Voddie nodded. "She's a quick learner, that one. F'lorna—F'lorna is her name. It will be hard for me to not think of her as my Morfie."

"With her two sets of youth memories, I think she will always be both F'lorna and Morfie," the old sage said. "Ra'ash does work in very interesting ways."

"The children in both East Basin and the Highland Cliffs are already singing songs about Morfie—how she ran away from the Highland Cliffs Chieftain, causing the waters to swallow up her trail. I knew there was so much inside of her. I even told Morgo that songs would be sung about her one day, and I was right!"

The old sage took a bite of his bread and chewed slowly while in thought. Once he swallowed, he took a sip of water and looked back at Voddie. "She is a strong and resilient young woman who has a deep trust in Ra'ash. I don't doubt that the songs about her have only just begun."

WRITER

Alisa Hope Wagner loves deep simplicity. She is home most days, but if you do see her out and about, you may actually be face-to-face with her extroverted identical twin sister. More than anything, Alisa adores being a wife to her high school sweetheart (Daniel), mother to her three awesome children (Isaac, Levi and Kiki) and daughter of the Most High King.

After hours of writing and editing at her computer, Alisa cannot wait to workout in her garage gym. When the day's work is finally done, she listens to smooth jazz and gets creative in the kitchen. But before she begins to write each morning, she sits with her Bible and journal and chats with God, letting the Holy Spirit encourage, correct and guide her.

Alisa is an award winning writer of Christian fiction and non-fiction books. She has been writing for 14 years and has written and published over 20 books across all genres, including her speculative fiction books, the _Onoma Series_. She lectures at churches and colleges about her four favorite topics: faith, family, fitness and fiction. Additionally, she writes about the topics on her blog, www.alisahopewagner.com.

Alisa competes in bodybuilding competitions and is a retired MMA fighter. She shares her health passion and knowledge in her 2 fitness books. She can be found on Instagram, Twitter, Facebook and Goodreads with her username: @alisahopewagner.

Alisa is the creator of _enLIVEn Devotional_: a writing ministry that brings the words of diverse writers together in order to support world missions. She and her co-coordinator, Holly Smith, produce devotional anthologies with proceeds going to the poor and needy of this world. You can find out how to get involved in this ministry at www.enlivendevotionals.com.

The most important thing Alisa would like to tell her readers is that God loves you so much that He sent His Son into this world to claim you as His brothers and sisters. No matter who you are or what you have done, Jesus loves you and died to have a supernatural relationship with you in this life and the next. Don't waste one single day. Ask Jesus into your heart, make Him your Lord and Savior and begin really living!

ARTiST

Albert Morales is an accomplished illustrator and painter with credits spread across the art board. He was a nominee for the 2018 CARTOON CROSSROADS Cartoonist of the year, where this year his strip joined the BILLY IRELAND CARTOON ART MUSEUM's collection of original art since the 1900's. His work is now curated and collected next to the likes of Charles Schultz (Peanuts), Bil Keane (Family Circus), and Bill Watterson (Calvin and Hobbes) to name a few.

Albert's creator owned comic strip SUPER IMPACTO VS. THE WORLD has also been recently published in a collection along with fellow cartoonists entitled TALES

FROM LA VIDA by THE OHIO STATE UNIVERSITY.

Albert has had the opportunity to work with the HERO INITIATIVE on several of their 100 book projects including: Wolverine 100, New Avengers 100, Fantastic Four 100, Walking Dead 100, Hellboy 100, and TEENAGE MUTANT NINJA TURTLES 100.

Wrapping up his run with MARVEL / UPPERDECK as an official MARVEL - UPPERDECK artist (with SPIDER-MAN: Homecoming and FLEER ULTRA X-MEN), Albert is continuing doing creative projects in the way of publishing creator owned books. Slated for 2019 and already catching fire is his new book ANNIHILATION JONES and his just announced illustration duties for ALISA HOPE WAGNER'S new VIOLET MOON SERIES starting with *F'lorna of Rodesh*!

You can find Albert Morales at the following social media sites.
artwise310@hotmail.com
https://www.instagram.com/angryroosterstudios/
https://www.facebook.com/albert.morales.5477

e

ALISA'S OTHER BOOKS

Onoma Series:
Eve of Awakening
Bear into Redemption
Mark within Salvation
Hunt for Understanding

Violet Moon Series:
F'lorna of Rodesh
Chieftain's Daughter

Children's Book:
Spreading Her Wings: Butterfly Princess Book 1

Fitness Books:
Fearlessly Fit
Fearlessly Fit at Home

Vessels Series:
Imperfect Vessels
Broken Alabaster Jars
Gathering Empty Pitchers

Following God Series:
Following God into the Cage
Following God onto the Stage
Following God across the Page

One Year Devotional:
Slay the Day: Your Daily Dose of Victory

Faith Books:
Our 6 His 7: Transformed by Sabbath Rest
Why Jesus: A 50 Day Holy Spirit Experience
Proverbial Tweets: 10 Years of Public and Private Faith

Devotional Books:
Simple Musings
Aroma of Faith

Devotional Anthologies:
Granola Bar Devotionals: Spiritual Snacks on the Go!
*Get to the Margins: A Devotional Anthology of Writers
on the Edge*

If you love this book, please leave a review on Amazon and/or Goodreads. Your words will help other readers to discover F'lorna and her family and friends, so they too can experience the unveiling world of Rodesh.

Made in the USA
Columbia, SC
15 March 2020